LOST KEY

A SHARK KEY ADVENTURE

CHRIS NILES

The author appreciates your time to read this work. Please consider leaving a review wherever you bought this book, and please tell your friends who might also like it. The best way for a reader to find new favorites is still a recommendation from a trusted friend.

Cover by Shayne Rutherford at Wicked Good Book Covers

Edited by Staci Troilo

For Adam

I'm proud of you.

PROLOGUE

October 1931

Tommy and Gigi started making plans when the judge replaced the whole jury.

For weeks, Al Capone's crew had worked to guarantee every juror was on their side. Even if twelve brand new jurors sat in the box, the Outfit would find a way to win them over, too. The Boss would beat these charges. He always beat the charges.

But this time was different. And Tommy and Gigi knew it.

When the jury announced their verdict, runners sprinted down the streets of Chicago. Every boy in town wanted to be first to shout the inconceivable news. "Hey! The jury found him guilty! They're takin' him straight to jail. The Boss is goin' to jail!"

In the Lexington Hotel, a young boy's breathless

cries echoed through the sweeping marble lobby. Barrel-chested henchmen looked up from behind their newspapers, shook their heads, and waved the boy away. No one believed the feds could make anything stick to the great Al Capone.

When Scarface walked the streets, children flocked to his side. He built schools so neighborhood kids could get an education. Later, after the market crashed, he built soup kitchens so they wouldn't starve. He created jobs and protected his employees. Charmed the women, joked with the men. Paid his employees well for their loyalty. Chicago belonged to him.

But as the news trickled in and people realized it was true, men gathered in twos and threes, then more. Working girls ran down to the lobby wrapped in robes — none of them would be doing any more business that night. Company cars filled the street in front of the building and the alley behind as Capone's guards and enforcers congregated at the Lexington headquarters. The crowd grew louder, and everyone speculated about the future of the organization.

In the chaos, Gigi slipped into the lobby wearing a simple dress. She clutched three small shopping bags in one hand and grabbed Tommy with the other, then tugged him into a narrow stairwell.

"It's time, baby. We gotta do it now, or we may never get another opportunity."

Tommy followed her down the steps into the basement. The two dashed through a maze of brick corridors. Mildew stank up the cool damp air, and Gigi stopped to sneeze.

"Gigi, shh!" Tommy scurried around the corner into Capone's storage vault. He pushed aside a stack of crates holding empty bottles. "It's still here. Babe, there's a latch beside that big mirror. Feel it? Up a little ... yeah, there."

Gigi jumped as the mirror swung aside to reveal a hidden staircase. She climbed through the hole in the basement wall then ran up the steps, reappearing seconds later. "There's a delivery truck right outside, and the alley is clear for now. Hurry!"

Tommy handed her his Thompson machine gun, then Gigi stood watch in the alley while he rushed up and down the stairs, lugging crate after crate and stacking them in the vehicle. Finally, he slammed the alley door behind him. After flinging the last crate into the back of the truck, he ran around to the cab. "Get in!"

Gigi leapt into the passenger's seat while Tommy started the engine.

They cleared the alley onto 21st Street then zig-zagged through the narrow streets toward freedom. The two drove through the night, Gigi singing songs to help Tommy stay awake. When they ran low on fuel, Tommy hid the truck down a wooded side road, and the two lovers curled together under Tommy's jacket to wait for morning.

"I think we made it, kid." Tommy tucked a curl behind Gigi's ear.

"How much do you think we got?"

"I dunno, but I know my arms are gonna hurt tomorrow." Tommy peeked through the window, counting the heavy crates lined up on the floorboards in the back of the truck.

"We can count it later, baby. Right now, I want to get some sleep. In the morning, we'll get gas, then get as far away as we can."

For the next three months, Gigi and Tommy wound a path throughout the eastern United States. Tommy taught Gigi to drive, and they kept moving, stopping in small towns along the way. He built a false floor in the truck to hide their cargo. Gigi counted the crates. She counted the gold coins and gemstones inside the crates. Then she counted them again, just to make sure.

"We're rich. Tommy. We'll never have to work for anyone else, ever again."

Tommy kissed the top of her head. "I never liked you workin' the way you did. But we need to be careful. We gotta hide this loot. We can't go throwin' it around. Boss might be in prison, but he still got a lot of friends in a lot of places."

"But babe, I want nice things. I want a big house and new hats. I want to ride the Queen Mary to Europe and meet dukes and princesses."

"You're all the princess I need, Gigi. We need to

watch our backs. If we dump these all at once, or even in big batches, we'll be dead within a week. We gotta lie low a little while longer. Just be patient. When the coast is clear, I promise I'll buy you the most beautiful house with the most beautiful view in the whole world."

Tommy sold off a few of the smaller stones one by one — for less than they were worth but more than enough to fill the truck with gas, pay for meals and rooms along the way, and build up a little cash reserve. But living on the run wasn't Gigi's cup of bathtub gin.

One evening, in a hotel in Chattanooga, Tennessee, she pressed up against him. "Baby, you need to buy me a real home, or one morning me and that truck are gonna be gone."

"I should have never taught you to drive."

She wrapped her lips around his earlobe and teased it with her teeth. "Buy me a house and you'll never have to worry about a thing."

The next day, Tommy found a buyer for ten coins — the most he dared sell at one time. He tucked $200 in his front pocket then drove south 'til the road ended.

CHAPTER ONE

Present Day

KATE KINGSBURY BRUSHED a sopping hank of curly bangs from her forehead. Her sports watch beeped. She wouldn't make the Olympic team, but the little screen showed her heart rate was right on target.

A school bus idled with its lights blinking in front of Shark Key Campground and Marina. As children climbed off the bus and ran across the highway, the driver waved out the open door at Kate. She crossed in front of the bus then paused at the driver's window.

"You coming out for sunset?"

"Not tonight, hon," the driver replied. "Rick's working late all week. Gotta take all the overtime we can get since the rent went up again."

She reached up high and patted the orange panel below the window, hot under the late afternoon sun.

"We'll miss you, but I understand. Do what you gotta do, Lily."

Kate jogged across the highway. After passing a little boy, she spun, jogged backward alongside him, then waved. "Good day at school, Colton?"

"It was, Miss Kate! I had 'Panish today with Señora Royse!"

"Oooh. Make sure to come by and teach me three new words at sunset, okay?"

The little boy nodded before running to join the group of kids waiting beside the little resort's faded sign. The bus's blinking red lights extinguished, the stop sign folded back against its side, then it proceeded up the road.

Kate turned and jogged up the lane. For a hundred yards, stands of mangroves crowded both sides of the narrow road like a runway to a magical land. Just as Narnia had its wardrobe, and Wonderland had its rabbit hole, the long stretch of nature separated the little island from the troubles of the outside world. The thick trees muffled the sound of traffic behind her, and the scent of the brackish water replaced the exhaust and blacktop of Highway One. Shark Key was Kate's sanctuary.

Where the mangroves gave way to open grass, the gravel lane serpentined left then right. A wooden gate hung open, worn by the salt air and wind, secured to a post with a frayed length of old gray dock line. Farther along, a couple travel trailers and a fifth-wheel that

hadn't moved since she'd been at Shark Key sat
between widely set posts. The campsites ended where
their low seagrape hedges met the shallow azure waters
of the Gulf of Mexico.

Across the lane, a series of narrower sites lined a
small lagoon, and beyond it, another row of oceanfront
spots stretched along the east coast of the long island.
Palm trees dotted the low landscape. Shark Key was
home to a few full-time residents, many with permanent decks, satellite dishes, and small storage sheds, but
in the off-season, nearly two thirds of the sites sat
empty. In another two months, after the heat broke and
the snowbirds flocked south for the winter, it would fill
to capacity until spring.

A few minutes later, Kate jogged past the sturdy
concrete shower house and laundry. A guy in his early
twenties with shoulder-length dreadlocks was covering
the little building with a fresh coat of bright white
paint.

"Justin!"

"Hi, Kate!"

She pointed to the eastern sky. "That storm's gonna
wash all your paint off."

The young man shrugged. "Nah, it's just a little
pop-up cloud. It'll blow off to the south. Besides, I'm
almost done."

"Suit yourself."

She crossed the crushed coral parking lot then
bounded over the seawall onto an ancient wooden

dock. With each footfall, her steps echoed off the still water below. The marina's owner, Chuck Miller, had been planning to update all the marina's docks to aluminum planks, starting with the bigger, deeper slips on the sunrise side of the island. Eventually he'd get to Kate's on the cove side, but she was glad hers was last on his list. There was something about the weathered wooden planks that felt peaceful, like a secret refuge — a haven from a bygone time.

Most of the empty slips would stay that way for another couple months, just like the campsites. A sixty-foot Hatteras named *Tax Shelter* gleamed at the end of the long dock. In the two years she'd lived at the little marina at the tip of Shark Key, the *Tax Shelter* had only left its slip twice. She'd heard the owner was a developer from West Palm, but no one she knew had ever seen him. A few slips closer, a pile of dive gear sat on the dock. Steve Welch was scrubbing the deck of his flats skiff, which he had tied up beside a bright white catamaran that had arrived a couple days earlier. Steve normally kept the skiff alongside his custom dive boat on the deeper side of the island, but the water was calmer in the western cove.

Kate waved at Steve, then trotted toward *Serenity*, her 46-foot steel-hull houseboat. Not long after she'd arrived in Key West, she used most of her savings to relieve a disillusioned midwestern couple of their little money-pit. She'd lived onboard ever since. Her slip was nearly impossible to pilot a boat into, so shallow the boat's hull rested on the bottom at low spring tide. But with *Serenity*'s blown engine, sailing those waters wasn't even an option. She'd had to have her new home towed into the cove, then Steve and Chuck had helped her pull it into the slip with ropes. But the upside, as Kate saw it, was she only had to do it once. And it helped that Chuck refused to take any slip rent.

She hurdled the low gate to the boat's stern deck. Whiskey, her seventy-pound German Shepherd, rose from a shaded spot by the door to nuzzle her, tufts of his loose hair sticking to her sweaty belly.

"Hi, buddy. Let's get you some dinner, okay?" Kate grabbed Whiskey's empty bowl from the deck and slid the glass door open with her foot. No need for locks with Whiskey aboard.

Watching intently, he waited as Kate shredded fresh meat from last night's rotisserie chicken then mixed it in with his kibble. She set the bowl on a stool in front of him. He held her gaze. She waited until she saw a good puddle of drool on the vinyl tile below him, then she nodded once. Whiskey tore into the bowl like it was a delicious, coconut-covered criminal while she wiped his slobber from the floor.

Kate grabbed a Modelo and a slice of lime from the fridge, packed two more in a small cooler, then climbed to the roof deck. A single zero-gravity lounge chair sat near the port rail. She pulled a tattered Travis McGee paperback from the dry box beside it before settling in. A soft breeze rustled through the mangrove leaves behind *Serenity*'s stern, carrying the familiar briny sea scent in off the flats to the north.

Home.

She smelled Whiskey's dog food breath as he climbed the bow stairs. He ambled to the back of the deck, spun around three times, then settled beside the rail with a clear view up to the parking lot and down the dock. Whiskey had never really taken to retirement.

Kate sipped her beer and read until the sun dropped low on the horizon. As the sunset blazed and the shadows lengthened, her dog jumped to attention, barking once at the sound of footsteps approaching on the dock below.

"It's okay, Whiskey. Just me," Steve said. "Ahoy, Captain! Permission to come aboard?"

Kate laughed. "Come on up! You boat people are so formal, I might never get used to it."

"Only pirates and police board without the captain's permission. I'm neither." He climbed the stern ladder then leaned against the west-facing railing over *Serenity*'s bow. "You might have the worst slip, but you've got the best sunset view in this blessed place."

"I knew you had an ulterior motive, stopping by like this. Beer?" She opened the cooler beside her chair.

"Don't mind if I do." He popped the cap and took a long pull. "Got a charter on Wednesday, if you wanna work it."

"Will I want to?"

"Long day. Starting at the Vandenberg. Photographers, and they want to take a few lobsters when they're done."

Lifting her eyebrows, she gazed over the top of her sunglasses.

"Okay, okay. It's three fifty-something midwestern dudes with about ten dives between them. They'll be awful, but they pay well."

"Then why did you even ask me?"

"Because I always ask you, even though you almost always turn me down. Hope springs eternal."

"Justin will be glad for the work."

"He will. And they'll love him. But he couldn't tease a lobster into a bag if he was starving."

She laughed.

"Ya know, Kate, I envy you. Sure, your boat don't run, but you only work when you feel like it and you never run low on beer or dog food."

"Here's to living the dream." She clinked her beer bottle against his.

The two faced west and watched the horizon pull the sun under.

CHAPTER TWO

MID-MORNING SUNLIGHT FILTERED through the thick hedge of seagrapes, dotting *Serenity*'s stern. Whiskey lay curled against the sliding door, one eye half-open facing the transom gate, while Kate repaired the utility sink on the boat's fish-cleaning table. She leaned hard against the wrench, then it slipped through her sweaty fingers.

"Ffff-Fox Mulder!" Kate squeezed her left toes, hopping and cursing the heavy tool. As the sting subsided, she tested her weight on the foot. Satisfied it wasn't broken — probably — she gingerly returned the wrench to her toolbox.

After tapping her phone and watching a few seconds of a how-to video, she examined the leaky faucet, its parts spread out on the threadbare green rug on the stern deck she referred to as her back yard.

"Ahoy!"

Kate toppled backwards. "Dammit, Steve."

Captain Welch leaned over the transom to offer her a hand. Kate waved him off, tucked her feet under her, then pushed herself up, wincing a little.

"You might want to get some ice on that." He pointed at her swelling left middle toe.

"I'm good. It's nothing a little time and a long run won't fix."

"Tough girl." He scanned the parts strewn everywhere. "You really could let me help you replace that."

"No, I can get it. But thanks."

"Really, Kate. I don't have a charter today, and I'd like to help. I replaced the deck shower on the *Hopper* a couple months ago. Me and boat plumbing are old buddies."

"It's just a washer. I've got this." Kate turned back to the array of parts. She picked one up.

"Try that one." Steve pointed at a section of pipe with a flange at the end, then reached over the low railing to pick up the length of plastic. He ran his finger along the edge of the flange, then pulled out a half-disintegrated rubber washer. "This might be your problem."

Kate sighed and flopped into a deck chair. "Thanks. I guess I'll run up to West Marine and grab one this afternoon."

"Chuck might have one in the hodgepodge he calls a shop. Check with him before you make a special trip." He rested his hand on the gate's latch and looked at her with a raised eyebrow.

"Really? Fine. Come aboard already."

He sat in the other deck chair. Whiskey eased up and moved to Kate's side, positioning himself between Kate and the visitor.

"What's going on? Are you okay?"

"I'm fine. Just annoyed. Seems like everything on this bucket is breaking at the same time."

"I can take care of it for you."

"I appreciate the offer. I really do. But I'm on my own now and I need to learn to take care of things myself."

"But you're not on your own, Kate. We all look after each other around here."

"I know. I do. And I'm grateful, but it's not the same as having a hus— it's just not the same. People can't always be there. Sometimes you have to do for yourself. *I* have to do for myself. So it's best I learn how. Besides, YouTube lasts forever. And it usually gets me there in the end." She rubbed her bare toes.

"Well, Captain Steve's first rule of boating is that something is always broken. So, get used to that. Second rule? Never try to repair anything in flip-flops." Steve laughed at his own joke and pushed himself up out of the deck chair. "Seriously, if you change your mind, I'll be polishing the rails on the skiff. Just come get me." He latched the tiny gate behind him then ambled down the dock.

Kate dropped back down to the rough turf. Whiskey nuzzled her, and she wrapped her arm around his neck. She fished through the parts then grabbed the one Steve had pointed out as well as another marred by a long crack. Then she dropped both into the deep pocket of her cargo shorts.

"Guard, Whiskey."

The dog's ears straightened, and he squared himself off directly opposite the gate, his back against the sliding glass door. With a full view of the boat's stern and the approaching dock, Whiskey had the perfect vantage point. Kate stepped over the transom then crossed the dock to the seawall. She passed through the thick hedge that encircled the whole island, limping up toward the low block building painted the hue of sunshine that housed the marina's office and workshop. An old bell, corroded by the salt air, jingled when the door opened.

A long counter covered in stacks of yellowing paperwork and fronted with fake wood paneling divided the room. Behind it, a cash register sat on a low bookcase below a plate glass window. Against the far wall, Chuck's 1940s-style metal desk rested against the wall. A high bank of jalousie windows invited a breeze to pass through to a matching set on the opposite wall. The right half of the room was fitted with mismatched shelving units displaying island necessities like toilet paper, coffee filters, and cases of bottled water. A rusting cooler groaned in the back corner, filled with soda, Gatorade, milk, and a small selection of canned beer. Sunlight battered the blistered tinting film that coated the wide front windows.

The boy from the bus stop stood at the counter with a half gallon of milk, writing a note. Kate peeked over his shoulder.

Colton Dawson. Milk $1.25. Thank you, Mr. Chuck.

Colton waved at Kate, hefted the milk into the crook of his arm, then ran across the parking lot toward his mom's Winnebago with four flat tires.

Kate crossed the room and peeked through another doorway into a dark, cluttered workshop.

"Chuck? Are you back there?"

A man's voice drifted through a doorway across the room. "Kate, is that you?"

"Yep. You missed Colton. He stopped in to pick up some milk."

"Didn't miss him. I saw him waiting in the bushes. He's embarrassed to ask for groceries when his mama can't pay. So we have this little system. I see him, I come back here, he comes in and gets what he needs, and leaves me a note. It works for him."

"He shops for them? He's in second grade."

"His mama works three jobs. Makes a kid grow up quick. Babette and I both keep an eye on him, and he knows to come up here if he has a serious problem. Sometimes after I close up the shop, he comes up to the house to keep me company. Does his homework at my kitchen table and watches *Jeopardy!* with me. He's a good kid." Chuck lived in a little concrete block house just behind the shop.

"You're a softie, Chuck."

"Soft is what my old body is getting. Come in here and help me get this pump down, will you?"

Kate paused, letting her eyes adjust to the darkness. Shelving units piled with random supplies and parts stretched from the concrete floor to the ceiling joists, blocking what little light streamed through the shop's dirty windows. Damp hung in the air, and the smell of mildew blended with oil and dust into a distinctive Florida-mechanic's-shop scent. Kate closed her eyes and pictured a wider, tidier shop with the same smell. In her memory, an antique Indian motorcycle sat propped up on jacks, its engine spread across the gleaming floor. She shook off the memory then turned to see Chuck struggling with an oversized pump on a shelf high above his head.

"What are you doing, trying to get that by yourself?" Kate's calves burned as she stretched up on her toes to pull the pump down for the older man.

"Thanks." Chuck placed the pump in a little wagon and rubbed his shoulder with a tanned, leathery hand. "Sometimes I forget I'm not quite as young as I used to be." He winked at her before tugging the wagon back into the front office.

"But you're not old yet. How's your shoulder doing?"

"Better, thanks. Most days it feels fine, as long as I don't try to reach for anything over my head." He glanced up to the empty spot where the pump had been. "They released me from physical therapy last week. Doc says this is probably as good as it'll get. Says swimmin' is good for it. Maybe I'll get Steve to take me out lobstering to keep it moving."

Kate smiled. "That's a good way to keep in shape for sure. You still using that antique regulator?" She nodded at the small pile of dive gear resting on a cluster of tanks.

"Kept me alive this long. No reason to change now."

"He's got a group going out to the Vandenberg on Wednesday."

"I heard. Justin's gonna go since someone here didn't want the ride."

"News travels fast, huh? You know tourists and I don't mix well."

"You picked the wrong place to live, kiddo. Ain't nobody makin' it around here without 'em."

"I'm doing fine, thanks."

He raised an eyebrow as the corner of his mouth ticked up in an impish grin. "Well, yeah, since you ain't got slip rent to worry about."

"You'd be miserable here without me. Your place'd get broken into every other day without Whiskey keeping people honest. Besides, you'd never get anyone else to give you three dollars for that mudhole you call a slip anyway." She winked. "So, I need a couple lengths of PVC and a washer for my deck sink. Got anything along these lines hiding back there? Save me a trip to town?"

He looked at the parts in her hand, then shuffled off to the back room muttering to himself. He returned with a faucet kit box in his hand.

"Chuck, I just need the pipe and a washer."

"Take the whole thing and make some room in my shop. Please."

Kate slapped a twenty-dollar bill on the counter. It was all she had in her pocket. "I'll give you more after Danny's check comes in."

He pushed the bill back toward her. "It was collecting dust back there, anyway. Take it."

"No. You let me dock here for free, and I appreciate it. But if I need a part, I'll pay for it."

"Kate, honey, I don't 'let' you anything. The Good Book says care for the widows and orphans. This is my way of doin' that."

Kate squirmed.

"Besides, you're right. Ain't nobody givin' me a cent for that slip, anyway. But the ponies were rough on me last weekend, so if you insist ..." He winked at her and tucked the twenty into his pocket. "Oh, hey. Got a new guy name of Branson Tillman playing on the deck tonight, and whatever's fresh'll be on the grill."

"Save me a seat at the bar." Kate tucked the box

under her arm then started toward the front office. The door jingled as a wiry form filled the doorway.

Chuck tensed.

Kate glanced at the new arrival. The man's hairline was receding, and brand new Oakleys perched on the bridge of his narrow nose. From his perfectly-starched open-collar to the smooth leather dock shoes, the man screamed Miami. She hadn't been a cop's wife very long, but Danny had taught her to size people up quickly and slot them into Friend or Foe.

And nothing about this guy looked friendly.

CHAPTER THREE

Kate rubbed her shoulder where the stranger had bumped her on her way out of the office. The sun warmed her skin, but the thin blonde hairs on her arm stood on end. She shook it off.

Not my monkey, not my circus. That sink isn't going to fix itself.

As she started across the parking lot, she scanned the back of the faucet box, hoping for a link to installation videos. But she couldn't put Miami Guy out of her mind. Chuck clearly recognized the man but didn't introduce him. She sensed neither of them had wanted her to know who he was.

Kate figured she should respect that and just go fix *Serenity*. Chuck's business was his business, like hers was her own. One of the things she loved most about the Conch life was the special culture among the full-time residents. When storms came or disaster struck, the little community took care of each other without hesitation. But a lot of locals had come here running from something. So no one asked questions they didn't need the answers to, and they didn't get involved in anyone else's business unless invited. And asking for help wasn't really Kate's way. Or Chuck's.

But the lanky visitor nagged at her. She stole another look back toward the marina office. Through the wide front window, she saw the two men arguing. Her hairs still on end, she turned and followed the hedge along the edge of the parking lot and around to the side of the sturdy little office building. She crouched below the open jalousie window.

"I notice you seem to have a little *problem*." The stranger's voice was the kind that couldn't be quiet if he tried. And he wasn't trying.

"I just ... I ... I need a little more time, that's all."

"You've had time, and yet you're falling further behind."

Kate heard a stack of papers crash to the floor. She shook her head and crept away from the window to the line of low cocoplum bushes that separated the office from the adjacent bar and restaurant.

She released a low whistle. Moments later, Whiskey appeared at her side. Kate led the dog back to her hiding spot below the window. She tuned out the dog's low pant and listened.

Chuck's voice shook. "Been running this place almost forty years and never had this problem during off-season before. I overpay during season so I can miss a few when it gets slow. That's what everyone does."

"I don't care what everyone does. Only what you do. Your loan documents say your payments are due on the first of every month. Every month, not just the months when tourists are here." He paused. "This doesn't have to be a problem, though." Kate noticed the man's voice carried an uncomfortable tone as he lowered it.

"I'm not selling."

"That's an unfortunate choice for you."

"This place has been in my family for three generations. It's rightfully mine, and I'm keeping it."

"I'm afraid that's simply not possible. Either you sell or the bank will file for foreclosure."

"My lawyer says—"

"I care about your lawyer even less. He even thinks about getting in the middle of this, and he'll be giving the gators indigestion before the sun sets."

Kate leaned her head against the cool concrete block. *What have you gotten yourself into, Chuck?*

After a moment, Chuck's voice carried out the window, tinged with desperation. "I'm sorry. I'll be caught up again soon. I know all the slips are empty now, but I've got reservations. Every slip will be full two months from now, and I'll pay everything I owe and more."

"You don't have two months. You barely have two weeks. Sell to me now, and you can walk away with enough to get a little trailer on the mainland. Miss the next payment, this place belongs to me. And you'll get nothing."

"'I've got deposits. I can come up with some now ...'"

Kate heard a crash, and the hair on Whiskey's shoulder's bristled. Chuck yelped.

She crept down the wall and around the corner, Whiskey sticking close behind. Staying low, she peeked through the glass door. The intruder had shoved Chuck against the counter, holding his bad arm wrenched behind his back. She spotted a bulge at the small of the man's back in the waistband of his crisp khakis. Kate cracked the office door for Whiskey to slip his nose in.

"Go," she whispered. The powerful dog burst inside.

"What the ..." The man released Chuck and spun around at the sound of the jingling bell as Whiskey launched up and over the counter, latching onto the man's arm. Arms and tail flailed. The intruder stumbled back into the open space toward the door, knocking down a shelf filled with marine toilet paper and sunscreen.

"Get off! Get him off me! Let go, you bastard!"

The harder the intruder fought, the tighter Whiskey held. As Whiskey tugged the man toward the center of the room, Kate called, "Whiskey, leave it."

The dog released the man and returned to Kate's side. Kate examined the interloper.

"You're not from around here, are you?"

"I'll call animal control!" The man clutched his arm, his shirt stained with blood and drool.

"No, you won't. Assault, intimidation, carrying an unlicensed firearm? You're nowhere close to legal here, so we all know this didn't happen. Now take your brand-new shoes and shuffle your tail out of here. As for the dog, he's had his shots. Take two aspirin, and don't call in the morning. Don't call, ever. Now go, or he'll find a more vulnerable spot to bite next."

Whiskey growled as the man scuttled out of the office. He piled into a shiny silver Mercedes before speeding away, tires squealing. Kate ordered Whiskey to stay by the door. She picked her way through the clutter then helped Chuck to a tattered office chair.

"What was ..." she paused. "You know, I don't want to know. You okay? Want me to call the police?"

Chuck shook his head and rubbed his shoulder. His gaze locked on the dog. "You're right. You don't want to know. And no, I don't want the police involved. They'd never make anything stick, and it'd create problems for you and Whiskey. But thanks, anyway."

"It's good for him to get a little taste of jerk human every now and then. Keeps him on his toes. Just don't make this a habit, okay?"

Chuck nodded and shooed Kate out of the office. "Flip the sign on your way out, wouldja please?"

The door jingled again, then a black sign swung back and forth, its bright orange block letters announcing the office was closed for the day.

CHAPTER FOUR

"Morning, Capt'n!" Kate looked up from the parts strewn on her deck and waved at the lean black man approaching her stern.

Beyond the few skiffs and dinghies tied up along the dock, a white forty-four-foot catamaran sparkled in the mid-morning sun. She'd met the captain of the *Knot Dead Yet* and his wife when they arrived a few days before. After they had settled in, they invited Kate up the dock to share a burger and a bottle of pinot noir. The couple were slowly cruising through the Keys, moving a few miles every couple of weeks. It had been the standard first night conversation, with talk of their early retirement and their travels. While the people chatted, Whiskey met their very spoiled Shih Tzu, Muffin.

They'd asked Kate how she'd gotten *Serenity* into the shallow slip. The *Knot* was almost scraping bottom at low tide at the deeper end of the dock. But they'd wanted a slip with a sunset view. Sunset in the Keys is as close to religion as a lot of Conchs get, with many stopping wherever they were to pause and reflect on another day in paradise. This couple was no exception, and they seemed excited to share their first one at Shark Key with Kate.

Kate had grown to appreciate the loose social connections of marina life. When she moved onto the houseboat, she expected solitude. But she discovered something better. Everyone was friendly, but no one got too close. When a new boat showed up at a marina for the first time, cruisers swapped introduction stories over a drink and sometimes a meal. Whenever someone needed a repair, the others would surely pitch in and help. But eventually, after a day or a week or a month, nearly everyone moved on. They were a community for the moment, but no one got too attached, and that was fine by Kate.

"Been up for breakfast yet?"

Between liveaboards and day charter guests, the marina's restaurant did a brisk breakfast trade during tourist season, keeping a full staff of cooks and servers busy starting at 5:00 a.m. from December through April. But during the off-season, Chuck and his best friend, Babette Wilcox, usually handled breakfast and lunch on their own.

Kate glanced at her watch. Ten after ten. Her breakfast had been an orange and a protein bar three hours ago, and she was already starting to think about lunch. "I was up at the office a little bit ago. Chuck's tied up this morning, but I'm sure Babette can still whip you up some eggs and bacon."

The captain — Kate thought his name was Bruce, or maybe it was Howard — tapped his hat and nodded as he trotted past her stern and up the seawall to the parking lot. Kate turned back to the stubborn length of PVC. She tightened a fitting, flipped the water valve, then swore as it immediately started leaking again.

Ten minutes later, Kate tucked her toolbox into the storage compartment beneath the aft deck. She'd have to go to town after all, but it could wait. She stepped into the dark salon. Like most residents of the Sunshine State, she kept the blinds closed in the summer so the poor old air conditioning unit had a chance of keeping up. In another month or so, the weather would finally start to relent, but she was already looking forward to letting in a little more light.

She grabbed an old one-piece from the bedroom, changed, then launched off the bow of *Serenity* into the shallow salt water. She angled slightly to the north, settling into a steady freestyle pace across the channel, breathing every third stroke. Almost twenty minutes later, her hands scraped the sandy bottom of Halfmoon Key.

Kate pulled herself onto the shore and shook off. The small island west of Shark Key was uninhabited, and the waters around it were so shallow, only the smallest flats skiffs and kayaks could reach it. Its narrow beach faced east, nestled up against the low mangroves covering the uninhabited key.

Just inside the tree line, Chuck had placed a water-tight deck box to store basic beach gear. She lifted the lid then rummaged through it for a dry towel.

I'll swing by with a kayak later and throw all these towels in the wash.

Kate made a mental note, but she knew she'd forget at least three times and Babette would end up washing the towels. She always did. Across the water, she watched the white catamaran's mast sway as its occupants moved around it.

William! That's his name. William. William. William.

She knew she'd forget that, too.

Kate retrieved a red and green striped towel from the bottom of the box, sniffed it, shrugged. She shook out the wrinkles then spread the towel on the tiny stretch of sand.

When Kate first headed for the Keys, she'd imagined huge swaths of white sand. In time, she'd grown to love the rocky shores and heavy growths of mangroves and seagrapes, but she was also grateful for the few sandy, soft spots in the area to rest in the middle of her morning swim.

She stretched her body flat and focused on her breathing — the oxygen passing through her nose and down into her lungs, the slow exhale through pursed lips. Her belly rose and fell in time with the water lapping against the shore. After a few grounding breaths, she drew her knees up to her chest, rocked side to side, then rolled up to sitting. She eased through a series of yoga positions, her body shifting from pose to pose by habit.

Kate ended the routine flat on her back, staring up at the clouds. Closing her eyes, she soaked in the briny smell of the salt on her skin. Tiny waves lapped against the shore, and the mangroves rustled in the light breeze.

Her thoughts drifted. A different, smaller sky filled her mind. In her memory, she looked up a short concrete driveway leading to a vinyl-sided house where, at the end of a narrow sidewalk, its dark green front door hung ajar.

Floating through the memory, Kate stepped through the door then across a small ceramic tile foyer. In the family room, a ceiling fan slowly spun, and an athlete sprinted across the TV screen. A rusty, metallic scent coated the roof of her mouth. She tried to will herself back outside, but her memory took her toward the hallway.

Kate forced open her eyelids. The mid-morning Florida sun burned into her retinas. She jerked her head toward the thick bushes behind her and scanned for movement. An iguana scurried up into the shade and froze. Her gaze searched the empty shore then landed on the lizard. She pulled a deep breath of sea air into her lungs, held it, slowly pushed it back out. Kate counted every breath, every leaf on a seagrape bush. She counted driftwood chunks resting at the tide mark then dock pilings across the channel. Eventually, her heart rate dropped and her breathing steadied. She'd been running from the same nightmare for two years. No matter how far south she ran, it found her.

Kate gazed back toward the marina. Whiskey sat at attention on the roof deck of her boat. They'd both grown comfortable at the marina, but the morning's trouble was bound to throw both of them back into old memories.

She gathered up the towel, shook it free of sand, bundled it back in the dry box. Took in the wide view of the west shore of Shark Key. It was a good place to stop running.

Kate waded to where the water was waist deep, dove in, then swam back to *Serenity*.

CHAPTER FIVE

Vincent Holt wiggled his car into a spot against the curb a block from The Dollhouse. The car alarm chirped as he dragged his feet up the cracked concrete sidewalk. He hadn't walked five yards, and his Hawaiian shirt was already dripping with sweat. Lush tropical plantings around all the historic vacation rentals taunted him behind their white picket fences. Shade for the rich tourists. Hot pavement for Vince.

He'd done a lot of jobs for Monty Baumann over the years, and if he'd learned anything, it was that loyalty was his boss's love language. And the man inspired it not by great leadership, but by threats and intimidation. Baumann owned enough of the Keys and the people living there that saying no to him was simply not an option. So when Vince's phone chimed with a text summoning him to meet Baumann for a late lunch at The Dollhouse, Vince knew he'd be sitting at the booth ten minutes early.

He stepped into the cool, dark bar. Settling into his usual booth near the back, he scanned the thin crowd. Two new girls twirled on the bar above a row of empty stools. A few men and two women sat at tables scattered around a tiny stage. In the center of the room, a group of rowdy twenty-somethings waved dollar bills at the dancers. A particularly loud one seemed hell-bent on convincing a redhead that he was chosen as Best Man because of his talents with the women.

Vince nodded at the bartender. Two minutes later, a blonde appeared at his table. She teased the long neck of a beer bottle up and down between her massive fake breasts before resting it on a cocktail napkin in front of Vince with a wink. He felt both stirred and revolted.

"Do you think I'd ..." He looked her up and down, eyes landing in her deep cleavage.

"I thought maybe." She dropped her chin and tried to catch his eye.

"You should know by now."

"Always a first time, once a guy gets lonely enough."

"Who's to say I'm lonely?"

"You got the look, honey. I see 'em all here. A guy's got someone at home but wants a little spice? He's got a certain look. A guy's lonely? It's in his eyes. You've got lonely eyes, Vince. Someday, it'll be too much. And when that day comes, you know where to find me."

Vince stared at her chest. "Not likely." He slipped a five-dollar bill into her cleavage then patted her back as she drifted away. The door opened. A thin, sallow man in a linen jacket walked to the bar then ordered a bourbon and water. After Vince caught his eye, the lanky man joined him. One of the new girls sauntered over to offer them a private dance. Vince tucked another five in her g-string and told her to get lost. Then he looked at his tablemate. "Little hot for a jacket, isn't it, boss?"

Baumann shook his head and swirled the ice in his glass. "I've got something for you."

"I'm listening."

"Nothing fancy, but it's important it's done fast and right." Baumann's pocket buzzed. He held one finger up and answered the call. It was more consideration than Vince had ever seen from the man.

"He WHAT?" Baumann's shout startled a waitress three tables away. He dropped his voice and slid deeper into the tall booth. "He still in the lockup?" He tapped his fingers on the rim of his glass while he listened. "Okay. Get a message to Axl. Tell him to take care of it before the arraignment." He tapped his screen then dropped the phone into the inside pocket of his jacket.

"Everything okay?"

"Dumb-ass new kid working security for a site up

on Big Pine got yanked early this morning, and he thinks he's on Law and Order. Spilling his guts, trying to get a deal."

Vince cringed.

"Kids these days have no sense of loyalty. Now, you? You get it. You'd never flip on me. Right, Vincent?" Baumann lifted his glass and leveled his stare directly across the table.

"Of course not, sir. I'd take a bullet for you. You know that." Betraying Baumann was unthinkable. But Vince was starting to get tired of living under the threat.

"You know that old man who runs the marina on Shark Key?"

Vince jerked his attention back to his employer and nodded.

"I need you to sit on his place. Two things. The main gig is the owner. We had a bit of a disagreement this morning, and I need him to see his way clear to understand my point of view. The second is some meddling bitch lives on a houseboat there. Her dog did this." Baumann slipped his jacket off his shoulder to expose a bloody, torn shirtsleeve barely covering a thick bandage wrapped around his arm. "She needs to understand that no one touches Monty Baumann."

"That's it?"

"That's it."

"Just understanding? Not out of the picture in a more permanent way?"

Baumann took a slow sip of his bourbon. "Don't get excited. You'll only make things worse. Keep it simple. Deliver the message."

Vince laughed. "Where's the fun in that?"

"If it was fun, it wouldn't be a job."

Vince clinked his bottle against the man's bourbon glass then turned his attention to the girls.

CHAPTER SIX

As THE SUN drifted lower to the west, the sound of an acoustic guitar floated across the cove. Kate's stomach grumbled. She had a small grill on her top deck, but no matter what she did, she'd never match Chuck's prowess with fresh fish.

She unlocked the top drawer of her desk, retrieved a narrow accordion folder, then thumbed through sections labeled "Groceries," "Phone," "Fun," until she found the one labelled "Eating Out" and pulled out a ten-dollar bill. She flipped to the one labelled "Beer" but found it empty. She glanced at the calendar and counted. Danny's pension deposited on the twentieth. Three more days. She could go three days with what was already in her fridge. She moved the remaining cash from "Groceries" into "Beer." Then she moved it back.

She tucked the ten in her pocket, locked the desk

drawer, nodded at Whiskey. Pulling himself up into a lazy stretch, he grunted, then wagged his tail once and trotted out the door behind her.

Kate picked up a chunk of driftwood and threw it for him as they made their way up the lane to the wide deck at the north point of the island. Branson Tillman was still setting up, and about a third of the tables were occupied, mostly with locals. It was a busy night for off-season. Kate dropped onto a stool at the bar. Whiskey curled onto the floor at her feet.

"Hey, Babette."

The broad-shouldered redhead turned, a huge grin revealing gaps where two of her teeth should have been. Babette and her husband used to live down the lane on the sunrise side of the Key in a used fifth-wheel with a wide deck. He died of a massive heart attack a few years back.

"Katie!"

Kate closed her eyes for a beat. "Only you, Babs."

"I'll call you what I want 'til you sic Whiskey on me." She winked at Kate and planted a cold Kalik on the bar.

"Oh, sugar! Babs, I'm sorry. I'm drinking water 'til my check comes in."

Babette waved it off. "On the house. So's your grouper platter. Chuck told me what Whiskey did for him this morning. Thanks for watching out for him. Old man wouldn't last a day on his own, would he?" She winked, but the smile had left her eyes.

"He's not *that* old. Look, Chuck's business is his business and none of mine. I'm just curious. How bad is it?"

Babette's face dropped, and she shook her head.

"Hey, sweetcheeks!" A tourist a few seats down called out over the din of the sound check.

Kate threw a glare down the bar and started to climb out of her seat.

"Katie, no. I got this." She turned to the sunburned man. "Hold your horses. I'm coming!" She patted the bar in front of Kate and shrugged. "Chuck will figure it out. Always does." Then she fluttered down the bar and got back to work.

Ten minutes later, a massive plate and a fresh Kalik landed on the bar in front of Kate. She stretched her nose over the plate and slowly sucked in the aroma. The grouper had been swimming in her backyard that morning and was on her plate tonight. Tidy grill marks stretched across the dense flesh of two huge filets resting on a toasted bun with a bed of fresh lettuce and homegrown tomato and a pile of steaming french fries. The filets were dusted with a hint of garlic, cayenne, and allspice. Just enough island jerk to bring out the fish's meaty flavor.

Kate pulled a chunk off one filet and held it an inch above Whiskey's nose. The dog sat tall, drooling and trembling. She bobbed her chin, barely more than a twitch, then he snatched the morsel. It disappeared with one gulp.

"Still don't know how he does that." Chuck settled on the barstool behind Whiskey and scratched the dog's ear.

"Training, that's all. He knows who's in charge, and he respects the chain of command."

"Thanks again for this morning. I'm sorry to have gotten you two involved in my mess."

Kate shrugged. "Your business is your business."

He looked around the bar, his gaze landing everywhere except on Kate. She took a huge bite of her grouper sandwich and waited.

"Well ..." he started, then paused.

Kate offered a fry to Whiskey.

"I've got a problem," Chuck finally managed.

Kate raised an eyebrow.

"Look, this isn't how I like to do things. Shark Key has been in my family for three generations. My grandfather came down here from Chicago when the railroad was the only way to get this far. He helped build the Overseas Highway. I've lived on this land my entire life, and I've never been further north than Hialeah." He squirmed. "I've had offers on it from time to time — good offers — but this is my home. I was born on Shark Key, and I'll die on it, too. It's gotten a little tight the last few years, though, what with the repairs from the big one a few years back and new building codes and taxes and all. I had to take a loan against the property, and, well ..."

Kate listened as Tillman drifted into a Bob Marley tune.

"A big-time developer from the mainland wants the Key. He wants it bad, and he smells blood in the water. He's the guy Whiskey got a taste of this morning. I'm sure you heard some of it. And yeah, I missed a couple payments. I've been skipping or shorting them during the off-season for years, and it's always been fine with the bank. I pay ahead when I can, and they let me slide when it's slow. But this year is different. This guy is on the bank's board, and he's pushing them to call the loan if I miss the next payment. Which I'm gonna miss. Until the tourists start showing up in a couple months, I'm barely making enough to cover food and utilities and pay Babette and Justin. I hate even having to say this out loud, but I need help."

His eyes pleaded with Kate. She sat stone-still while her mind charged into a thousand dark corners.

"Kate, your business is yours and mine is mine. I know you've needed space to deal with your demons, and I haven't asked you any questions. But I know a little about where you come from. The trust fund and all."

Kate pulled a long breath through her teeth.

"Do you think your parents would be willing to invest? I'd keep all the risk, all the responsibility. They'd get it all back by the end of next season, and after that, it'd be gravy for them. I just need a little bridge."

Kate counted the bottles standing in rows behind the bar.

"God, I'm sorry." Chuck suddenly looked down at his flip-flops. "I don't want to get into your business, Kate. I just ... Remember I met them that one time they came down? He mentioned he was in real estate?" He let the reminder hang.

"Yeah. The time they came down." She focused on the smell of the grouper on her plate. "The time they spent three minutes on *Serenity*, then told me I was wasting my journalism degree? That I needed to get a real job and quit being selfish? Or the time my mother said she was ashamed to tell her bridge club her daughter lived on a broken-down boat in the Keys? Or maybe you mean the time my father told me if I married a cop, I'd better take his name because he wouldn't consider me a Kingsbury? Yeah, Chuck. I remember." Her already-dry voice flattened to bitter. "I'm sorry, but I'm afraid they aren't really an option."

Chuck rested a hand on her arm. "I'm sorry, kiddo. I didn't know."

Kate pulled away from him and stuffed a cold French fry in her mouth. After a pause, she managed to meet his gaze. "It's okay, I guess. I chose this. After ... it happened. After Danny ..." She shrugged. "I figured out what was important. Life is short and it's precious. I'm not going to waste it as a slave to my parents' expectations, and I'm not going to waste it getting bound up for anyone else. Ever. That's all. So yeah, there's a price for everything, right?"

Chuck slowly nodded. "Yeah. There is."

The two sat in silence as the guitarist sang.

As Kate handed the remaining fish down to Whiskey, she noticed Chuck staring at a framed photo of an elderly man on the north point of the key, where the edge of the deck stood now.

"Who's that?"

Chuck scanned the deck. "Who's who?"

"The photo. Up behind the bar."

"Oh. That's ... Come to think of it, maybe there's one more option."

CHAPTER SEVEN

KATE SIPPED her beer and waited for Chuck to continue.

"When I was a kid ... This already sounds like a crazy old man story. I'm not a crazy old man. I'm not even sixty yet. Let's get that right from the start?"

She nodded, but in her mind, the jury was still out.

"I was born on this island. My mom and dad were high school sweethearts. They married right after graduation, and my grandpa built a house for them as a wedding gift. Same house I'm in now. They loved the flats, and all they ever wanted was to stay and help Gramps run the place.

"Anyway, it was the sixties. Vietnam was heating up, and in the beginning, people believed in what we thought we were doing there. So Dad drove down to the recruiter's office and enlisted. He was able, and it was the right thing to do. I had just turned six. Like so many did that year, he came back in a flag-covered coffin. And like so many widows did back then, Mom just fell apart."

It was familiar territory. And all too fresh and raw. Every muscle in her body clenched. Whiskey pulled his body against her leg, and she started counting bottles.

"Oh, Kate. I'm sorry. I didn't ..." He waited.

After a few seconds, she turned back to him. "It's okay. Go on."

"Well, Mom started spending more and more time in the bars. Gramps tried to get her into rehab, but she couldn't stay clean. I was nine when they found her body in a flophouse. Gramps buried her with Dad in the cemetery downtown, and then it was just him and me."

Chuck stood and hitched up his pants. "Come here." He took Kate's hand and led her to the south edge of the deck. Low, thick mangrove hedges stretched down the shore on either side of the long, narrow island. Beyond the lush greenery, tips of masts bobbed in the current.

"Every year or so, we'd put in one more new thing." He pointed around the property as he talked. "Longer docks. Camper hookups. We added a kitchen to the bar. New fuel pumps. Little by little, we built this place together, Gramps and me. I hated going to school, not because I didn't like studying, but because I loved helping him here more."

Chuck gazed down toward the line of docks on the sunset side where *Serenity* sat with her hull skimming the sandy bottom. "He was old when my dad was born. Older still after Mom died. No man in his seventies should have to raise a kid. But he did it, and he never complained. Not a word to me or to anyone else for that matter. Sometimes I'd find him sitting out at the end of the sunset dock — right out by your slip — sipping on a beer and watching the water. I always imagined he was thinking about what life would have been like if things had been different. If Grandma hadn't run out on him. If Dad had come back from 'Nam. If Mom had stayed clean and raised me. If he'd have been able to retire and just watch the tide flow in and out. But every now and then, maybe two or three times a year, he'd take off in his boat for a couple days. Never told me where he went, and I never asked. Seemed to be something he needed to do. And it seemed right to let him have that because mostly he just worked hard around here."

He turned around and leaned on the deck railing. "By the time I graduated, he was getting up there. And he wasn't thinking quite straight anymore. He'd get confused about who'd paid their slip fees, or he'd accidentally quote someone a rate from the fifties. So I kinda took over. I don't think he really noticed. Just did less and less until mostly what he did was sit on the porch over there in his rocker and watch the tide."

She followed his gaze and waited. Just like she had

painful baggage, so did he, and in her experience, people sometimes needed a minute to find the strength to carry it.

Chuck stared across the water, then pushed back off the rail. Then together they ambled back toward the bar, Whiskey trailing behind them.

"As I took over the books, we hit a wall growing things around here. Seemed we were only taking in enough to keep up, not enough to cover new projects like Gramps had before. And there was always something needed fixin'. The walk-in or the air conditioner would die. Dock boards needed replaced. I never quite figured out how he'd managed cash flow. To be honest, I didn't think all that hard about it. Not as hard as I should have, anyway. I just started borrowing when I needed to. Like when I put in this deck a few years after he died. Even though I paid ahead when I could, I still kept falling further and further behind til I had to mortgage the place to cover the new fuel tanks the thieves at the EPA made me put in."

Chuck pulled two more beers from the cooler and handed one to Kate. She took a pull, then picked at the label, waiting for him to go on.

He drained half the bottle before continuing. "Still nags at me. He always prided himself on giving locals the lowest slip rates in the Lower Keys — especially the native Conchs. He always tried to help widows, and during the war, he always hired the boys who'd lost their daddies in 'Nam. We never had a lot, but we always had enough. So how'd he keep up with all the new projects around here?" He shrugged and turned toward the stage where the guitarist was just wrapping up his set. As the crowd cheered, Chuck led Kate up to the stage.

"Hey, Branson. This is Kate. She lives aboard the old houseboat at the end of the west dock."

Branson stretched his hand over the body of his guitar and shook Kate's. "Nice to meet you, Kate."

"Likewise. Your music is good. How long have you been playing?"

He rested his guitar on a stand. "Down here? About three years. Came down from Maine when my boss decided he didn't want to run a business anymore. I figured it was time to take my fate into my own hands. Literally. Packed up the six-string and headed south, and I've never looked back."

"Well, it was a good decision. They love you."

"I've been lucky to develop a few good fans who help spread the word when I play somewhere new." He turned to Chuck. "You've got a great place here. Thanks for letting me play." He nodded his farewell, then drifted down to greet the crowd.

Chuck looked across the deck out to the water. "You probably don't remember much of the eighties, do you?"

"Where'd that come from?" Kate laughed. "I was born in eighty-six, so not too much, no."

"Well, back then, we didn't have such thing as

reality TV. We had reality, period. Anyway, back then, live TV shows were a big event. And one of the biggest was when Geraldo Rivera made a huge deal of opening up a secret vault that had supposedly belonged to Al Capone."

"I think I heard something about that. But what does that have to do with anything?"

"The whole thing was a huge fiasco. They'd promoted the hell out of it, and they expected to find piles of money or dead bodies ... something dramatic. When they opened it, it was totally empty. A complete anticlimax. But Gramps was crazy over it. He was pretty out of it by then, but every time an ad for the show came on, he went nuts. He'd point at the TV and laugh his head off. And he kept reminding me to make sure we were in front of the TV before it started. He didn't want to miss a minute of it."

Visitors were drifting to the west railing to watch the sunset. A greasy Magnum wannabe in a Hawaiian shirt and a baseball cap scooted down to make room, then they all stared at the blazing orange ball sinking toward the horizon.

Chuck dropped his voice to nearly a whisper, picking up the story as if he'd never stopped speaking. "I figured Gramps was trying to connect with his youth. He'd been in his twenties during Capone's heyday. He was originally from Chicago, and he'd met Grandma in a speakeasy, so I was sure it was a reminder of all the fun times. But when the show started, it was like he knew it was gonna be empty. Everyone expected them to find *some*thing. Everyone except Gramps. He started pointing at the screen before Geraldo opened the vault. And all he said was, 'Gotcha, you sick bastard.' Then he just laughed."

Kate watched the horizon. It was too hazy to hope for a green flash, but she quietly watched as the last sliver of the sun faded into the sea.

"He died not too long after that," Chuck continued. "His reaction to the empty vault struck me as odd, but with everything else going on, I pretty much forgot about it. He had some weird notes that referred to Capone in his old papers, but I never bothered to dig any deeper. I figured it might be fun to research after I retired or something. But now, maybe it's my last chance. Kate, it's a long shot, but I think maybe he took whatever was supposed to be in that vault and hid it."

She stared at him. Then she busted a gut. "Dang, Chuck. You nearly got me. That was a long way to go for a laugh, man. How long have you been working on that?" She laughed so hard, she crouched down and buried her face in Whiskey's fur.

Chuck gently rested his hand on her shoulder and pulled her back up.

"Oh." Kate met his gaze, then turned her attention to her ragged flip-flops. When the silence stretched between them, she looked back up. "You're not joking, are you?"

He shook his head.

"You know it sounds insane, right? Al Capone's lost fortune?"

"Yeah. It sounds crazy. But it's all I've got." Chuck's body began to shake, and he started back toward the bar. "I need to come up with a couple million bucks in two weeks, or Baumann is gonna snatch this place out from under me and build some stuffy gated community and fru-fru resort. You and me? We'll be scrapin' up rent money swabbing Steve's deck and kissing tourist butts. I was born on this island. I can't let that bastard steal it from us. You gotta help me, Kate."

CHAPTER EIGHT

VINCE TRACED a pattern through the tiny droplets on his beer bottle. He ignored the crowd and watched as clouds floated above the western horizon. Every nightfall, tourists and locals alike gathered against every west-facing railing in the Keys. And even the cloudiest sunset in the Lower Keys was better than a sunny day in New Jersey. At least, the part of New Jersey he was from.

The sun peeked beneath the cloud cover on its path beyond the horizon. Within moments, dusk settled over the deck. Tiki torches took up the slack, and the thin crowd drifted back to their tables, a few of the tourists shooing stray seagulls from their half-eaten dinners.

Vince returned to his table near the bar then kicked his feet up on the chair opposite him. He sipped his beer slowly and picked at a thread on his shirt.

He'd watched his primary gig — the bar's owner — drift around for the past half hour, checking in with patrons. Finally, the man had paused to speak intensely with a woman sitting alone at the bar with a giant German Shepherd at her feet.

Who brings a filthy animal to a restaurant?

With what he'd overheard during sunset, it could be his lucky day. Just needed to get the chick and the dog out of the way, then figure out how to use this Al Capone-thing to his advantage. Vince drifted up to the bar to eavesdrop, near-empty beer bottle in hand. The dog lady sounded skeptical.

"Chuck, that's a hell of a story, but if I were you, I wouldn't bank my future on it."

"I think it's the only option I've got left. I can't let it go without at least trying."

"What about other banks? Refinancing? You've got to hold enough equity..."

The bar owner shook his head. "Tried 'em all. Cash flow isn't good enough, especially right now. But once I get the docks upgraded and put in new fuel pumps, I can ..."

The man droned on. Vince fought down a sneer — a month from now, this whole island would be bull-dozed and Baumann would be laying the foundation of his newest playground for his rich friends.

Can't build it without me. Won't let me near the place once it's open.

Vince watched the bar owner while the woman

yapped. "Don't you just need enough to get caught up on your payments?"

The man's shoulders dropped even further. "It should be that easy, but this ain't no home loan. Baumann is on the board, and he wants this land. After they foreclose, he'll buy it from them for four times what I owe, which isn't even a quarter what it's worth. The bank wants me to default as much as Baumann does. They're in bed together to steal this place out from under me and make a killing."

"Why didn't he just try to buy it from you?"

"He did. Shark Key isn't for sale. But apparently it's available for the taking."

Baumann already owned half of the Lower Keys, and he was maneuvering to buy the other half, one twisted arm at a time. Vince's job was secure — he'd done everything from construction site cleanup to running cargo across the Strait to taking care of problems like this Miller guy — but only as long as he delivered. His fingers teased the thick gold chain around his neck. He almost felt sorry for the guy. Baumann was a world class tool. The man would sell his daughter to seal a deal. Probably had. Her slimy dirt-bag husband never could have landed such a rich, hot blonde without paying for it in some manner.

"Kate, I've got nothing left. I know it sounds crazy, but this is my last chance, and I can't do it alone. Please?" The guy sounded like a little kid begging his mom to stay up because there was a monster under his bed.

But this time, the monster was standing at the bar wearing a Hawaiian shirt.

The woman shook her head. "Steve had a really good season. He was planning to upgrade his compressor and nav station. Maybe he can put it off a season and float you a loan?"

"He might, but it's too little too late. Look, Kate. I know you prefer to keep to yourself. I know you don't get in the middle of other people's messes. I know you have your own baggage you're hauling around, and it makes that broken-down boat of yours sit really low in the water. I stay out of it and let you be. But kiddo, this is your home and your haven as much as it is mine. You could find another slip, easy. But going rate would cost you nearly a thousand a month, even with the long-term discount. And you'll be stuck around four-story dry storage and forklifts and concrete. You'll have to go all the way down to Smathers Beach or the community pool for your swims."

Vince looked down the bar for the toothless fat chick. This conversation was more pathetic than he was getting paid to listen to. And it kept getting worse.

"I don't want to sound like your dad or anything, but honey, you'd have to get a job. That little bit you've got coming in from Danny's pension is barely enough for you now. I don't want be a jerk. I don't want to sound selfish. I just need you to see that saving this place is as important to you as it is for me. Kate, please. You need this, and Gramps is our last hope."

The idea of hidden treasure was insane. Vince had seen too many crazy northerners come down searching for Spanish gold and long-lost shipwrecks. He'd crewed for some of them and found a few stray trinkets on the floor of the Straits, but enough rich men had invested more than enough money for Vince to know that there was nothing left for the random explorer to find.

But the old man seemed convinced. Vince nursed his beer and wandered down toward the docks. He was tired. Tired of standing around, watching and waiting. Of threatening and roughing up people whose only crime was enough bad luck to get on the wrong side of the boss. Of evenings at The Dollhouse, then waking up alone.

Flipping on Baumann could cost Vince his life, but if the grandfather had really hidden something valuable enough to save the island, it could be enough to buy a new life away from all this. He was ready for a change, and maybe his best chance was to let Chuck lead him to it. But first, he needed to deal with the woman.

CHAPTER NINE

Kate slipped off the barstool then tapped the side of her leg. Whiskey jumped to attention.

Chuck took her hand. "Please. Just think about it."

She shook her head and squeezed his fingers. "I can't, Chuck. I can't." When she walked away from the bar, Whiskey followed her down the steps.

Melodic steel drums faded as she crossed the small, crushed-gravel parking lot. Warm, humid air hung heavy and still. Just another week or two, then the heat would break, leaving the locals about six weeks of pleasant weather before the snowbirds began to migrate south to their campers and condos. The money they brought with them made life in the Keys possible for most of the residents — there was little industry there that didn't spring from tourism in some way or another. But the footprint the interlopers left behind every spring lingered longer each year. The newspaper was filled with stories of drunken tourists befouling their island paradise, and the streets were littered with yesterday's newspaper.

At first, the Keys were simply a place for Kate to escape, and she had come to love the quiet haven she'd found. The idea of a bully taking this spot to build another gaudy money-trap and running out native Conchs like Chuck was appalling. But Kate had come to the Keys to avoid drama, not to get mired down in someone else's problems. She'd seen enough trouble on the mainland to last her a lifetime. And then some.

She picked up a chunk of driftwood and held it up in front of Whiskey.

"What do you think, buddy? Our home sweet home isn't going much of anywhere. Maybe we pack what can fit in the car and just start driving? Feel like a road trip, boy?" She tossed the wood toward their dock. Whiskey bolted after it. He met her halfway across the parking lot, and she tossed it again, landing it on the dock a few feet from where *Serenity*'s stern line was tied off. The boat sat low in the water below the dock, leaning a little as the port side hull scraped the shallow bottom on an extraordinarily low spring tide.

The dog ran for the driftwood but pulled up short, his hair bristling and a deep growl forming in his chest. Kate drew up behind him. In the shadows of the full moon, she noticed a form settled into one of the folding chairs on the deck outside her door.

She patted the dog on the neck. "Can I help you?"

As she drew closer, she saw a walking cliché — the Hollywood version of a New Jersey mobster in all his Godfather glory. He was thin and swarthy, with dark, slicked back hair and a chunky gold chain. Instead of the ubiquitous pinstriped suit, he wore a tacky Hawaiian shirt. But it was the way he moved that told her he wasn't a wannabe. The man held himself like every enforcer she'd met covering organized crime back in New York.

Crap.

"If you're here about the dog ..."

He stood then took a step forward.

Whiskey quivered beside Kate, anticipating his release command.

"Stay."

The dog held in place in the parking lot, watching closely as Kate approached the man standing on her boat. She stopped on the dock near the stern cleat.

"Thing's a menace." He rubbed his arm as if he'd been the one Whiskey bit. "Mr. Baumann has every right to report him and have him put down."

"But he won't."

"We haven't decided that yet."

Kate looked him up and down. "Yes, you have. Your boss doesn't want any more attention on his business than I want on mine. That's why you're here and not the cops. So let's settle this now. Why are you trespassing on my boat?"

"I just came by to share a little friendly advice.

CHRIS NILES

Stay out of Chuck Miller's problems." He stepped over the transom then climbed up onto the dock. "You seem like a nice young woman. I'd hate to see anything happen to you or your sweet little pooch over there."

"I appreciate your concern. But my relationship with Mr. Miller is not yours to worry about. And you might want to reconsider that threat."

"Threat? No one is threatening anyone here. I love animals." He took a step toward Kate.

Whiskey launched down the dock and flew at the man. The intruder anticipated the attack and spun off just before the dog made contact. Whiskey's momentum carried him across the dock and into the water of the empty slip beside *Serenity*. Whiskey scuffled to get a foothold, but he was stuck in the water and out of the fight.

Kate planted her feet and dropped her weight lower. "You need to leave."

The man laughed. "I recommend you go ahead and start packing. You won't have a slip for much longer, and this bucket ain't goin' nowhere, darlin.'"

"Go."

"Or what? You'll make me? Is this middle school?"

"Go."

The intruder shrugged, then charged toward Kate. Just as he reached her, she ducked and spun out of his path. Grabbing his arm, she leapt to her feet. His body twisted, landing face down on the dock, his arm wrenched behind him. She dropped

68

her full weight to her knee planted in the small of his back.

"Interesting." His voice was muffled by the rough wooden boards. He powered his body up with his free arm and stood, flinging Kate onto her back. She tucked, rolled backwards, then bounced back up onto her feet. Whiskey barked as he swam around the end of the dock to the shoreline.

"It's okay, boy. I've got this."

The man laughed. Then he charged her, grabbed her by the throat, pressed his thumbs against her airway.

The force of his charge pushed Kate backward. With only a few seconds to break free from the man's powerful grip, Kate dropped her weight onto her back foot. Crossed her arms. Swooped them up between his. She twisted her hands in front of his face, pressed her arms out and down to break his hold. In one fluid arc, she circled her arms around then clapped her open hands against his ears.

He buckled.

Kate slammed her knee upward into his gut. He dropped down hard on the wood planks. Grabbed his head with one hand and his belly with the other, struggling to suck in a breath.

Training dictated the next step was to run and scream for help, but she never expected anyone else to fight her battles for her. She backed down the dock. When her heel hit the first concrete step, she climbed up onto the more solid ground of the seawall. Whiskey pulled himself out of the water then crouched beside her, growling, the salt water dripping from his fur.

While she and Whiskey huddled together panting, she managed a demand between gasping breaths. "You need to leave."

The man reached into his pocket then waved a sand-colored handle. His thumb flicked a lever, releasing a four-inch blade that snapped into place.

Whiskey froze, mid-growl.

The man grinned at Kate. "I'll leave when I'm ready."

He leapt up the two steps to the seawall.

Kate dropped and spun, grabbing his wrist as he came at her. She pushed his arm across his body and crossed her foot in front of his. As the man struggled for balance, Kate clenched her right fingers into a fist then swung. Her knuckles landed against the side of his face three times before he planted his back foot against her weight.

She clutched his wrist with both hands then twisted it backwards. Dropping low and using her body for leverage, she jammed his forearm up into a wrist lock, twisting him onto his back and forcing the knife from his hand. Kate rammed the handle of the knife down into his face. He grabbed his nose with both hands as he rolled onto his side. Blood gushed between his fingers.

Kate kicked him once in the ribs, then backed into the parking lot. "Leave. Now."

He struggled to his feet. Tugged his shirt over his head to mop the blood from his face. "Dumb bitch. I wanted to give you a chance to get out of this. But you've chosen your side. Better watch yourself."

She shifted behind a car as he gingerly moved through the parking lot. Once he passed her, she stepped back down to the seawall then crouched beside Whiskey, still frozen in place.

"Whiskey, buddy. It's okay." Kate held both hands open in front of him and continued whispering words of comfort until the dog relaxed. He shook the remaining saltwater from his thick coat then gingerly stepped toward the dock.

"Come on, boy. You need a nap, and I need a beer."

CHAPTER TEN

Two Years Earlier

THE SUDDEN CLANG of the doorbell jerked Kate back to reality. She pressed her body hard into the back of the chair. Her head flew from side to side, checking for threats. Sunlight streamed through high skylights onto the pale carpet that still smelled of disinfectant.

The doorbell chimed again. Kate peeked through a small fisheye lens in the center of the green steel door. Pete and Jennifer stood on the front step holding a casserole dish covered in tinfoil. Kate froze. If she was still enough, they'd turn around and leave.

"Kate, honey, we know you're in there. We saw your shadow moving. Please let us in for a few minutes? I promise we won't stay long."

Inch by inch, Kate slowly drew her body into a tight ball on the floor in her tile foyer.

"Kate, please."

She clutched her knees to her chest and shut her eyes, praying they'd leave.

"Kate, don't make me use the key."

Crap. The key. Kate had forgotten Danny gave his partner a key the last time they'd gone away for a long weekend. She unclenched, uncurled. Pulled herself to her feet. And after a fortifying breath, unlocked the door.

Jennifer passed the dish to her husband then gently wrapped her arms around Kate, who stood on the white tile, arms at her sides, allowing the hug without returning her friend's affection.

Pete stepped over the threshold, shut the door, then locked it behind him.

Kate met his gaze and gave a curt nod. It was all the acknowledgment she could spare.

He set off for the kitchen, casserole in hand.

She didn't want him in there, but then, she didn't want them in her home, either.

Pete came back then led her to the couch. As they walked to the living room, he glanced at his wife, then back to the kitchen.

Kate hadn't washed a dish since it had happened. The thought of her friend seeing the state of the kitchen was unbearable, but the words wouldn't come to stop her. Jennifer quietly stepped around the corner. Moments later, the utilitarian sounds of running water and clinking dishes drifted to the front of the house.

Curling against the corner of the couch, Kate stared at her bare toes.

Pete wrapped a soft blanket over her shoulders. "It's okay to cry, Kate." He pulled a handkerchief from his pocket and tucked it into her clenched fist.

She shook her head.

"I miss him, too." He pulled her small body against his side. "They tried to give me a new rookie, but I'm not ... I ... I miss him, too."

Kate held her breath. She tipped her head back to keep the tears from spilling down her cheeks.

"It's okay." Pete's lie felt like twice the betrayal in his soft, gentle voice.

"No," she whispered. "It'll never be okay."

He squeezed her shoulders. "Fair enough. How about this? What happened to Danny will never be okay. But you? You can be okay again. It might take a long time, but you can. I promise."

Kate sat limp in his arms as gravity tore the tears from her puffy eyelids, leaving wet trails on her cheeks.

When her friends left an hour later, her kitchen was clean and her stomach was full. She locked the door behind them, went to the hall bathroom, then threw up.

It would never be okay again.

Jennifer stopped by every few days. Kate still couldn't bear to enter the master suite, so Jennifer brought shampoo and a toothbrush to the hall bathroom for her.

She would have ignored the gesture, but Jennifer waited until Kate showered. She also made Kate eat, and after Jennifer left, Kate threw it all up again.

Then she retreated to the corner of the couch to resume staring at the wall.

Eventually, Jennifer brought Pete back.

"Katie, you can't stay like this."

"Do. Not. Call. Me. That."

Pete's mouth twitched into a stifled smile. "At least you care about something. Look, you have to snap out of this. You've got to get back out there and start putting the pieces together for yourself. We can't do this for you forever. You have to eat on your own. You have to think about hygiene." He lifted her chin. "Kate, you have to live for yourself."

She slowly focused on him and nodded. "I think you need to leave now."

The next day, Kate put a For Sale sign in the front yard. The real estate agent brought a team in to clean and stage the house. Kate slept on the couch. She ate cereal and made sure to put the bowl and spoon in the dishwasher when she finished. While she waited for the house to sell, she made herself busy. Took Krav Maga self-defense classes to refresh her skills. Trained hard. Toned up. Won every sparring match.

She still had nightmares.

Then the department asked if she would adopt a retired police dog named Whiskey. She thought maybe he'd make her feel safer, so she said yes.

Two days later, she accepted an offer on the house. She signed a power-of-attorney, packed Whiskey into her Civic, changed her phone number, then headed south.

CHAPTER ELEVEN

WHISKEY SAT on the dock while Kate nestled her last few bottles of Yuengling into a small cooler filled with ice. She climbed the stern ladder to the roof deck, settled into a lounge chair, and snapped her beer cap into a bucket across the deck. It rattled and landed in a deep pile of its brethren.

The dog climbed onto the bow and up the stairs. He nuzzled against her arm then turned three times before curling up beside her chair. His eyes remained alert and trained on her.

Kate scratched behind his ear. "Well, that was something, boy. I don't get to upstage you very often." She tipped her bottle toward him. "Here's to Krav Maga."

Footsteps thudded on the dock.

Whiskey jumped to his feet, shaking.

"Ahoy! Permission to come aboard?" Steve called.

"Jeesh, it's after nine. You're still here? How has your wife not divorced you yet?"

"And give up my paycheck? Why would she do that? She's already got the house to herself."

"That woman is a saint to put up with you."

A high, musical voice drifted up to the roof deck "Yeah, I am, for sure."

"Susan!"

Steve climbed the ladder, his wife right behind him. He reached into the cooler and pulled out two bottles of beer. After opening one, he handed it to his wife, then dropped the cap into the bucket.

Kate gave him the side-eye. "You ask permission to set foot on the boat, but you've got no problem helping yourself to my beer?"

"If you bought better beer, maybe I'd ask."

Kate laughed. "Rookie cop pension doesn't go far enough these days, but my beer is your beer, Captain, whatever it is."

"If you'd work for me more often ..." He let the offer hang in the thick, humid air.

Kate climbed out of her lounge chair and offered it to Susan.

"Thanks." The slight woman perched on its edge. "We can't stay too long, but we were headed to the truck when we heard some commotion over here. Are you okay?"

Kate laughed. "It was a misunderstanding. It's fine. I can take care of myself pretty well."

"Yeah, but it doesn't mean you have to do it alone, either." Steve patted the small of his back.

"I shouldn't have to do it at all. But as long as you're here ..."

Steve sat on the dull, pitted railing and leaned his elbows on his knees.

"Has Chuck mentioned any ... trouble to you?"

"No, but I've noticed a couple of Stock Island's finest scumbags milling around a little more than usual. I wondered if something was up but figured Chuck'd say something if he needed help."

"Well, he's said something to me."

"Go on."

"He's fallen behind, and a developer is pressuring the bank to call in the loan. He's got a couple weeks, tops, to come up with it."

Steve let out a low whistle.

"Yeah. He's got some harebrained story of a hidden treasure from his grandfather he wants me to help him find. I told him I was staying out of it. But that bastard ..." Kate nodded her head toward the parking lot. "He just made it personal."

"Hidden treasure? For real?"

"I don't know. Chuck seems to think there's something to it. His grandfather had some connection to Al Capone or something. Look, I like him. And I love it here. I've got it pretty good, cheap beer notwithstanding. But I'm not interested in getting into someone else's problems."

"I don't know. Sounds like his problems are our problems, too. Regardless, if we can help, shouldn't we?"

Kate shook her head. "What happened just now down on my dock? I handled it. But it's what I came down here to get away from. And it's bad for Whiskey, too. He's been doing great, but then he saw the guy's knife and freaked. I got lucky, but I'm not interested in pushing that luck much further."

"Whiskey freaked? He's the most badass dog I know."

"I never told you the story of how he got retired, did I?"

Steve shook his head.

"I don't know a lot of the details, and honestly, I don't want to know. It pushes a few of my triggers, too. But Whiskey and his handler were out on a call one night when a junkie came at them both with a knife. Whiskey made it. His handler didn't." She crouched down and gently patted the top of the huge dog's head.

"Big guy here was in the vet hospital for three weeks, but he pulled through. They tried to pair him with another handler, but he wouldn't respond. Refused to take commands. Froze up. They couldn't put him back to work. It happened right around the time I lost Danny and ..." Kate looked across the little cove, focused on a point far past the horizon.

Steve and Susan waited.

After a moment, Kate shook her head and rejoined

the group. "So they thought we'd be good for each other, you know? And I guess in a way, we are. We understand each other."

Susan nodded. "Who knew dogs could get PTSD."

"Most people don't ever have to think about it, but yeah. It happens. Dog and handler usually bond really closely. Most of the time, the handlers adopt the dogs when they retire, but sometimes the dog's trauma makes it hard for them to be with a family."

"Well, I'm glad you two found each other. How old is he?"

"He was five when he retired, and it's been two years, so he's seven now. He's starting to feel it a little in his hips, but he's got a lot of spunk in him for an old dog."

"Yeah, our two cockapoos are fourteen and they still play like little puppies. When they're not sleeping, of course." Susan laughed and raised her beer. "To the dogs."

"To the dogs. Cheers."

The three clinked their beer bottles together then drank to man's — and woman's — best friend.

CHAPTER TWELVE

THOUSANDS of tiny bulbs twinkled in the twilight like stars — the only kind Tina would see, since the glow of the boiling city across Biscayne Bay blocked the real ones from view. Delicate strains of classical music from a string quartet drifted on the breeze, mingled with the sound of salt water lapping against the seawall. Guests seeking to escape the crowd on the broad patio meandered in twos and threes around the sweeping lawn.

Behind a tall hedge, beside a droning air conditioning unit, Tina Ransom passed a tray of half-empty glasses and half-full plates to a husky young man wearing a blank stare. "Take those straight back to the kitchen and don't drop any of them this time!"

"Mama, I know. I'm not a idiot."

"Did you know when I handed you the last tray, Lucas?"

The boy nodded.

"But you dropped the last tray. And the one before it. Drop this one, and you'll get fired. And I'll get fired for bringing you along. And then both of us walk outta here with nothin'. You want that, boy?"

Lucas shook his head. "No, Mama. I do not." He slowly turned then squeezed between the thick hedge and the air conditioner to the kitchen's service door.

Tina straightened her narrow black tie, heaved a tray of freshly-filled champagne glasses onto her left forearm, then floated back onto the lawn. She scanned the crowd. Instead of looking for nearly empty glasses, she looked for Rolexes and bluster. She'd never had a dry spell last this long, and she intended to change her luck tonight, if for no other reason than she wanted to never have to risk her reputation again by bringing along a worthless lump of a son. But rent money was rent money, and the end of the month was closing in.

She made her way through the crowd, weaving and pausing between clusters of aging women — the lucky few who enjoyed the temporary upgrade from mistress to wife. Of course, a new mistress would eventually unseat each one, but they'd all walk away with settlements big enough to buy a small Caribbean island. Tina both loathed and envied them.

"I couldn't believe the nerve. The little trash at Hermès refused to show me a Birkin. Stupid little whore treated me like—"

"Oh, you mean that fat one with the straw hair and the spray tan? What's she, like a size six?"

"At least. She might be an eight. I don't know why they don't fire her."

Tina smoothed her polyester slacks down her hips and moved on, trading full glasses for empties, taking orders for cocktails, and, if the price was right, discreetly directing a guest or three to the second-floor restroom where they might happen to stumble across a line of cocaine that someone might have accidentally left on a tray behind a large silk flower arrangement.

She drifted past a cluster of men holding glasses of clear amber scotch.

"Can always tell a novice. They love Macallen 12. It's worth the price to just see their faces when they get their first taste of lowland peat."

She moved on, remembering there might be a little Jose Cuervo left in the bottle on top of her refrigerator, as long as Lucas hadn't gotten to it first. The conversations were all the same.

"...had a four handicap, and almost drove the cart into that water hazard on fourteen..."

"...hired a Dominican batting coach, if you can believe..."

"...next project should be opening to investors by November. I'm closing a great deal on Shark Key in a couple weeks..."

Tina stopped short and almost toppled all the glasses on her tray. Grandma Gigi's gravelly voice echoed in her head. *Shark Key, my shriveled ass.*

She leaned in toward the clump of men. The one

speaking was dressed in a white dinner jacket, black slacks, and a black bow tie. Had a receding hairline, narrow nose. "...closest undeveloped island east of Key West. It's a little over sixty acres, and all that's on it right now is a rundown campground, marina, and local dive bar. The owner is a schlub named Miller. Been in his family for generations. I'm on the board of the bank that's holding the note, and he's about to default. I'm getting it for a song. If you come in on it now, there's no way you can lose..."

Miller. Shark Key. Tina shoved the last four glasses of champagne from her tray into the first empty hands she saw then scurried back behind the hedge. She pulled a soft pack of Marlboro reds from her pants pocket, and had to press the side of her palm against the cement block wall to steady her lighter.

Mama said Grandma Gigi's stories were nothing more than the lies of a crazy, washed up dancing girl. But they all started in Prohibition-era Chicago with Al Capone and ended at Shark Key — colorful tales of secret vaults and stolen trucks and a mad road trip covering most of the eastern part of the country with her first husband, a guy named Tommy Miller.

Tina leaned her back flat against the concrete wall and sucked another drag off her cigarette. If Tommy Miller and Shark Key were real, then so was the loot they took from Capone's vault. And if Grandma Gigi had risked her life to steal it, then Tina had every right to her share of it.

She stomped out the cigarette, left the butt in the sandy soil. Sweeping down the hedgerow, she caught Lucas coming out of the kitchen, grabbed him by the collar, then pulled him into the parking lot.

"We've got a new gig, kiddo. Ever been to Key West?"

CHAPTER THIRTEEN

KATE TOOK a deep breath and stretched. The moon hung high over the calm little cove at Shark Key by the time Steve and Susan climbed down the ladder and dropped their bottles in the blue recycling bin at the edge of Chuck's parking lot. She watched their car creep between the seagrapes through the campground then down the gravel lane toward the highway.

Shark Key was exactly the paradise Kate had needed when she fled to the Keys after Danny died.

She drew in the heavy humid air. The distinctive low-tide smell of saltwater with hints of sweet gardenia and dead fish comforted her. Her rundown boat tucked into this tiny cove should have been the perfect space to escape her bad memories.

But the nightmares had followed her.

She'd spent the last two years learning to live for herself. These Conchs were a friendly bunch. There was always someone happy to share a beer or watch a sunset. Babette was always behind the bar and good for a laugh. Either Chuck or Steve could usually be counted on to help lift anything heavy. And she could turn to Susan whenever her computer or phone needed an upgrade.

But none of them knew what was inside her head. They didn't know what she saw when she closed her eyes — the blood clumping in strands of cream-colored shag carpet, Danny's glassy eyes staring at the hall ceiling.

Kate shook off the memory and used the tail of her light flannel shirt to open the last bottle of Yuengling. She imagined a spark of light igniting in her chest, watched it gently expand into an invisible dome surrounding her. Surrounding *Serenity*. Let it push out across the parking lot until it burst with a loud scream.

Whiskey jumped to his feet.

Kate slipped the bottle into the cupholder of her lounge chair then stood to get a clearer view over the hedge. Two figures struggled in the light streaming from the restaurant's kitchen doorway.

"Whiskey, go ahead!"

The dog stayed rooted on the roof deck.

Crap.

Kate slid down the ladder then launched up the dock. She crouched low and crept between the cars dotting the gravel lot, finally taking cover behind a dark sedan a few spaces down from the back of the kitchen.

"No one has to get hurt."

"Take my purse. Just let me go."

Kate froze at the sound of Babette's plea.

"I don't want your purse. I need you to pass along a message since your boss isn't here."

The growled demand came from a familiar voice — the man she'd had chased off earlier. Bastard was nothing if not dedicated to his job. Kate peeked around the rear bumper. The thug had his left arm around Babette's neck, dangling her body against his chest. Her feet kicked at his shins.

"Put me down!"

"You need to tell him two things. One, get rid of the bitch and the dog tomorrow. And two, sign the deal with Mr. Baumann. He comes through, and we'll make sure he's got enough left to get a little place on the mainland and live out his days in peace. He doesn't, and all hell will rain down on him."

Babette kicked her heel backward between his legs, but only caught the back of his thigh.

"Don't."

He shifted to balance against Babette's thrashing. As he turned, light glinted off a chef's knife pressed against Babette's belly.

Kate reached into her pocket for the KA-BAR she'd taken off of him a couple hours earlier. She slipped it out, snapped the blade into place. Crept closer in the shadow of the hedge.

"Let me—"

Kate froze. Babette's shout abruptly changed to a gurgling moan.

"Dumb bitch." There was a heavy thunk as the man dropped the woman's body to the dirt. He leapt into his car, fired up the engine. His tires sprayed tiny bits of coral as he spun out of the lot.

Kate dropped the knife and ran to Babette. The woman lay curled on her side, her arms wrapped around her belly. A pool of blood soaked into the sandy dirt beneath her. Kate pulled her friend into her lap. She tore her flannel off and pressed it against Babette's gushing gut.

Chuck came running out his back door, phone in his hand. "I called 911." He slid to the gravel beside Babette then pulled her close, taking over the pressure on her abdominal wound.

Kate jumped to her feet.

"Don't—"

Kate sprinted to her car, dropped the keys from the visor, then whipped the little car down the winding lane. A cloud of dust still hung above the drive, and she followed it, speeding around the curves, the Civic drifting each corner like a sprint car on a dirt track. As she whipped to the right onto the final straightaway through the mangroves, she realized she was too late. Vehicles sped past in both directions on the Overseas Highway, and she had no idea which way the attacker's car had turned.

She looked hard down the highway in both directions, hoping to see a car driving erratically, but all she spotted was the ambulance, its lights and sirens blaring. Kate turned around, waited for it to make the turn, then followed it up the mile-long island road.

Moments later, the ambulance skidded to a stop beside Chuck and Babette. Within minutes, the parking lot was filled with emergency vehicles and flashing lights.

Kate dropped onto a concrete parking bumper beside Chuck and tugged at her blood-soaked tank top. He wrapped his arm around her bare, shivering shoulders.

"Why do they want this place so bad?" She leaned on his shoulder, her head bobbing when Chuck shrugged.

"Money. There's not much open space left around here, and there's millions to be made off of rich tourists."

"Then why don't you sell?"

"Because this is home. Not just my home. It's your home. It's home to the people who dock here for a day or a month or stay here forever. It's home to the old couples who drive their motorhomes down for the winter and to the newlyweds who can only afford to stay in a tent for their honeymoon. It's home to the single moms who can't afford the rent in town. I don't need to be rich. I need to be here."

"This guy." She tipped her chin toward Babette to indicate her attacker. "He was waiting on my boat when I got home from dinner. He came at me and Whiskey. Said he had a message from the guy who was in your office earlier. I thought I'd gotten rid of him, but clearly, I underestimated him. Seems like no matter where I go, people get hurt."

"Babette said he was looking for me. Said to tell me to back off. You know me, Kate. I'm pretty laid back. Live and let live. But the only way to stop a bully is to stand up to him. I have to find Gramps's money and end this for good. I'm sorry you've gotten so involved. If you want to go, I'd understand. I know a guy with a tug who owes me a favor. He can give you a tow, and I'll talk to some friends who might have slips further up the Keys if that's what you want."

Kate stared into the seagrapes, counting leaves.

"Kate?"

She pulled away from Chuck and watched across the parking lot as the paramedics loaded Babette into the back of the ambulance.

"No. I'm done running. Let's shut this bastard down."

CHAPTER FOURTEEN

Vince's lungs ached in the thick pre-dawn mist. Clutching a steaming coffee in one hand, he pulled a cigarette from the pack with his lips then flicked a flame from his lighter. His face throbbed with each drag. Skinny little blonde had caught him off guard, and that'd never happen again. His nose was black and blue, but on the bright side, she hadn't been strong enough to break it.

He started across the empty highway, looking down as he crossed the dotted white line between lanes. This time of morning, the only people on the road were the locals who worked the flesh from their fingers to create a vacation paradise for people with enough money to forget about the real world for a few days or weeks at a time.

His feet hit the sidewalk on the north side of the

highway and carried him toward the sound of lapping water to his right. A layer of dew clung to the waxy leaves of hedge insulating the lush golf course and tidy little townhomes from the Overseas Highway's constant traffic and the shantytown trailer parks of Maloney Avenue beyond. Vince imagined scheduling tee times and slowly walking the course. Buying cold beer off the back of a golf cart from a busty girl. Berating his caddy for recommending the wrong club. He was ready to be on the other side of the transaction.

He passed a gas station on the corner, its sign still shredded from the previous year's hurricane, and made his way around a low stucco wall. A barren construction site sprawled before him. He slowly paced to the end of a long dock stretching out into the sound beside the first empty lot. Vince had been watching the sunrise from this dock as long as he'd lived on Stock Island. Long before Baumann had even bought the land he sat on. By next summer, it would be torn out and replaced by one more wealthy snow-bird's brand-new boat lift. Maybe flanked by a set of matching his-and-hers jet-skis or a stand-up paddle board for the wife and her dog.

Yes, Vince was tired of being jealous.

As he sat at the end of the dock watching the sun peek over the horizon, Vince replayed the worst bits of the night. His orders were to keep Miller from catching up on his payments, so he'd planned to rough him up and tell him to get rid of the broad before going home to watch the Packers and Falcons. Should have stuck with the plan. But he got greedy and impatient, and now he was paying for it. He didn't expect the little broad to bust his nose up. And the fat one had caught him by surprise.

Vince crumpled his foam cup then tossed it into the water below him. His legs ached as they lifted his body back up off the dock. A seagull who'd landed on a piling beside him startled and flapped away.

"I'm getting too old for this crap." Not quite forty, his body felt like it belonged to the plaid-pants golfers twice his age. Life as Baumann's errand boy wasn't conducive to one's health, and it was a job with a limited lifespan. He needed to find a way out. And as crazy as Miller sounded about Al Capone's empty vault, wouldn't it be even crazier to miss out on a chance to take it all right out from under him?

The sky brightened as the sun climbed higher. Traffic on the highway across the water picked up during Vince's quiet time at dawn. His thoughts drifted to life somewhere — anywhere — else, financed by Chuck Miller's grandfather. He just needed to stay close, keep Baumann at bay, and wait for Miller to find the loot. Then he'd swoop in and take what he wanted.

But he had an errand to run first. He glanced at his watch. The property appraiser's office opened soon, and he would be there when they unlocked the doors.

Less than an hour later, Vince leaned across a bouquet of fresh flowers resting on the dull yellow Formica counter, his hair slicked back and his most charming smile spread across his face. Bess had been in Baumann's pocket for years, so favors were expected. But Vince suspected she lived with six cats in a studio apartment over someone's garage, and over time, he'd learned she was far more cooperative when he dripped honey. And flowers.

"Shark Key ... Shark Key ..." She muttered as she thumbed through worn folders with faded labels. "Here we go. Looks like the computer was right. I only have one transfer for that parcel. Looks like it was from the estate of Thomas Miller to a Charles Miller in 1986."

"Anything on when the old guy picked it up? Who had it before him"

"I'm sorry, sugar. Looks like he probably had it most of a lifetime. Anything older than the winter of 1941 was lost in a hurricane. I got nothing before that as far back as our records here go."

"I just need to know when he came south and who was with him. Baumann is trying to make sure no one's gonna crawl out from under a rock and tank this deal."

"Maybe you'd have better luck at the historical society? They have the best collection of information about the early days down here, way back before Flagler built the railroad."

Vince fought the heartburn climbing from his belly up through his chest. This should have been simple. But it was beginning to feel like fitting a harness on a wild iguana. He put on his best syrupy tone, thanked Bess, then stomped out into the humidity.

CHAPTER FIFTEEN

DUST SWIRLED in a wide beam of morning sun. Kate sneezed.

"God bless you!" Chuck pulled a tissue from a faded box on the nightstand, and a new plume of dust whooshed through the air. He handed the tissue to Kate.

"Thanks, but I think that might do more harm than good."

He pulled two more tissues out and handed her a clean one. Dabbing at her nose, she took in the room.

"Have you even been in here since he passed?"

Chuck laughed. "I'm sorry it's not the tidiest. I use it as a guest room every now and then, but to me, it's still Gramps' room. No one's been here for a few months. I guess I should get in here and dust, but I'm a bachelor. Dusting isn't really something I dwell on."

Kate drew a finger along the top of the dresser, tracing a deep trough. "I can see that."

The room was wide, furnished with a carved double bed, a single nightstand to its right, and around the corner, a matching dresser with a speckled, cloudy mirror. Atop it, a hunk of bleached coral rested beside half a pitted bronze nameplate from an old ship. On the opposite wall, a blue flag hung above a narrow closet in the corner.

"That's the official Conch Republic flag, you know."

"Official?" Kate raised an eyebrow at her friend.

"Well, it was mostly a joke. But back in the early eighties, the Border Patrol set up a roadblock just this side of Florida City. Since that's the only road in and out of here, it was a pain in the ass for both the locals and tourists. And of course the smugglers used boats and went right around. Someone mentioned seceding from Florida in protest, and it sort of became a thing. It wasn't meant to be serious. We know where our bread is really buttered, and we're nothing if not pragmatic down here. But we also like to speak our minds. So the Conch Republic became a way to get our voices heard, even if we were speaking the language of snark."

"How'd the folks on the mainland take it?"

"Eh. They mostly ignored it. Patted us on the heads and handed us another case of rum. But they did remove the checkpoint, so maybe it wasn't so crazy after all." Chuck shrugged and turned to a small drop-front desk beside the closet. Above it hung a huge marine chart of the Keys extending all the way out past the Marquesas. He jutted his chin toward it. "Gramps marked all his favorite fishing holes. See here..."

Kate peered at the chart, and Chuck pointed to a spot about a mile northeast of where they stood. "This is where he landed the bonefish that's mounted over the bar."

She noted a symbol beside *Winter, Neap Tide* in shaky handwriting beside the location. The map was covered with similar notations. "Looks like Gramps got around." Kate's fingers brushed the map as she followed his notes to the east through what is now Marine Sanctuary. "Are any of these locations possibilities for him to have hidden the treasure?"

"All of them and none of them. Gramps was a crafty old dude. If he hid something, he would have meant for it to stay hidden."

"I don't mean any offense, Chuck, but why wouldn't your grandfather have told you where he hid the money? He knew you were taking over the Key. He was getting older and had to have known he wasn't going to last forever."

Chuck sighed. "I only found out about his time with Capone from some stuff I found after he died."

"Like what?"

"Old photos. There was one in particular, Gramps looked so young. But it was him and three other guys in pinstripe suits and fedoras. They were standing in front of a black, open-top car, and they looked like they were dressed up like gangsters for Halloween. But the Tommy guns they were holding looked a little too real."

"Tommy guns? That's serious."

"Yeah, and there were some newspaper clippings about Capone, too. The photos were faded, but it looked like Gramps standing in the background in a couple of them. He never talked about his past, and I guess that's why." Chuck paused, his finger hanging in the air. Suddenly, he snatched a tissue from the box and sneezed.

"Gesundheit."

"Thanks." He wiped his nose and continued. "Anyway, near the end, his mind went a little quicker than either of us expected. Looking back, I suspect he had a series of small strokes, although we didn't know what to call it at the time. One day he was doing the crossword in the paper, and the next day he couldn't read a clock. I'm sure he meant to tell me. He just waited too long."

"That sucks. I'm sorry."

"Yeah, it wasn't much fun. The worst part of it was how frustrated he got when he couldn't keep his normal routine. It seemed like he knew something was wrong, but he couldn't put his finger on it. He'd always been so independent. Self-reliant. He had been in charge all my life. And then one day, I realized our roles were reversed."

Kate brushed her fingers over the brittle map, its

surface dented from the ballpoint pen Thomas Miller had used decades before.

"I'm sure there were a lot of things he meant to tell me. I wondered for a while, but I was really still a kid. I wasn't as self-absorbed as most of the twenty-some-things of the day, but I was still trying to figure out who I was. When Gramps got bad, that existential crap got set to the side. We had a business to run, and he needed someone to take care of him. So that's what I did."

"I can't imagine taking all that on at twenty-six."

"Well, you do what you gotta do, right?" He squared his shoulders and turned to the map. "He used to keep all kinds of notes. I'm sure he referred to some of these spots, but I gave all his old things to the Key West Historical Society after he died. They had all of it on display for a while, but I'm pretty sure they put a bunch of his stuff storage to make way for new exhibits."

"Do you think we could get it back?"

"I could request it, but as a former member of their board, I can tell you they love red tape even more than the government. There are piles of forms to fill out, and we don't even really know exactly what we're looking for. Baumann'll have this place plowed over before we could get it all approved."

"Let's at least go by and see what they've got. What do we have to lose? I'm free this afternoon, and so are you."

"I'm happy to take you down there, but I doubt we'll find anything."

"So you're saying all we have is this map? There's no way we can check out every one of these sites in time. Where would we even start?"

Kate took another look around the room and sneezed.

CHAPTER SIXTEEN

A SPRAWLING GUMBO limbo tree stretched up from the curb, its tiny leaves forming a canopy over the narrow street. Kate ducked her head to dodge a low, twisted branch.

"Is it strange that I've been here for almost two years, and I haven't been much of anywhere but West Marine and Publix? Every now and then, I ride my bike to the used bookstore, but most of the time when I come to town, I've got Whiskey with me, so we just run in and then go home. I've never really walked these side streets or stopped to look at the gardens. It's all so different from anything you can see up north."

She tripped on a crack in the sidewalk. Chuck caught her before she hit the crumbling cement.

"I'm happy to be your tour guide. I grew up on these streets. Went to school about a mile back that way." Chuck pointed over his shoulder. "The old cemetery is right in the center of the island, and nearly ninety thousand people are buried there. Fun fact — you can bury up to five bodies in each plot — two underground and three above. My mom, dad, and Gramps are all in the same plot, and it's where they'll put me when I go, too. We're starting to run out of space, but it's still the cheapest real estate on the island."

They walked down the block past brightly painted little conch houses with wide porches, clapboard siding, and rusting iron fences, their tiny front gardens choked with lush tropical flowers and palms. Tiny speckles of sunlight streamed through layers of leaves shading the quiet street.

The thick foliage and tightly packed wooden homes harkened back to another era. The only concession to modernity were the small, battered cars parked bumper to bumper on both sides of the street. Without driveways or garages for many of the homes in town, Conchs parked their cars anywhere they could squeeze them.

Halfway down the next block, a narrow dirt lot opened up to their left. A giant kapok tree sprung from the center of the space, spreading its arms wide and shading the entire area. A brightly-painted taco truck was tucked into the back corner, and picnic tables lined the edges of the lot.

"Here we are."

Chuck waved to Steve and Susan, who sat together

at a table near a weathered wooden fence. Steve rose from the table. "How is Babette?"

"She's doing okay. Kate and I are going to stop by the hospital on our way back out of town this afternoon."

Susan's shoulders loosened, and a small smile drifted up her cheeks. "Hope you don't mind, we already ordered for everyone. The chorizo is amazing, and they tend to run out."

Kate glanced at the long line, stretching out to the sidewalk even though it was barely eleven. People waited patiently in the shade talking with other patrons, not a smartphone in sight. "Thanks. I still haven't gotten the hang of standing in line like a Conch."

Susan laughed. "We're all on island time, all the time. What's the point in hurrying, right?"

"Steve! Susan!"

Steve jumped up at the shout from the busy truck. Chuck helped him retrieve trays of food and sweating bottles of Corona, then they spread them on the picnic table family style, passing out thick paper towels to use as both napkins and plates.

Kate fumbled for her purse.

"No, no. On the house." Steve interjected. "I keep Tia's generator purring, and she keeps us fed. And fed well, I might add. Dig in!"

The four of them fell into a moment of silence, savoring their first bites. Kate picked up hints of island spices blended with traditional Mexican flavors. She chose the jerk chicken and chorizo with mango. Chuck offered her a bite of his traditional carne asada street tacos tinged with allspice and nutmeg. Kate had never tasted anything quite as delicious.

A stray rooster approached the table and stared at Kate, waiting for his share. She cocked her head to one side. The rooster mirrored her, tilting his head as well. She laughed and dropped a small chunk of meat from her taco to the ground for him.

He pecked at it and stared at her, leaving the meat at his feet.

"Oh. Ooops, sorry."

The others laughed.

"New tourist attraction — Key West's Cannibal Chickens!"

Susan smacked Steve's arm. "Leave her alone! But Kate, you do look a little like a tourist, feeding them and all."

Kate straightened up and took another bite of her chicken as she looked at the bird. Resigned to losing the staring contest, she turned back to the table. "So. We've got two weeks to find a sunken treasure that's been lost for eighty years, with no clue where to start searching. We need to get a look at Thomas Miller's old notes. Chuck and I are going to check out whatever's available at the Historical Society this afternoon, but he's thinking they're not just gonna give everything back. Ideas?"

Chuck stuffed the last bite of chili-glazed mango into his mouth and nodded. "Gramps loved to hide things in plain sight. One year when I was maybe twelve or thirteen, I think, my Christmas present sat on his workbench for the entire month of December and I never even realized it was for me. It was a new trolling motor for my little inflatable. I loved fishing from that little thing..."

"Chuck. Focus?"

"Yeah, yeah. I'll get there. Let an old man have his memories."

Steve snorted. "You're not that old, man. And I'm not so far behind you."

"The decade makes a difference, kid. Trust me. I got aches —"

"Hey! Old men, both of you." Kate tapped the table. "We have a problem to solve. If we're gonna do this, we've gotta do it."

"Heh, listen to the youngster, all focus and business. Lighten up. Patience is a virtue." Steve laughed and nodded to the ever-growing line for the taco truck.

"Patience, my tail feathers. The clock is ticking. We don't even really know what we're looking for, do we? Other than an old notebook, maybe?"

Chuck chimed in. "Gramps had a lot stuff, true. But it's not a regular notebook. He used to write his notes in the back flap of an old book. Said it was stupid to pay for a book full of blank pages when the books he already had on the shelf had plenty of space to write in.

We'll know it when we find it. So it's just a matter of finding it."

Steve took a swig of Corona. "You're sure it's not on exhibit?"

"I'm not sure, to be honest. They rotate things in and out, and I haven't been over there in years."

"And you're sure you can't just ask for it?"

Chuck shrugged. "I'm sure we could, but they made it pretty clear when I dropped it all off that while it still all belonged to me, it'd take an act of Congress to get anything back."

"Well, we need it." Kate huffed. "And if they won't give it to us, then we'll just have to find it on our own."

"A little dramatic, don't you think? We're not breaking in. We're not going anywhere we aren't supposed to. We're just checking to see what's on exhibit."

"I'm not sure that will be enough, Chuck."

"But you're not sure it won't. Let's just see what we find, okay?"

"I'm just saying maybe we should be prepared in the event that what we need isn't readily accessible." Kate tossed a scrap of tortilla to the rooster standing on the packed dirt behind her. "We'll check out the exhibits and see if the book is even there. And while we're at it, we can count security cameras and look for an alarm panel and a place to hide until they lock up. All the things responsible criminals check for before a job." She let her bottle drop onto the table. "Steve, you'll stay outside and keep watch."

"Watch for what?"

"Seriously? Do you people not think we need a plan?"

Steve laughed. "Kate. Relax. This isn't the Guggenheim. It's a tiny little local museum. Chuck will charm someone into letting the two of you into the archives, you'll find the right book, then you'll leave. Simple."

"Susan, a little help here?"

Susan shrugged. "Unlike the rest of you bums, I do have to get back to work at some point, and my job requires me to keep a clean criminal record. I'm counting on you to find a starting point without landing in jail. But while you lawbreakers go on your little reconnaissance mission, I'll make sure I've got bail money at hand." She winked at Kate. "Really, honey, you can relax. Everything will work out fine. I've got a good feeling."

CHAPTER SEVENTEEN

KATE PAUSED in a shady spot on the narrow sidewalk and shook the hem of her t-shirt to dry her sweat. Just ahead, visitors flowed through the intersection at Duval Street in both directions, pushing against each other like salmon swimming upstream.

The shaded back streets of Key West's Old Town were quaint and peaceful, but even in the off-season, when the cruise ships were in port, Duval Street was a maelstrom of sweat and sunscreen, garish flowered shirts, baggy white shorts, fanny packs, tennis shoes, and sandals with socks.

Chuck's steps slowed behind Kate as they approached the crowded intersection. "I've been here all my life, and I still sometimes forget what this end of town is like when the ships are in."

"Maybe the locals hate the crowds down here, but I love the energy. If you think about it, every day we have thousands of people trying to get just a tiny taste of what we take for granted every day. And because they get so little of it, they appreciate it that much more."

"Steve, the tourism ambassador."

"It's better than biting the hand that feeds me, I think. I can choose to resent them all because of the few obnoxious drunks throwing trash on the street, or I can choose to see the best in the many more who appreciate our little paradise."

"Well, I prefer them in smaller groups, and I prefer them drinking at my bar."

"Hey, I do my best to bring them your way, old man."

"And I appreciate it."

Kate left the men in the shade and approached the river of humanity, pausing a few feet from the current. As she looked back to check on her friends, a rooster scurried across the sidewalk between them.

"Heh. Why did the chicken cross the road?" Chuck called out.

Kate watched the bird peck at the bottom of a freshly-painted picket fence. "Because he's a rooster, which means he's a man, and men do whatever the hell they want. Now both of you get a move on. We've got work to do!"

The trio wove their way through the crowd, across the packed traffic on Duval Street, and into the narrow streets of Bahama Village which was lined with bed and breakfasts and short term rentals. Lush tropical gardens surrounded tiny front porches with quaint tables and chairs offering the perfect little escape from plodding everyday lives of dreary gray skies and kids' events and eight-to-five jobs. Every week, a new flock arrived to escape their humdrum routine, and every week, they all returned their rental cars, shuffled through security at the tiny airport, then flew back to their responsibilities on the mainland.

Kate strolled up Whitehead Street and took a moment to appreciate her life. She could walk these streets any day she wanted. Her only expenses were food, gas, and her phone. She worked when she felt like it and didn't when she didn't. She had no need for a vacation.

The street curved to the right, and within a block, the lush jungle of apartments became tiny shopfronts offering t-shirts, coffee mugs, and every type of souvenir Kate could imagine and a few she couldn't. Then to the left, the tight streets opened out into a wide plaza surrounded by two- and three-story buildings. At the end of the plaza, where the land met the azure blue sea, a massive cruise ship consumed the horizon.

Steve led the way across Mallory Square and over a sturdy wooden bridge at the south edge of the plaza. "Margaritaville is up ahead here, and then the Historical Society is on the next block over." They reached the edge of the plaza. A wide pier stretched south along the water behind the resort.

He pointed out another smaller ship docked across from Truman Annex, just beyond a small basin with a jet ski rental operation, a few waterfront shops, and a row of docks where Steve's dive boat, *Island Hopper*, was tied up. "The big ship at Mallory Square will leave before sunset, but this smaller one isn't scheduled out until ten. It's a singles cruise, and they give the passengers more time to, um, appreciate the nightlife. I've got a sunset cruise booked for a group of them."

"I'll say a prayer for you." Before Steve left to return to the *Hopper*, Chuck patted him on the shoulder.

Once their friend was out of sight, they followed the pier around the basin then back toward the street. As they rounded the corner, Kate admired the sturdy red brick building tucked behind a row of tall, skinny palm trees.

"And here we have it," Chuck said. "The old Custom House was built back in the heyday of Key West in the late eighteen hundreds, and it handled almost half of the import traffic into the state of Florida. But that dried up during the depression and most of the business — and the residents — fled to the mainland. The government took it over for a while, but it sat abandoned until the nineties when the Art and Historical Society got the idea to restore it. I served on their board for a couple years, but, tell ya the truth, it was more cocktail parties and wooing donors than I wanted to do."

He led Kate around to the front of the building, citing bits of history — some accurate, some not so much — and noting points of interest couched in what seemed like a historical architecture tour. "Up on that roofline, you can see where they had to run cables along the outside of the brick during the renovation. To keep utilitarian clutter to a minimum, there aren't any cameras up there."

They slipped down the alley behind the building, quietly taking note of parking, cover, and exits, and hoping they wouldn't need to care.

CHAPTER EIGHTEEN

KATE FOLLOWED Chuck around to the front of the building, then they climbed the wide stone steps. The three-story red brick building faced east, surrounded by a wide veranda framed with massive arches. A common style in the late nineteenth century when the building was originally built, brick accents framed all the windows but the center one of the third story, which was capped with a high peak. Protected from the boiling mid-September sun, the deep wraparound veranda offered cool shade. They stopped to allow their eyes to adjust, and once ready, opened the heavy double door then stepped into the museum.

Chuck waved a membership card toward the young man at the admission desk as they stepped into the tall, cool foyer. A wide, wooden staircase rose directly ahead of them, with exhibit rooms flanking both foyers. "These house the rotating exhibits.

Gramps' stuff was upstairs, so whatever's still on display will be up there." They mounted the steps, climbing slowly to take in a collection of fifty-nine intricate pen and ink drawings by Guy Harvey illustrating the story of *The Old Man and the Sea*.

"You can't swing a six-toed cat around here without hitting Papa Hemingway, can you?"

Chuck shrugged. "True, true. And the ones doing the swingin' probably never read a one of his books. But he's good for business."

At the top of the staircase, a velvet rope barred entrance to the third floor. It bore a wood-and-brass placard reading *Archives: Visitation by Appointment Only*.

They returned to the second floor to the Early Keys exhibits. A detailed model of the U.S.S. *Maine* dominated the southeast exhibit room, with placards detailing how its sinking in Havana drew the United States into the Spanish American War. As they explored the exhibits, they found photographs and artifacts from Henry Flagler's railroad and learned the regular ferry service between Key West and Cuba was used to run bootleg liquor during prohibition. Other installations told the story of the Hurricane of 1919 which killed several hundred and wiped out a fleet of military tugboats and other vessels moored in Key West Harbor.

Chuck stopped in front of an information card with photos from the Labor Day Hurricane of 1935.

"Gramps used to tell stories of this one. He'd only been down here a couple of years when it hit. He was working on a crew in the Middle Keys maintaining the Overseas Railroad. For days, the weather had been getting worse, but it was the middle of the depression, and they were desperate for jobs."

"So, they kept working?"

"Yeah. By the time they realized how bad the storm really was, it was already between here and the mainland. The railroad was the only way out of the Keys. Even though the storm was raging, the government started piling people onto the train. Gramps brought as many of his friends and their families as he could back here to ride it out. He said Grandma hated having all those people around. She wanted them to watch out for themselves, but it's a good thing he gave them shelter. A twenty-foot wave swept that train off the tracks and killed about four hundred people, some of 'em men he worked side by side with. I sometimes heard him still prayin' to God to forgive him for not bringing all of them here with him."

Chuck picked at a cuticle as they continued around the room. "A lot of folks gave up and moved back to the mainland after that. Those who stayed were the resilient ones — the foundation of Conch culture. The New Deal created a massive project to rebuild the bridges, and Gramps found work and formed the first campground on Shark Key for the workers."

He pointed to an acrylic placard with photographs of letters and books resting on the same wooden desk Kate and Chuck had rooted through earlier that morning. A note at the bottom of the display read: *Artifacts on loan through the generosity of Charles Miller, Shark Key.* Another smaller notice on a clear sticker read: *Artifacts currently in storage and viewable by appointment only. Please contact the visitor's information center on the main floor to make arrangements.*

"Maybe we could just have them pull it and take pictures?"

Chuck shook his head. "We could. But we don't know exactly what we're looking for and we don't have a lot of time. If we miss something and have to come back, we might all be sleeping in our cars."

"Hey, that was my plan before you dragged me into this mess. But I guess if we're gonna find out what's up there, we may as well do it now. It's easier to beg forgiveness than ask permission, right?"

"Keep your voice down." Chuck nodded toward a museum volunteer in a maroon blazer standing in the wide entryway to the room.

"Even with her hearing aids, I'm not sure Mrs. Peacock over there would catch anything anyone is saying in here. Go distract her so I can get upstairs and look around."

"Huh? What do you—"

"Pull her in here around the corner. Ask about the hurricane or something. Maybe she was here for it."

"Wow, Kate. She's not *that* old."

"Just get her in here."

"I don't think this is such a great idea. Too many people know me. I'm pretty sure that's Madeline Hochstetter. I went to school with her son, and she worked in the school library."

"Jeesh, Chuck, is there anyone on this island you don't know?"

"Not really. Everyone who's been here a while is all connected. I just don't want them to put it together, seeing me here, then having Gramps' stuff come up missing."

"Would you rather move into a trailer in Hialeah?" She pushed him toward the docent. "Just catch her attention and keep her occupied."

Chuck plastered on a smile. "Mrs. Hochstetter? Is that you?" He led the old woman around to the model of the *Maine* as Kate casually wandered back out to the central hall. As soon as they were out of sight, she bounded up the third-floor staircase, climbed over the velvet rope, then stepped into the archive room.

Rows of file cabinets lined the walls of the room and fireproof cabinets filled the center, each labeled with a simple number. Kate scanned the room for any type of signage or system for the storage, but found nothing. The room snaked around, stretching the full length of the building, and then back around to the opposite side of the staircase. She slipped the tail of her t-shirt over her hand and tried the handle of the closest cabinet. Locked. Of course.

She wove her way through the maze of cabinets, trying random drawers and doors as she went. As she rounded the corner to the north chamber, she spotted a small computer terminal nested between two large cabinets. With a single tap of a key, the monitor lit up.

Kate typed M-I-L-L-E-R into the search bar. A list of artifacts appeared, a number beside each one. There were too many to memorize, so she clicked the "print" icon. A printer under the tiny desk spit out a few pages listing Thomas Miller's possessions.

She was reaching for the pages when voices echoed around the corner. Footsteps sounded to her left. To her right, a wide hall and open space loomed before the first cabinet big enough to conceal her.

No way out.

Kate scrambled to wedge herself low between two cabinets in a corner across from the terminal. As she pulled her arms in and tucked them beneath her thighs, she noticed the bright computer screen glaring back at her, displaying a complete list of Thomas Miller's possessions. But she didn't have time to clear her search.

She pressed back into the shadow. Slowed her breathing. Waited.

The visitor and the curator both donned gloves and began opening cabinets, examining pieces of art for an upcoming charity exhibit. Kate barely breathed.

Nearly an hour later, the two finally selected all their pieces. They locked the cabinets, dropped their gloves in a tiny laundry basket, then left.

Kate uncurled her body from the tight niche and shook the stiff ache from every joint. She scanned the printout, but no personal notes were on the list. In fact, no books were listed at all. She glanced at her phone and saw a text from Chuck.

Must have missed you leaving. I'm heading to the hospital to check in on Babette. Meet me there.

She flew down both flights of stairs then out the front door into the blistering heat.

CHAPTER NINETEEN

"There!"

Tina stomped on the brakes and followed her son's meaty finger to a faded sign tucked into a huge seagrape bush on the north side of the highway. *Shark Key Campground and Marina.* Her tires skidded to a stop. A horn blared, and the driver behind her extended a one-finger salute as he gunned his engine, passing her on the road to Key West.

"Can you believe that?" Tina cried, shoving her arm through the open window and flipping him off right back. She shouted at his taillights. "Relax and get some manners, jackass!"

"Is this it, Mama?"

A narrow gravel drive sliced through a thick stand of mangroves and squat palm trees, curving out of view to the left about a hundred yards in.

"Don't look like much." Pebbles and road grit

sprayed onto the highway behind them as Tina punched the accelerator and spun her car onto the lane. A chain of small, brackish, algae-rimmed lagoons lay on the right side of the gravel track, but as the car whipped around the left curve, the thick vegetation opened to reveal the sparkling Gulf water. She flipped down her sun visor and jerked the wheel, nearly missing the curve where the lane turned sharply back to the right and through a rickety gate.

Thick wooden posts marked campsites on both sides of the lane. The sites were sandy and spotted with palm trees. Dense hedges stretched along the waterline. Paths to the beach had been cut through the bushes at many of the sites, and kayaks leaned against the hedge in several spots. A few tents and small campers were set up, but many more of the sites sat empty. Beyond those, the lane opened into a wide parking lot of crushed coral. A few masts peeked over the hedge along both sides, and Tina saw water and wooden docks though several breaks in the foliage. At the north end, a cluster of low concrete block buildings and a wide deck stood between the parking lot and the shallow turquoise water of the Gulf of Mexico.

Tina parked the car, its engine ticking as mother and son climbed the steps to the wooden deck dotted with tables and chairs. A massive thatched roof extended over a bar and a small cedar-sided building. Aluminum shutters were lowered around the bar area. A sign scrawled in Sharpie on a piece of cardboard torn from a toilet paper carton announced the restaurant was temporarily closed for a staff emergency.

Lucas sighed and plopped himself down on a heavy bench in a patch of shade.

Tina lit a cigarette. "What now?"

"I'm hungry, Mama."

"You ate three sausage biscuits from the Burger King in Marathon not two hours ago. Did you forget that already?"

"I cain't help it. I'm big, and I get hungry a lot."

"Well, the restaurant is closed."

"Maybe..." the boy's eyes landed on a small lock in the center of a pair of shutters.

Tina glanced around the empty deck, then took a tentative step toward the bar.

"Ahoy!"

Tina jumped.

"I'm sorry. I didn't mean to startle you." A tall black man wearing a long-sleeved white shirt rounded the corner of the bar. "The owner had a little emergency and had to close up for the day. Can I help you with anything?"

"I don't know, maybe. We just got here this morning from Ft. Lauderdale, and my boy, he's a little hungry. We were lookin' for a bite to eat and maybe a cold drink."

The man glanced over at her faded gold Saturn, windows down and its body looking like it had barely survived a shark attack. "I can't offer you something from the restaurant here, but I could whip up a couple sandwiches and some bottled water if that would help you out."

"Oh, no. We—"

"I don't like no mustard on mine," Lucas interrupted.

Tina slapped him on the side of his head. "We could never impose on your kindness like that."

"No imposition at all. Make yourselves comfortable at one of the tables and I'll be back in a few minutes." The man disappeared through the hedge. Seconds later, one of the masts rocked back and forth as he stepped aboard.

"What. Are. You. Thinking. Boy? We ain't here to make friends or take charity. We have no idea who this man is or how he's connected with this place, but now we're obligated to him." She stomped through the maze of tables and pulled out two chairs near the railing that had a clear view of the water. She cranked the umbrella up then sat in the shade.

Lucas wandered over to the table and sat beside her. "What are we here for, Mama?"

"Never you mind. I'm still workin' that part out. You jus' keep your mouth shut and let me handle things. When I need your help, I'll ask for it."

"Will it be like last time I helped?"

Tina's jaw tightened. "No, baby. I told you then, and I ain't gonna tell you again. You forget about that and don't talk about it no more. Ever. You hear me?"

Lucas's forehead crinkled up for several seconds, his eyes flitting first to the right, then the left. Finally, he nodded slowly.

"Good. Now you stay here." Tina stepped up to the deck railing and examined the construction while admiring the view. She walked the perimeter of the deck, dollar signs adding up as she surveyed the restaurant, the office and workshop, and the sturdy little block house along the far shore of the island. The greatest value lay in nearly a mile of unspoiled, undeveloped solid ground. "Not bad, cousin. Not bad at all. Too bad your luck's about to change."

Grandma Gigi's stories rang in her ears. Tina loved hearing about Chicago. The nightlife and the bootlegging and gambling. When Tina was little, Gigi told the biggest stories, but as she got older, the tales got darker. More personal. How there was more money than they could ever spend—and how Gigi was willing to try but couldn't find where Grandpa Tommy kept it. How he promised to take care of her but insisted on building a ramshackle house with his own hands. How the house was nearly a mile from the road, and further still from any kind of civilization where Gigi could buy clothes or have a drink or go dancing. How she deserved rewards for putting up with it until it was just too much to take.

One night, when Mama was out late and Gigi had one more gin and tonic than normal, she told Tina a new story. One where she'd left a son named Paul with her first husband Tommy. Tina had forgotten until she heard the pinched-nosed man at the cocktail party.

It didn't take much digging to discover Paul had a son named Charles, and Charles was, in fact, the registered owner and mortgagee of this very property. A property which, even without Capone's loot, should have rightfully been half hers, if not for her cousin's bad business sense.

"By the way, my name is William Jenkins, and this is my wife, Michelle."

Tina jumped. The man carried a tray of sandwiches and a big bowl of slaw, and the trim woman beside him set a bucket filled with ice and bottled water in the center of the table in front of Lucas. William pulled out the other two chairs. "May we join you?"

Lucas tore into the food, grabbing the biggest sandwich and stuffing a huge scoop of slaw into his mouth straight from the bowl. Tina smacked his hand, and he dropped the sandwich on the table in front of him.

"Thank you for your hospitality." Tina scrambled through her mental catalog for a plausible story. Too broke for vacation. Can't say looking for family. "We came down looking for work and hoping to find a nice place to settle down for a while."

"But Mama—"

"Lucas here, he's strong and good with his hands, but he ain't so smart, so we need to find somethin' where I can stay close, you know? Make sure he's okay. That's hard to find up in the city."

Michelle reached for a half sandwich from the tray. "It's so nice to see a family stay close." She glanced over at William, who was dangling a piece of lettuce over the arm of his chair. A huge iguana stood frozen at the edge of the deck, its eyes darting between the tempting lettuce and the danger of humans.

Tina played to Michelle's family sensibility. "I couldn't bear to be apart from my precious boy."

"I see that. So, Lucas and ...? I didn't catch your name."

"Tina. Tina Ransom."

"Nice to meet you, Tina. Where are you staying?" Michelle wiped a non-existent crumb on a napkin and held her hand out.

Tina dropped her sandwich on the table and shook Michelle's hand, smearing it with a glob of mayonnaise and not caring in the slightest. "Well, we haven't got quite that far yet. We just came down this morning. Figured we'd sleep in the car til we find a cheap place in town."

Michelle looked past the parking lot and down the narrow lane. "When we docked a couple days ago, the owner showed us around. He mentioned having several open campsites with full facilities — a shower house and even a laundry room. Maybe you could stay here?"

"Ain't got a camper..."

"I think we might have an extra tent and some sleeping pads. Don't we, William?"

"Oh, we couldn't..."

"Nonsense! Of course you can. We're not using them, and I'd love to see them put to good use. Let me just go check right now. We'll text the owner, and we can have you all set up in no time. Come on, love." She tucked the final bit of her sandwich into her mouth and pulled her husband along behind her. As they crossed the deck, William tossed the leaf of lettuce to the iguana, who ambled forward, snatched it up, then scurried back into the shade of the low bushes.

Tina watched the two strangers walk back toward the docs. She couldn't have planned this better if she'd tried.

CHAPTER TWENTY

KATE STRUGGLED to stay perched on the narrow windowsill of Babette's semi-private hospital room. The warm afternoon sun only served to annoy her further. A thick blue curtain hung in the center of the room, and a low, steady tone beeped from the other side like a dripping faucet.

Chuck sat in the room's only guest chair, pulled up close to the bed, and held Babette's hand while she slept. Kate hadn't yet forgiven him for leaving her trapped between two file cabinets in the restricted area of the Custom House. She might not forgive him for a while.

"You stranded me there. Stuck." Her harsh whisper hissed through the still room.

Without turning, Chuck whispered softly, "I apologize. You were gone for a long time. I thought you left and I missed you." He just barely pronounced the word *missed*. Despite his efforts to be quiet, Babette still stirred.

"Who is watching the restaurant, Charles?"

Her voice was rough. Chuck lifted a small foam cup of ice water from her tray then held the straw to her cracked lips. "It can stay closed as long as it needs to. You're more important than a late lunch for a couple of boat bums." He glanced back at Kate. "Besides, the only person we feed regularly is right here, anyway."

Babette's bed shook as her body twitched and short breaths turned to coughs. "Oh, it hurts to laugh."

Kate glanced around the room, her gaze landing on anything that wasn't Babette. Since she'd arrived at Shark Key, Babette has become about the closest girl-friend she had. But the smell of disinfectant and the buzz of fluorescent lights were unbearable. If Kate had been a better fighter, Babette would be puttering around the kitchen at Shark Key instead of lying in a hospital bed with stitches in her side.

As Chuck and Babette chatted softly, Kate allowed her mind to drift to the sight of Whiskey, frozen on the dock. She had only heard the broad story of why Whiskey was retired. There'd been an incident. Whiskey had been stabbed, and his handler had been killed. She knew the dog had some issues on the job after that, but she had never seen him freeze up that way.

Her attention came back when she heard Chuck's voice break.

"I'm sorry. All this is my fault." He looked down at his fingernails. "That guy works for Baumann. He came at me earlier in the day, and Kate's dog got a good bite on him, and I guess it upset him."

"It wasn't Chuck's fault. If anything, it was mine." Kate shifted on the windowsill. "He was sitting on my boat last night when I got home. Whiskey froze when he pulled a knife on me. I got rid of him, but I could have done more. I should have done more."

"Both of you, stop—"

The door opened. Steve and Susan tiptoed past the blue curtains then crowded around Babette's bed. Susan rested a huge vase of bright red and yellow native blanket flowers on Babette's tiny side table before giving her an awkward hug.

The injured woman winced.

"I'm sorry, hon. How bad is it?"

"Doctor says I'll be sore for a while, and I can't lift anything or drive for a few weeks, but they should let me out in a couple of days, as long as Chuck can help keep an eye on me."

Susan perched on the end of the bed and rubbed Babette's feet. "We all will."

"I just hate being a burden on y'all."

"You're never a burden. You take care of all of us all the time. It's our turn now." Susan turned to Chuck. "So, how did it go at the Custom House?"

Babette raised an eyebrow. "The Custom House?"

"Yeah. Kate and I went to try to see if we could get our hands on some of my grandfather's old documents. I might have a way to get Baumann off our backs. Kate?"

Everyone turned just as Kate slipped off the windowsill for the thirteenth time. She gave up trying to perch on the little slab and began pacing the tiny space between the bed and the wall.

"Not great, if I'm honest. I got up into the archive area without being spotted, but I couldn't find anything in their database. Then I got trapped holding my breath between two file cabinets for an hour while two curators stood ten feet away. Chuck, on the other hand, left me there and had a leisurely stroll back over here." She glared at him.

"I said I'm sorry. But the big picture is that we're at kind of a dead end again."

The rough sound of a clearing throat shot through the blue curtain.

All five of them jumped.

"If you wanna get into the Custom House, I know just the girl to help."

Steve pulled back the curtain. On the next bed, propped up on pillows and peeking from a blanket pulled all the way up to her chin was a huge black face, topped with a Dolly Parton-level platinum blonde wig.

"I'm Kara. Sorry, I couldn't help but overhear your problem. Monty Baumann has been preying on any

Conch landowner he can get his claws into since I still thought I was a little boy, and honey, that's a long-ass time. He took one of my best dancers for all she had and then some. Anything I can do to help you stick it to that greedy bastard, I'm your girl."

Steve burst out laughing and held out his hand. Kara shook it.

"We didn't realize ..." Kate started again. "Why would you put yourself out like that?"

"Oh, don't be silly, little one. You must not be from 'round here. We stick together. When one of us needs help, all of us help. 'One Human Family' is more than just a bumper sticker, you see. I may be stuck in a hospital bed, but I'll do what I can from here to help. And when I get out? That piece of rooster dropping's gonna have to watch out for Kara Quinn."

She winked and reached for her phone.

CHAPTER TWENTY-ONE

JUST PAST SUNSET, Kate pulled the parking brake on her ancient Civic in the tiny parking lot behind the historical society.

Chuck reached between the seats and his seat belt snapped back against the window. "If I'd have realized it would be this easy, I never would have asked you to—"

"Don't. It's all good. We don't actually know what it is your grandfather hid, but if it's real, you're still going to need help locating it and getting it moved someplace safe. So, let's take this one step at a time. The first step is getting in there to find his notes. Kara said her friend would be here to meet us, but I don't see any cars in the lot."

"Right ... you never come into town. No one ever drives down here if they can help it." The two climbed the back steps of the Custom House and rapped on the door.

Despite the lingering heat, the hairs on Kate's arms stood straight out. "I've got a bad feeling about this, Chuck."

"Relax. You got in and out of the archives this afternoon, and you weren't supposed to be there. Now, we're just a generous donor and his friend, picking up a personal item that is rightfully his at the appointed time."

"Still." Kate rubbed her arms and waited while Chuck rapped again.

They heard a rattle. A blind in the adjacent window twitched, then a moment later, the heavy steel door swung wide. A short woman in her late forties with red glasses and a twinkle in her eye stood there, her arms laden with file folders, her short hair ruffled and dotted with dust and cobwebs. "Come in, come in. You must be Charles Miller. And ..." she shifted the weight of her load to stretch a hand out.

"Kate. Kate Kingsbury."

"Nice to meet you, Kate. I'm Amy. Kara told me you needed to liberate an item of yours that's on loan here, Mr. Miller?"

"Chuck, please. And yes, some of my grandfather's effects are here for the Early Keys exhibit. I need to see his books and most likely take one back with me."

"Normally there's an avalanche of paperwork

involved in returning items on loan. In fact, this is why we try not to take items on loan at all anymore. But Kara called and filled me in on a little bit of your current situation, and let's just say I'm sympathetic." She winked. "This adventure can just be our little secret!"

Chuck nodded.

"I pulled the catalog files from the basement for your grandfather's items. We're still gradually adding our older archived items to the computer, but we're only about a quarter of the way through them all. Most of your items haven't made it in there yet." She wiggled the pile of files in her arms. "Let's spread out on one of the work tables upstairs and start through them. I'll ask you to stop in the restroom in the hall and wash and dry your hands thoroughly, please." She skipped through the little vestibule then used the tip of her elbow to press the elevator call button.

Once in the archive room, they divided the file folders among them then began to sort through the information. Each artifact, down to the individual letter, had its own file, with photographs and descriptions detailing the contents and condition as well as a sheet cross-referencing it to other items in the collection. On the inside of each folder, a log indicated the item's current location and everywhere it had been.

Kate skimmed through folder after folder. Letters between Chuck's grandparents. His grandfather's World War I army uniform. A ukulele with worn spot on the body just below the sound hole. A small wooden recipe box.

Her stomach rumbled, and she glanced at the clock. It was past nine. She hadn't expected this to take quite so long.

"Mr. Mil— I mean, Chuck," Amy said. "Is this the book you're looking for?"

Chuck leaned over her shoulder to see a photo of a small, dark gray bound book, its pages jagged and yellow with age. He could barely make out the title, *Treasure Island*, embossed on the front cover. The photo below showed straight lines of faded, crooked writing on the inside cover.

"Looks like a good start."

"Great. It's in cabinet 405, and it looks like the other books are stored with it." Amy led them to a tall fireproof cabinet at the opposite side of the room. She pulled her keys from the pocket of her flouncy white floral skirt, slid a small one into the lock, then popped the heavy door open with a flourish.

Amy paused and sniffed the air inside the cabinet. "Maybe I'm crazy, but I love the smell of history." She pulled several antique books from the cabinet then laid them side by side on a nearby table.

"Dang, Chuck! These must be worth a fortune." The words burst from Kate's mouth before she could stop them.

He shrugged. "Maybe, but it seemed wrong to sell them to the highest bidder." He gently opened the cover of a first edition copy of *Treasure Island*. The brittle, yellow pages crackled as he turned them. He flipped to the back cover, its inside surface covered with cryptic symbols, numbers, and notes in small, scratchy cursive. "Hey, come look at this."

She rounded the table to stand beside him then pointed at one of the notations. "That symbol was on the map in your dad's room. Could the numbers be dates?"

"Yes. Dates, and a note of what he built." His finger skimmed down the page. "Look at this first one. '46 *e dock ext.* – 26. And here's another one. '60 *wed* - 25, *house* – 320. That's the year my parents got married. Wed could be wedding? And he's got to be talking about my house. He built it the same summer, so my mom and dad could have a place of their own. If I didn't know better, I'd think this looks like a bank book — his log of what he took out and what he used it for."

"If that's true, it looks like over the years, he used a lot. How much do you think could be left?"

Chuck gently flipped through the book's brittle pages. Thomas Miller had scratched notes in nearly every margin. Chuck shook his head, closed the book, and set it off to the side. He quickly checked through the remaining books, looking for any additional notes, but they were all pristine.

Amy slipped *Treasure Island* into a sturdy little box with metal reinforcements on the corners, then gathered the remaining books and reverently returned them to storage. "It is kind of a shame that they're just hidden away in here…"

"It is. Maybe you could put them back on display?" Kate brushed her fingers across the leather of another book.

She nodded. "I'll definitely be adding them to the potential exhibits list for our next review."

Chuck looked at the flat gray box. "We can take this, though, right?"

She pulled a set of forms from a yellow folder sitting on the end of the work table. "You can take the book. You just need to sign here. And here. And here, here, and here." She handed Chuck a pen and flipped through a stack of forms and releases, pointing at each place his signature was required.

"Thank you."

"Of course. Anything to keep more land in the family around here." Amy stacked the reference files together, heaved the pile onto her hip, then escorted them to the exit.

The door closed behind them with a heavy thunk. Kate glanced at her watch. "How were we in there that long?" She paused to tug her keys out of her pocket, and Chuck continued down the steps.

"It was a little surreal, seeing all his things catalogued like that. When they were at home, they were just random stuff. Now they're a part of history." He held up the book. "This—"

Out of what felt like nowhere, a tall form burst from behind the bushes and tackled him. Chuck's leg folded beneath him at an unnatural angle. The man pinned him on his back then delivered a sharp right hook to the chin, slamming his head into the pavement. He grabbed the book from the concrete beside the unconscious Chuck.

As he spun up, Kate recognized the bruised nose as the one she'd broken the night before.

He ran across the lawn, hurdled the short bushes, sprinted toward the water.

Kate bolted down the stairs, watching the garish floral shirt round the corner at the pier. She was torn between giving chase and tending to Chuck, but it was really no contest. She returned to her friend then crouched by his side. "Chuck! Chuck!"

A hand on her shoulder made her jump. She looked up to find Amy pointing down the pier. "I'll call for help. You go after him."

Kate nodded and sprinted toward the docks. Rounding the turn, she saw the man slow to a jog in front of the cruise ship. The loud blast of the vessel's horn vibrated in her chest. She charged for the water.

The man with the pointed, bruised nose swiped a card then stepped aboard the cruise ship.

Its hatch slammed shut behind him before Kate could reach him.

CHAPTER TWENTY-TWO

Vince jumped at the sound of the ship's hatch banging shut. The crew members scrambled around him, shouting orders and making preparations.

"Security to bridge. Last passenger aboard. Clear for departure."

A passing deckhand pointed him toward the bank of elevators off to the left, then fell in with the other crew. Vince punched the elevator button and cradled the box against his gut, trying to catch his breath.

A sunburned man in a red floral shirt and white tennis shoes climbed onto the elevator with him. "You okay, buddy? Do you need a doctor?"

Vince shook his head.

"You sure?"

"Yeah. Just ... thought ... late ..."

"You just barely made it, for sure. The ship is pulling out, but it's not worth an asthma attack, man."

The elevator dinged. Deck Five. Vince stumbled out into the crowded lobby, crossed the main promenade deck, then found his way outside to the railing. He clutched the little gray box and watched the city slowly drift into the distance.

His breath began to return to his lungs as he explored the ship deck by deck, finally finding a quiet corner and a soft chair. He opened the box, pulled out the book, and thumbed through the pages.

"What the hell is so important about an old book?" The pages flaked as he rifled through them, tiny bits of brittle hundred-fifty-year-old paper dusting his lap. He flipped to the back cover and ran his finger under the first line of scrawled notes.

"What are you reading?"

Vince jumped. A middle-aged woman held a hardback novel in the crook of her arm. Glasses. Pale skin. Polyester kimono covering up god-knows-what. He shook his head and returned to the book.

"Looks old, like an antique. If I had books like that, I don't know if I'd have the guts to bring them on vacation with me. I'd probably build some special sealed case for them. But I guess that's why I don't have any collectible books. No, it's the library for me. Or sometimes I'll pick something up at Half Price Books if I know I want to read it over again. I know some people like those electronic—"

"Lady, I get you're trying to be friendly, but I'm not really in the mood to make friends."

"But ... this is a singles cruise. I thought we were all here to make friends?"

Vince stared at her. "You mean this isn't a gay cruise? I'm gonna kill my travel agent."

"I'm sorry." The woman stammered and backed up a couple of steps. "I just thought, you being into books and all..." She stepped another step back and bumped into a bulkhead. "Just, well, good night."

The woman's cheeks flushed red, and she spun and took off down the deck.

He pulled out the card key he had lifted off a tourist in town. The man bore a passing resemblance to Vince — similar height, build, and hair. Vince had bought the guy a couple drinks and discovered enough to know he was traveling alone. Vince loved Singles Cruise days.

It had been easy enough to slip the guy's key from his pocket and leave him with another drink containing a special surprise. In the rush to get stragglers aboard, he looked enough like the guy to pass through security check and get onboard. The asthma attack didn't hurt either.

He walked back inside and scanned a diagram of the ship near the elevator. His room was on deck seven near the stern. Vince climbed two flights of wide, carpeted stairs, then walked the length of the ship until he reached the correct room. He slid the card key into the lock. With a soft click, a green light blinked and the lock disengaged.

"Mr. Lombardo!" A steward in a crisp white uniform waved from the end of the hall. Vince waved back and wrapped his fingers around the door handle. "How was your day in Key West? Can I get you anything this evening?" The steward jogged down the hall toward him. Vince lowered his head and motioned to his stomach.

"Not feeling well? I can bring up some medicine or call the doctor for you sir?"

Vince nodded and fumbled with the door handle until it finally opened. He slipped into the tiny state-room then slammed the privacy lock.

He collapsed on the narrow couch. An elephant made from rolled up bath towels stared back at him from the bed. His doppelgänger was a tidy man, shirts neatly hung in the closet and shoes all lined up on the shelf below. Vince loosened the collar of his shirt, kicked off his shoes, then stretched out on the bed with the antique book.

An hour later, still unable to decipher the scratched notes in the back of the book, Vince set it on the desk. He picked up the ship's brightly-colored itin-erary for the next day, which lay beside the smiling towel animal.

Cozumel. Of course. Vince had run variations on the cruise-ship gag a few times before, ending up in a variety of Caribbean locations. Cozumel, Belize, even once in Honduras. Ship security supposedly matched your face with a photo of the passenger, but when the lines were long and the ship was about to leave, they didn't look too closely. Vince had been Al Rizzo, Joe Agnoletti, and Tommy Ricci in the past year, and he'd gotten a few relaxing getaways out of it. He'd just need to get off and blend in with the crowd at the next port before his mark sobered up, reported his key lost, and booked a flight to catch up with the ship again.

Cozumel was a great place to blend in. As soon as they got into port, he'd send Baumann an update. In the meantime, there was no harm in spending a little time in the casino and picking up some company for the evening.

Vince selected a comfortable-looking outfit from Tony Lombardo's closet, took a hot shower, slicked his hair back, then ambled down to the ship's casino.

CHAPTER TWENTY-THREE

"CHUCK, that was the guy who put Babette in the hospital. Who is he? How would he ..."

Chuck sat on the steps of the Custom House, his head hung low. "Baumann is a scum, but I never imagined ..."

"Who knew where we were going to be tonight and why we were here? It was just you, me, and Babette, right? And the drag queen and this Amy woman." Kate pointed toward the street where the curator waited for the ambulance.

"Well, I mentioned it to Steve when I ran into him down at the fuel dock this afternoon."

"Was anyone else around? What did you tell him?"

"No one else, really. No one important. Just the Jenkins guy from the catamaran that came in on Saturday. Well, him and his wife. And the fuel guy."

"Jeesh, Chuck! Maybe next time you could broadcast it on the VHF."

"Well, I had just gotten back from the hospital and was telling Steve we'd be closed for a few days, and so I offered him and that mom and son who just took a camp spot this morning some of the stuff from the fridge, you know, that'd spoil before Babette is back on her feet."

"So those new people know, too?"

"Yeah. And I had the fuel guy deliver a little extra since I thought we'd be, you know, going out to search."

"And you told him this?"

"Kinda. I told him if all went well tonight, we'd be out a lot over the next few days, and he asked where I was going. I told him I didn't know, but I would after tonight."

"Oh, Chuck. You didn't."

"He seems like a good guy. He's been delivering my fuel for a year. It's not like he works for Baumann or anything."

"Chuck, anyone could work for Baumann. You said it yourself. He owns half the Keys and he's trying to steal the other half. It stands to reason he'd also own half the people." Kate sat on the pier and leaned against a concrete piling. "I knew this was a terrible idea."

"What was a terrible idea?" William Jenkins' baritone resonated across the little plaza. He and Steve climbed off Steve's *Island Hopper* and joined them, beers in hand.

"Nothing," Kate spat.

Chuck took a beer from Steve. "You know that little errand I mentioned this afternoon when y'all were at the fuel dock? Yeah, it didn't go so well."

She took the bottle from Chuck's hand then set it up on the concrete wall. "It went fine until we got ambushed when we left the building. The guy had to have been following us. Same guy that came at me yesterday and then attacked Babette. We came out, he tackled Chuck, grabbed the book, then ran for the ship. I couldn't get past security and watched them close—"

"Wait, he can't have been a passenger on that ship if he's the one who put Babette in the hospital?" Steve interrupted. "How can it be the same guy?"

"I don't know, but I busted his nose at Shark Key yesterday and I saw the same busted up nose board that ship tonight. I have no clue how he got on it, but he did, and it's gone. The ship. The guy. The book. Sorry to be the one to say it, Chuck, but I think you're screwed."

Jenkins waved Steve over toward Chuck, rested a huge hand on Kate's shoulder, and crouched beside her. "It's not that bad, is it?"

Kate noticed Steve checking out Chuck's eyes with the little flashlight he kept on his keychain. "I'm a monster. Chuck's the one that got tackled. He's the one who's going to lose the marina. I never should have agreed to get involved in this. He needs professional help. Lawyers. Police. Whatever. Not some random chick who lives on a broken-down boat."

"Katherine. Listen to me. We've tied up at dozens of marinas in our travels. We've met beach bums and washouts and retirees. We know the customs. Everyone's friendly, everyone helps out, but no one relies on anyone. Everyone eventually moves on. Right?"

Kate shrugged. "Yeah, that's how it works."

"What I've seen at Shark Key is different. You all are family. And not the kind of family you're stuck with. You're the family a person chooses. So if Charles turned to you for help, he must believe you're a person he can trust and the help he needs."

She stared as the ambulance's flashing lights preceded it into the parking lot. "Family. All family gets you is ..." She pushed his hand off her shoulder then stomped off.

"Wait!" William caught up to her and spun, jogging backward. "What did I say?"

"Never mind. Trusting people is just BS, that's all." She reached her car, opened the door, climbed into the driver's seat. "Maybe all those people at all those other marinas are on to something. Quit trying to make it all better. Just. Don't." Kate slammed the door of her Civic then peeled out of the parking lot.

CHAPTER TWENTY-FOUR

SERENITY'S SALON door slid shut with a crash. Kate caught Whiskey glaring from inside the glass.

"Sorry, bud. Maybe next time. I know it's late, but I'm running way farther than you can keep up." The big dog pawed at the door as she flopped on a storage box to tie her running shoes.

"Kate!" William's voice rose over the sound of tires crunching across the parking lot. "I'm glad I caught—"

"Don't."

"They're keeping Chuck overnight, but he's going to be fine."

"Good for Chuck. Maybe y'all can help him now, since my help just gets people hurt."

"That's ridiculous."

"What do you know? You don't know me. You don't know anything about me."

William checked his watch. "You have a point.

How about I grab my shoes and get to know you better?"

"No, thanks."

"How about I just grab my shoes and we can run in silence? It's a little late for a young lady to be out alone."

"I appreciate it. Really, I do. But I run out here at night all the time. Besides, you never know. You could actually be the dangerous one."

"Not everyone is a threat." He paused, his dark face difficult to read in the sodium orange of the dock lights. "Please? I'll just be a second." He ran down the dock to his catamaran.

Kate tightened the laces and started down the lane at a comfortable jog. Just before she reached the highway, she heard William's steady steps behind her. They turned east on Overseas and he matched her pace.

Two miles passed in silence before Kate spoke. "Why do you care?"

"Nothing better to do, maybe?" They jogged on. "Michelle and I retired a few years ago when we sold an app she developed. We went a little crazy at first. Fancy cars, big house, swank cocktail parties with movers and shakers. But it got boring fast. None of our friends cared about anything but how they looked. After a while, that's all we seemed to care about, too. And what we thought was more money than we could imagine seemed like not enough at all.

"One day I looked at her, she looked at me, and we realized we'd become strangers. We didn't know each other anymore. So we sold it all and bought the boat. We stayed two weeks in Havana. A month in Cozumel. Worked our way around the coast, with a few weeks of diving in Curaçao and Bonaire before hopping our way back up the Windward and Leeward islands. We move when we feel like moving. And everywhere we go, we make a point to get to know the locals. Get a feel for the real culture of a place beyond what they show the tourists. We haven't been here long, but I can tell you folks on Shark Key are a solid little family."

"I don't do family."

"Chuck sees you as family. The closest he's got, anyway."

"Sucks to be him, then."

"Look, Kate. What happened tonight wasn't your fault. Chuck's going to be fine. And it's not the end of the road. We checked, and that ship is headed to Cozumel. The guy isn't going anywhere until it docks at noon tomorrow, so all we have to do is beat him there."

Kate laughed. "And how do you propose *we* do *that?*"

"We fly."

Kate flapped her arms at her sides. "With these great big wings?"

"I have a plane. I called a buddy, and he's bringing it down first thing in the morning."

"Of course you do. You have fun with that."

"Kate, it's not like that. Look, Chuck is in the hospital. Babette is in the hospital. You're the only one who can recognize this guy."

"They're both in the hospital because of me."

"You've seen him three times now. We need you in Mexico."

"And how do you possibly think this will work?"

"The only way he could have gotten on that ship is with another passenger's ID. Somewhere on this island, there's some poor tourist passed out drunk somewhere and missing his card. Tomorrow morning, that guy wakes up and raises holy hell with the cruise line. If our guy doesn't get off in Cozumel and stay off, he'll be in a world of hurt. So Cozumel is our place to catch him before he boards a flight or rents a car or charters a boat to heaven knows where."

Kate ran faster.

William matched her pace.

"I'm sorry. If you really want to go, I'll give you a description."

"A description won't be enough."

"Then I need to fix this for Chuck myself. My check comes in a couple days. I guess I could book a flight to Cozumel in the morning and chase this guy down."

"On your own?"

"Yes."

"He'll be long gone."

"You don't know that."

"Let's say you find him. Then what?"

"Then I get the book back from him."

"That's the dumbest thing I've ever heard."

Kate stopped. "It's all I can do. I don't have the money to give him. You say I can't get the book back for him. I don't see a way to fix it, and my only other option is to start looking for a new slip for my boat."

William turned around and jogged in place. "No, it's not. Steve has military experience. I have resources. I hear you're pretty badass yourself when you need to be. We go together, we find the guy, and we deal with him."

They ran together in silence for another twenty minutes.

"I came down here after my husband died."

William slowed, but Kate kept her pace. He caught up. "I didn't know. I'm sorry."

"Don't be. Not yours to be sorry for. Anyway, our friends tried to help me, but what did they know about it? I was so angry. Angry at myself for leaving him there alone. Angry at the jerk who killed him. Angry at him for being vulnerable. He was a cop. He wasn't supposed to get cut in our own house by some punk who wanted our DVD player."

"Kate, I'm..."

"I came down here to start fresh. To build a life on

my own. To not need anyone and for no one to need me. Just me and my dog. That's all."

"We're not meant to be alone. We're pack animals. We do better when we're together."

"You might. I don't."

"You do. You don't like how it feels when things go sideways. I get that. But I promise if they go sideways and you're all alone, it's a thousand times worse."

They turned up the lane to Shark Key. She looked over the low seagrape bushes at the moonlight glinting off the rippling water.

William finally spoke. "It's beautiful out here. I hate bullies, and I'm not willing to let some greedy developer steal this place out from under Chuck. Neither are you. I'll pick you up at seven. Bring your passport." He jogged up the dock then climbed aboard the *Knot Dead Yet*.

Kate let Whiskey out. He ran up to the hedge and did his business while she stretched her aching muscles. She'd pushed a faster pace than she was used to, and Jenkins kept up as if he was walking.

She whistled to Whiskey, then went into the boat's salon to find her passport.

CHAPTER TWENTY-FIVE

AT 6:55 A.M., Kate's boat rocked. Someone rapped on the sliding door. She threw a lightweight plaid shirt over her black tank and khaki shorts, slipped into her shoes, then grabbed a small day pack.

She pulled a can of tomato juice and an apple out of the nearly bare refrigerator before opening her door.

"Good, you're ready." William looked like he'd been up for hours. "The plane'll be here in about twenty minutes, so we need to get over to the airport. Do you mind driving? Save Steve the trip out here to pick us up?"

Kate pulled her keys out of her bag.

Fifteen minutes later, they parked outside the General Aviation terminal on the southeast end of Key West. Steve waited, his legs stretched out in a tiny chair in the cool, tiled office. Susan sat in the chair beside him.

"Thanks for coming, Kate."

"Don't you have a charter tomorrow?"

"Yeah, but I've got a good feeling about this. We'll be back tonight. And if not, the keys to my boat are in the office. Justin can moor up at a dive site well enough, and hopefully one of his dive-master buddies is better at lobstering than he is."

William joined them and pointed through the window at a sparkling white single engine plane taxiing toward them. "All fueled up and flight plan filed. Let's rock and roll!"

Kate hitched her bag over her shoulder, pushed open the door, then led the others out to the small airplane. A tall, lean man in cargo shorts and an olive polo shirt climbed down from the pilot's seat. He perched his aviators on top of his sandy blonde hair and shook William's hand.

"She's a beauty."

"Jake, thanks for bringing her down for me."

"No problem at all. Been meaning to run down here for a while now, anyway. I saw a property just listed that looked interesting, so it's a great excuse to spend a few days. You saved me a tedious drive, my friend." The pilot grinned. "If you're not going to be back by the first of next week, just give me a call."

"Oh, I expect we'll be back tonight. But stay as long as you like." The men shook hands again, then William walked all the way around the plane, touching and caressing it like it was his wife. Steve climbed up into the front seat, and Kate and Susan settled in the back behind him. As William completed his preflight checks, Kate adjusted the headset over her ears.

"Have you ever flown out of here on a small plane?" Even through her headphones, Steve's voice sounded as giddy as a boy who'd just gotten his first Red Ryder BB gun.

"Nope. First time."

"You're in for a treat. William, we're good on time, aren't we? Let's head out over the Marquesas and past Fort Jefferson."

"Roger." William tapped the push-to-talk button. "Key West Clearance Delivery, this is Cirrus Two-Five-Zero Charlie Delta, IFR to Cozumel, with information bravo, clearance on request."

A crackly voice burst from Kate's headset. "Cirrus Two-Five-Zero Charlie Delta, Key West Clearance Delivery, you are cleared to Cozumel International as filed. On departure climb and maintain two thousand, expect one-zero thousand within ten minutes, departure frequency one-two-four point zero-two-five, squawk two-seven-three-four."

"Does that—" William popped his hand up between the seats, and Kate cut her question short. William repeated the entire confusing sequence back over the radio.

Finally the plane began to roll. As they taxied, William glanced toward the back seat. "Sorry, Kate.

We'll have time for questions later, but I need to keep the radio clear until we get to cruising altitude."

Kate gave him a thumbs-up between the seats just as the plane drew to a stop and the radio crackled again. "Cirrus Two-Five-Zero Charlie Delta is holding short of runway niner, ready to go."

"Cirrus Two-Five-Zero Charlie Delta, Key West tower, fly runway heading, wind calm, runway niner, cleared for takeoff."

"Okay, cleared for takeoff runway niner."

Seconds later, the little plane shot down the runway, then its nose slowly began to rise. It gently climbed over Stock Island and into the bright morning sun.

"Cirrus Zero Charlie Delta, contact Navy Key West Departure on one-two-four point zero-two-five. Have a great flight."

"One-two-four point zero-two-five for departure. So long."

As the island fell away, the plane banked around to the northwest, giving Kate a birds-eye view of the Lower Keys. Susan tapped Kate's shoulder then pulled her headset down around her neck and shouted over the whine of the engine. "You can't see it, but Shark Key is off to the east over there, then as we come around you'll be able to see the whole island of Key West."

Kate peered out the window. As they passed north of Old Town, Susan pointed across the water. "Sunset

Key sits just ahead, with Christmas Tree Island just this side of it, and then you can see the shallows running a few miles out. In a couple minutes, we'll be out over that area and coming up on the Marquesas Keys. Even if you've taken a boat out there, it looks totally different from the air."

"Yeah, I've been out there a couple times, but don't know those sites as well as the reefs to the south."

"This area just below us now is a wide swath of quicksand. It just looks like sand from up here, but back in the eighties, the wreck of a Spanish Galleon, the *Atocha*, was found there, half buried."

Steve pulled his own headset off as he twisted between the front seats. "The site stretches across forty square miles, and I'm sure there's a lot more down there no one has ever found."

As William took direction from the air traffic controllers and continued to climb, Susan and Steve continued the guided tour until their voices grew hoarse. They flew over Fort Jefferson, built during the 1800s to protect the shipping lanes into the Gulf of Mexico. "If you haven't been out to the Fort yet, it's a fun trip. Make sure to take the tour with Hollywood. You'd never know it looking at him, but he's the best storyteller in Key West. And that's sayin' something."

As the fort fell away behind them, William adjusted their course to the southwest. He tapped his headset, then pointed to each of them. Kate slipped it back over her ears, tucked her feet beneath her on the light gray leather seat, rested her head on the window, and immediately fell asleep.

After what felt like ten minutes, William's voice rattled back into Kate's headset. "Ladies and gentleman, we are beginning our final descent into Cozumel. Please make sure your tray tables are stowed and your seat backs are in their upright position."

CHAPTER TWENTY-SIX

I'M way too old to sleep on the frickin' ground. Tina pulled her knees toward her and rolled over to twist out the muscles in her lower back.

"Ow!" The lump of blankets beside her cried out as she kneed Lucas in the kidney.

"Then get out. Git." The blankets fell still. Tina rolled to her other side then fished a five-dollar bill from her purse. "Here. Go take this up to the office and see if they got some coffee made."

Lucas crawled through the tent's low vestibule then clambered to his feet. He only made it two steps before screaming because a huge sandspur embedded in the arch of his right foot. Hopping on his left foot, he tried to pull the spiky seed without impaling his fingers. When his left foot landed on another sandspur, he collapsed back on his butt, both feet stuck in the air, and wailed.

"Cheese and crackers, Lucas! What's your —" Tina's fully-grown son was rocking on his back, feet and arms flailing, screaming like a child.

She tugged on a pair of cutoff shorts, pulled a threadbare tank top over her head, slipped on her flip-flops, then she climbed out into the morning heat to help him. After she had tugged the spurs from both his feet, she ordered him to stay while she crawled back in the tent to find his shoes.

A few seconds later, she returned with them. "Here. Put these on, idiot. You lived in Florida all your life. You know better."

Lucas rubbed the bright red pinprick wounds on his feet, put on his shoes, then carefully pushed to his feet. He retrieved the money from the sand before lumbering up to the concrete block office building.

Tina popped the trunk lid then dug through her bag for a light long-sleeved shirt. She pulled one out for the sniff test. It barely passed, and with a shrug, she tied it around her waist. Next she took a toothbrush from the side pocket, then walked to the long concrete-block building with the "Comfort Station" sign in front.

The entrance to the women's side faced north, on the east end of the building. The men's room sat on the other end, and the laundry room backed up to it from the south. When she'd visited the bathrooms the night before she hadn't bothered with the lights. But in the bright morning, she noted that the white tile and cotton shower curtains were cleaner than her bathroom at home. She quickly brushed her teeth, spit a little blood into the gleaming porcelain sink, then headed back to the campsite. Lucas had returned with coffee and left her a foam cup on the weathered wood picnic table. The heavy sound of his snores drifted from the tent. *At least he's good at sleeping.*

She plopped down on the top of the table and listened to the rustle of the palm fronds in the light breeze. Low hollow thunks and metallic clangs sounded from beyond the hedge as the boats tied to the dock rocked in the gentle surf. The salt air smelled fresh, tinged with the scent of fish but with none of the city smells she was used to — exhaust fumes, garbage, or the sour mildew funk that spread under the carpet of every apartment she could afford.

Tina allowed herself to imagine for just a few seconds what it might have been like to live here if Gigi had stayed and kept her claim to the place. She saw herself as a kid, swimming in the little lagoon and learning to sail like a proper rich girl, meeting a wealthy developer's son and being a guest at all the parties she'd had to work instead. But Gigi left, sealing her fate. Now was Tina's chance to reclaim her birthright. She pulled her phone from her back pocket then typed "Key West Marriage Records" in the Internet search bar.

Two hours later, she scraped a huge white Ford pickup truck as she squeezed her Saturn into an illegal spot near a two-story white office building on Simonton Street. She slipped the long-sleeved shirt over her tattered tank before stepping into the cool, dry air conditioning of the vital records office.

"Can I help you?" A tall, slim woman with auburn hair met Tina at the long counter. The nametag pinned above her breast pocket read: TREVA.

"Sure, Treeva."

"It's actually Treva. The E is short. Like *Treh Vuh*."

"Whatever. I need some old marriage records. Nearly a hundred years back. Thomas and Gigi Miller. I think they were married here in nineteen thirty-some-thing. How long will it take to get that?"

Treva's forced smile stopped at the corners of her lips as her fingers tapped the keyboard. "The fee is $5 for the first copy, and $4 for each additional copy. I'll need your name, address, valid ID, and payment to start the search for you. How many copies will you need?"

"Lemme get this straight ... you want payment before you start the search? And you want an ID?"

"Yes."

"I thought these were public records?"

"They are."

"Then why ain't they free? And why do you need an ID?"

Treva shrugged. "Just the policy. If you don't want to provide an ID, I can't give you a certified copy of the record. If you just need the date and an unofficial copy, these are all on ancestry.com. You might be able to get help with that at the library."

Tina balled her hands up but held them tight at her sides. "The library. Where's that?"

"Oh, it's not far at all. You just go a few blocks up Simonton here, then go right on Fleming. It'll be on your right. You can't miss it."

"Can't miss it, huh?"

"Nope. It's pink with white shutters, and it takes up the whole corner. I promise you'll see it. Can I help you with anything else?"

"You didn't help me with what I came for, so I doubt it. Thanks for nothing."

"Well, you have a nice day, now."

Tina stomped out of the office. *Even the public servants down here are annoying.* She stomped out of the building then turned right on Simonton. After three blocks, she stopped a scruffy man on a bike. "Do you know where the library is?"

"Long walk the way you're goin' now, for sure. Shorter if you turn around. Few blocks up that way, you'll hit Fleming. It'll be a block to the right." He raised a bottle wrapped in a paper bag, took a long pull, and rode off down the street.

Tina spun around then stormed back up the street. The old man at the library's information desk was only slightly more helpful than whatever-her-name was — tree-something — but he eventually managed to find a record of the marriage of Thomas Miller and Regina

O'Halloran on June 30, 1932. He printed the web page for her before returning to his sudoku puzzle.

Her sunglasses fogged up when she stepped back out onto the wide library steps. She paused a moment to get her bearings then headed west on Fleming Street. Halfway down the block, a brazen rooster flapped out from behind a flowering vine with heart-shaped leaves and white flowers. Tina's heart raced, and she screamed as she kicked the squawking bird away. The same scruffy drunken biker who had given her directions was riding by.

"They're everywhere. They don't hurt nobody."

"What kind of friggin' barnyard is this island? How do people live here?"

"You get used to them eventually. I swear." He pulled a bottle wrapped in a brown lunch sack from the basket of his bike and held it out to her. "You look like you could use a drink."

"It's ten-thirty in the morning."

"Is it that late already? You're behind." He nudged the brown sack closer to her. She glanced at the rooster staggering away down the sidewalk and took the bottle.

"Thanks." She twisted the cap off, took a gulp, and nearly choked. "What IS this?"

"Kombucha, of course. What did you expect, rum? We're not all drunks down here! Only half of us."

Tina took another sip and shrugged. "Thanks, I guess."

"You're welcome, I guess." He rode off down the street then parked his bike in front of the library.

She sipped the kombucha and strolled down the shaded sidewalk, looking at the printout. Tommy and Gigi had been married in 1932. They'd had one son, Paul, who'd had one son, Chuck.

Gigi had told her she'd left Key West just a few months before Tina's mother, Bridget, had been born, but she never divorced Tommy. So Chuck and Tina were cousins and equal heirs to Tommy's estate. Shark Key might be on the verge of repossession, but Tina would still make sure she got her fair share of whatever they'd stolen from Al Capone.

When she got to her car, a parking ticket lay folded under her left wiper. She pulled it out, tore it up, then left it on the street for the wind to scatter.

Can't find me if the car doesn't belong to the tag and the tag doesn't have an address.

CHAPTER TWENTY-SEVEN

KATE RUBBED HER EYES.

"What time is it?"

William laughed. "It's almost ten-thirty We'll be landing soon."

"Did I miss the inflight snacks and beverages?

Steve passed bottles of water between the two front seats. "You were snoring pretty hard back there. I didn't want to wake either of you."

Kate peered out the window at the azure sea. From their altitude, she could see the island of Cozumel ahead of them and the Yucatan peninsula beyond it. Tiny whitecaps dotted the sea east of the island. The shallow waters between the island and the mainland glowed bright greenish blue, dotted with dark shadows of reef.

"Should have brought our dive gear. I haven't been down here since—"

She and Danny had come here for their honeymoon. A full week of sun, diving, and matrimonial bliss. Her heart sucked like a vacuum in her chest. She rested her forehead on the window and counted the whitecaps below them.

Moments later, William gently guided the plane to the ground and taxied to the small private terminal.

"*Hola, Señor* Jenkins!" A stout uniformed man trotted out to greet them. He pulled William into a half-hug, and Kate thought she saw William slip something into the man's shirt pocket.

"You look well, Luis. How's Marguerite? Still feeding you plenty, I see."

"Good, thanks. See for yourself when you join us for dinner tonight."

"Thanks, friend, but we can't. As much as I'd love to catch up, we're in a bit of a hurry. This is just a day-trip for us." He held up their passports, with a completed immigration and customs form sticking out of each.

Luis glanced at the paperwork then waved them on through the terminal as the local FBO crew tied down the plane and began refueling.

Steve flagged a taxi just outside the terminal. As he climbed into the back seat, Kate spotted a distinctive bulge at his waistband. She leaned over to William. "Was that ... is he ... are you ..."

William patted her hand. "Yes, yes, and no. One is enough for what we need to do today, I think."

The taxi whipped out of the airport toward the oceanfront highway. As they turned left, Kate glanced north up the highway. A tall stucco hotel stretched high above the trees. She spotted a sign near the road. *Playa Mirador. A Kingsbury Resort.* Kate's breath caught in her throat. It finally released once the taxi was moving south.

Racing down the narrow lane, the driver narrowly dodged parked cars and beachgoers unloading for a day in the sun. Off to their right, calm blue water sparkled under a clear mid-day sky, and shadowy reefs dotted the shallows. As they drew closer to the town of San Miguel, the sidewalks grew thicker with ambling tourists who pointed, nudged their companions, and drifted in and out of the open shops along the east side of the road. The cab jerked to a stop behind a line of traffic, then they only traveled three blocks over the next five minutes.

"I think we can walk from here." William pointed out a big white building a few blocks further south. He handed the driver a fistful of bills, then the four of them spilled out of the hot cab.

"Do you always carry pesos around?"

"A man can never be too prepared." William winked at Kate. "Michelle and I have been in and out of Mexico a few times in the past year, so yeah, I keep a little local cash handy. I raided the supply as I was packing this morning. But a lot of the shops catering to tourists here actually prefer to trade in dollars. They can often get higher prices out of tourists, and the locals get a better exchange rate with the banks, too."

Kate leaned over a thick, shell-encrusted wall to admire the clear, shallow water. Small boats dotted the harbor, and a few clusters of snorkelers explored the reefs. Further down the narrow beach, she saw a small group of tourists climbing from a low dock onto underwater scooters. Across the street, the shaded sidewalk was crowded with tourists milling in and out of the tiny shops.

The foursome walked south along the sun-soaked route with Kate in the lead. William dodged tourists and nodded to the many locals setting up vending carts or selling wares from the trunks of beat-up cars. Kate stopped one and bought a floppy white hat to keep the sun — and her target's eyes — off her face. Steve and Susan brought up the rear, just a typical tourist couple holding hands as they enjoyed the tropical sun.

To their right across the harbor, a small cruise ship approached the downtown pier. Dockhands scurried up and down the pier, throwing thick ropes to secure the huge vessel. Doors opened as the ship's crew arranged the barricades, small podiums, and monitors used in each port to check guests on and off the ship. Within minutes, the first passengers began disembarking.

Steve pointed to the crowd crossing the long walkway. "He'll be in the first crowd off, and he'll want to get clear of the area pretty quickly, so let's stay on our toes."

Kate adjusted the brim of her sun hat. "I'll go ahead and get as close as I can. When I see him, I'll signal you and fall in behind him. You all close in from both sides, then we'll herd him into a corner." She nodded toward Steve's waist. "I sincerely hope you don't plan to use that."

"No plans, no. But after what that guy did to Chuck, I want an undisputed advantage when we finally meet."

Kate slowly made her way down the pier toward the ship, shifting her day pack and trying her hardest to look like a woman who can't find her sister. She waved off the cruise photographers who kept framing her with the ship in the background and kept her eye on the stream of passengers heading toward her.

CHAPTER TWENTY-EIGHT

Morning sunlight streamed through the open curtains of the small stateroom. Vince rubbed the crust from his eyes and slipped out from under the thick arm of the playmate he'd picked up at the casino. After wrapping a towel around his waist, he grabbed a pack of cigarettes then stepped out onto the balcony.

The ship was due into port at noon. He had three hours to get rid of his guest, order coffee and breakfast, fill a bag with a few of Lombardo's finer things, wipe the room clean, then get off the ship with the first crowd of eager tourists.

He flicked his cigarette butt out into the wind then opened the sliding door, returning to the stateroom just in time to see the hall door snap shut. The bed was empty. He smiled and picked up the TV remote. With just a few clicks, a pot of coffee, eggs Benedict, and extra crispy hash browns were all on their way to his door.

Vince grabbed a quick shower then sorted through Lombardo's clothes, selecting two days' worth and stuffing them on top of his own dirty duds in a small daypack he found in the closet. He wiped every surface of the room, tucked Thomas Miller's copy of *Treasure Island* into the pack, then perched a straw hat atop his slicked-back hair. On his way out the door, he winked at his reflection.

The crowded elevator stunk of shampoo and sunscreen. Vince backed into a corner to avoid bodily contact with fellow passengers who chatted with each other about swimming with turtles and the island Jeep tour that ended at a tequila tasting room. He envied their enthusiasm but just wanted get off the boat and blend into the crowded little town.

He slid Lombardo's keycard into the reader at the security podium. Tipped his hat at the tiny woman sitting behind the screen. Sauntered down the pier. Home free ... until he spotted her.

How could that meddling blonde possibly be here in Cozumel?

No way at all. Except there she was, right in the middle of the pier. And worse yet, she was waving a big white sun hat at someone near the shops. What Vince had thought would be the easy part just got complicated. He dodged two overly aggressive ship photographers and ducked into a group of rambunctious cruisers who'd started the day's partying a little early.

Vince stuck to the group through the maze of stalls and shops, his gaze darting back and forth as he searched for an exit. Beside him, a drunken woman carrying a huge beach bag staggered along the edge of the crowd, pointing at various items in each shop they passed. Vince had just mapped his route to freedom when the woman stumbled into a wide terra cotta platter. It crashed to the floor, drawing way too much unwanted attention. He scurried out onto the street, leaving the ruckus behind him.

As tourists flowed across the avenue to Señor Frog's, Vince peeled off into the small shopping plaza, wiped the card key clean, then dropped it in a nearby trash can. From there, he blended into the loose crowd of shoppers walking toward the town square.

Halfway down the first block, he slipped behind a tall display of tie-dyed sundresses and surveyed the street. No sign of the blonde or her big white hat. He stepped back out to the sidewalk and waved at a taxi careening up the avenue. It sped by, so he flailed at the next one. And the next.

This is worse than trying to hail a cab in Manhattan.

Vince ducked into the next shop. It was shallow, with every bit of its white walls crammed with displays of brightly-colored ponchos, sarongs, and dresses. The shopkeeper had positioned racks of straw hats and sunglasses between them, and tables stacked with souvenir t-shirts filled the center of the shop. Vince pulled a batik dress from the wall and held it wide in front of him to block the view from the street. He hoped the shopkeeper would think he was inspecting the merchandise while he actually checked for the blonde who was bound to catch up with him.

As he worked his way up Avenue Rafael E. Medgar, the four-lane boulevard running the length of the city, he repeated this process in shop after shop — duck into a shop, block with a piece of merchandise, check for a tail.

Three blocks north of the cruise pier, Vince spotted a second-story rooftop cantina. He surveyed the crowd of tourists. Surrounded by a cacophony of color and sound from the shops and the stream of people making their way up and down the avenue, few of them ever looked up. It was the perfect hiding place to stop and come up with a plan.

After ducking up the narrow terra cotta staircase, he settled himself at a tall table with a view of the avenue and opened a menu. Only then did he breathe a little easier. He pulled his hat low then sent a text to Baumann.

Moments later, his phone rang. Baumann. Vince tapped the screen to send the call to voicemail. Then he scanned the crowd on the street, looking intently for the blonde.

"*Buenas tardes, señor.* Can I bring you a beer?"

Vince admired the young Mexican waitress packed into a tiny bright halter top and even tinier jeans shorts. Typical tourist joint. If the food was good and the drinks were strong, the servers wouldn't need to show more than they hid to make tips.

"Corona, *por favor*." He set a ten-dollar bill on the table then weighted it down with a heavy clay ashtray. After the woman turned back toward the bar, Vince pulled the battered copy of *Treasure Island* from his pack while scanning the crowd on the street below.

He opened the book, pored over the faded ink in the margins, then turned to the back page. The tight scrawl was barely legible. It seemed like a ledger of some sort, but the entries didn't make any sense.

When the waitress returned with a sweaty bottle of beer, he snapped the book shut then stuffed it back in his pack. He nodded his thanks, turned, scanned the crowd on the sidewalk below. Amid the pudgy, sunburned horde, he spotted her.

White hat. Blonde hair. Sunglasses.

Pointing straight at him.

CHAPTER TWENTY-NINE

FINALLY, she found him. Even under a woven straw fedora and baggy green shirt, his beady eyes and bruised nose were unmistakable. Kate turned and waved back up the pier at no one, hoping he wouldn't spot her. She let him pass by before falling in behind him. Staying a few yards back, she scanned the crowd and spotted the top of William's head at a shop several stalls behind her.

The crash of breaking pottery pulled Kate's attention to a group of tourists ahead. She spun just in time to see the straw hat — and therefore the creep wearing it — round a corner. Fixated on the space where his straw hat disappeared, she slammed face-first into the crowd building around the broken terra cotta.

"¡Va a pagarla, señora!"

"Get your hands off—"

"I ain't payin' for no—"

Kate pushed her way through the screaming crowd, but when she emerged around the corner, the man was gone. She flopped against the wall and swore.

"Hey, now."

"I thought we had him, Susan. We almost had him."

"It's a small island. We'll find him."

She waved at the crowd streaming through the little market. "How?"

"I don't know. But we will. We have to." William wrapped his arm around Kate's shoulder. She started to shrug it off, but to her surprise, if felt oddly comforting.

"How about this?" William mused. "We can cover more ground if we split up. I'll take the south end — I know a couple guys with shops down that way, and I can move quicker by myself. You three stroll up the street toward the north and see what you can see. Sound like a plan?"

"Better than standing here feeling sorry for ourselves."

They found their way out of the maze of shops to the wide boulevard. William turned right, and they watched him disappear into the crowd. Kate followed Steve and Susan across the street where they joined the cruise passengers ambling up the sidewalk lined with tiny open shops. Most storefronts were small, single rooms with one cashier, little more than a market stall. With crowds like this, the tiny shops kept every patron visible and easy to monitor. But a few of the larger shops catering to tourists took longer. They were deep, meandering stores, stocked with high shelves of Mexican crafts. Steve walked to the back of one, leaving Susan and Kate pretending to shop near the front.

"It's not that much different than Key West, really."

Kate spun around. "Looks pretty different to me."

"Sure, the history and language and culture are different, but in some way or another, nearly every job on this island is made possible by tourism. Dive operators, shopkeepers, the guys who run the Jeep tours that circle the island. Those are the obvious ones. But the schools teach the kids of those people and the utilities serve their homes. The grocery stores and gas stations are kept afloat by the tourists, too, just like ours are. And everyone speaks enough English to haggle with the visitors."

"Hadn't thought about that. And I do see the similarity in the crowds. Can't stand 'em here, either." She shrugged and turned into the next dimly lit ceramics stall, watching the street.

"These are cute." A husband wore a floppy, khaki-colored hat with a thick cord around his chin. He was dressed for an African safari more than a Caribbean island.

His wife, pale and sunburned, shifted a plastic sack to her left hand and examined a bundle of ceramic fish. Each one hung from a thick length of twine, and they jangled against each other as she lifted the bunch. "Nice catch."

Out of the corner of her eye, Kate noticed the shopkeeper rolling her eyes at the tired joke.

"But where would we put them?" The wife continued to hold the fish above her head, spinning them back and forth.

"Maybe the guest bathroom? Or the porch. There's that bare spot beside the door."

Kate slipped back out onto the street and joined Susan. They continued down the crowded avenue, checking stalls and milling through shops, with Steve following a few paces behind. Each time they stopped, one kept watch while the others swept through the store.

Several blocks north of the cruise terminal, Kate caught a glimpse of a man with dark, slicked-back hair in a deep green collared shirt.

"There!"

She pushed through the crowd, with Steve overtaking Susan behind her. The target ducked around a corner. Moments later, Kate and Steve rounded the bend into a crowded plaza lined with small stalls. No sign of the green shirt.

"Hey Amigo, come look. I make good deal."

Kate ignored the aggressive market vendors and pushed her way through the crowd. She checked between stalls and under tables, but the man had disappeared again.

"Dammit." She plopped down on a concrete bench in the shade of a low palm tree. The soothing sound of a huge fountain in the center of the plaza only served to annoy her further. "It was him, and I freaking lost him. Again."

Steve bought three bottles of water from an elderly woman sitting beside a cooler filled with ice, a wide piece of cardboard proclaiming "Ice Cold Agua. $2.00"

He started to check the caps on both bottles. The woman stopped him. "Wait, *señor*. No. No. Here..." She reached into a second cooler behind her and handed him fresh bottles, seals intact, and returned the refilled bottles to the ice.

Steve handed one of the bottles to Kate and snapped the seal on Susan's as she caught up to them. "We'll find him. This city just isn't that big. He knows we're following him, but he doesn't know William's got the pier covered. All we need to do is get upwind and start herding him back that way. Piece of cake."

Kate wiped a bead of sweat from her neck. "Piece of cake? None of this would even be happening if I'd been paying attention last night."

"Don't be so hard on yourself."

"He just came out of nowhere, Steve. He burst from the bushes behind the building, beat the crap out of Chuck, then ran. It was like he knew exactly where we'd be and what we'd have. How could he know?"

Steve leaned back and scanned the crowd. "If he's

Baumann's muscle, then he's keeping tabs on Chuck."

"But the ship?"

"Key West is small, and there's only one road out. If I was a scumbag, and I was near the port, and I needed to get clear, fast, then sure. I'd roll a tourist who looked like me and take his sea pass. If you think about it, it's almost genius. No one without a pass can get on the ship, so it gives him a perfect getaway. Get off at the next port then blend into the crowd. Exactly what he's done."

"But he'll have to get back to Key West eventually, right?"

"Sure, eventually. But remember, he doesn't know the significance of the book, so he doesn't need it like we do. His only job is to keep it away from us. By now, the guy from last night will have reported it so all the ships will tighten their security. If I was him, I'd be looking to—" Steve hopped to his feet. "I know where to find him."

He pulled his phone out and dialed. "William? Meet us in the plaza as fast as you can get here!"

Ten minutes later, William climbed out of a cab. As he walked toward them, Steve shouted, "He'll be looking for a boat."

Kate scanned the seawall across from them and the clear water beyond. The beach was dotted with dive shacks, jet ski rentals, and parasail operators. "No shortage of boats here. He could be halfway back by now."

"He could be, but he's not." Steve sounded confident. "It's not as easy as snagging one of those little dive boats and chugging east. First, he'd need something with enough range to make the crossing. If he's smart, he's not headed straight back to Key West anyway. He'd never make it back through immigration."

"You're assuming he'll check in when he gets back to the Keys," William countered. "Sure, the Coast Guard is on their toes, but you come in at the right time, it's not too hard to blend in with the traffic and claim you were just out fishing."

"But what he won't do is bee-line straight back," Steve said. "And without the right stamps in his passport, he'll need to be careful where he goes."

"Maybe this is a dumb question, but I'm new to this international escape business." Susan shrugged. "What's to stop him from just catching a flight back?"

"Passport stamps," William replied. "Even if he has his passport on him, which is unlikely unless he's smarter than he looks, he won't show as having entered Mexico legally. Without record of entry, he won't get past immigration to exit. And if somehow he did, he'd have a hard time making it through U.S. immigration when he got back. That's all computerized now ... he'd have a lot of questions to answer."

"Okay, so he's got all the time in the world, he's got Baumann's money, and he won't be able to fly."

"Right. A boat will take longer, but it'll be a lot

easier."

"So, we need a bigger boat."

"Already on it." William tapped at the screen of his phone. "I know the harbormaster at a big marina north of town. There are only a couple places we could charter a boat with enough range to make the crossing, but there might be a few options that aren't official." He tapped a couple more buttons. "I just sent you the details for every operator in town who might have boats that meet his—"

Kate pointed up at a rooftop bar just beyond the next intersection. "Wait, is that him? It's him."

William followed her finger and nodded. "Maybe."

The man suddenly ducked low and scrambled out of view.

"He's bolting!" Steve sprinted down the block, then darted into the street as a white taxi entered the intersection. It screeched to a halt, but not in time. Kate winced at the loud thunk as his legs slammed into the front quarterpanel, then he flipped across the hood from the momentum.

Susan rushed into the street, and a crowd of tourists surrounded them.

Kate pushed through the onlookers until she reached her friends, then crouched beside them on the pavement.

"I'm fine. Go after him!" Steve was already rolling to his knees. Kate shoved through the crowd, broke free, then ran.

CHAPTER THIRTY

VINCE TRIED TO STAY COOL.

The blonde pointed from the street below. A tall black man followed her finger, his gaze landing at Vince's table in the rooftop cantina. Another heavier man and a woman he'd seen around the Shark Key marina looked up, as well.

Vince grabbed his pack then ducked into the enclosed stairwell, catching his waitress as she hurried past.

"Is there a back door? Another way out?"

"No, *señor*. I'm sorry. This is the only way down onto the street."

Vince shoved her aside, flew down the steps. He ran halfway up the block, his head swiveling to see if the blonde was following. There was a commotion near the corner that had to be them.

Ahead, he spotted a teenager climbing onto a small motorcycle. As the engine fired, he tackled the kid, shoving him off the seat. Then Vince swung his leg over and kicked the stand backward. He tore out onto the avenue, cutting off a speeding taxi.

A cloud of exhaust from an ancient blue four-door choked him as he passed it on the right. He barely squeezed between the car and a parked white taxi van, then he leaned back into the center of his lane. Vince passed the next car on the left, scraping the high curb of the median. From there, he wove in and out of traffic until he came upon a side street. Leaning hard to the right, he fishtailed as he made the bend. Tourists scattered in the crosswalk as he careened down the road.

He zig-zagged through the narrow streets, doubling back several times to be sure he'd lost them. When he was certain they weren't following, he pulled the bike into an alley near the north end of town and left the keys in it. After carefully checking the avenue, he stepped onto the street then flagged down a cab.

"Airport."

The airport was less than a mile away, and they arrived within minutes. Vince slung his pack over his shoulder as he stepped into the small, modern airport terminal. He started toward the ticket counter. Twenty yards to his left, at the entrance to the security screening area, he stopped short and patted his back pocket, even though he knew it was empty. A large sign was mounted on a stand ahead of him. *Passports and boarding passes required past this point.*

His passport was still in his sock drawer back on Stock Island.

Vince pulled the pack from his shoulder and sank to the floor, his back against a cool white pillar. A small chameleon paused near his knee. The little animal met the man's gaze and tilted its head to the side.

"I can't wait to hitch a ride with one of the boss's rich buddies this time. I need to get off this god-forsaken island today."

He scanned the bright terminal. Wide murals of clear turquoise water and bright tropical fish covered the walls. Pictures of happy vacationers in snorkel gear, sitting on the swim platform of a luxurious cabin cruiser—

That was it. If he couldn't fly off the island, he'd just have to find a boat.

He counted all the cash he had with him. Across the terminal, he stuffed a credit card into a cash machine and pulled out the maximum amount the machine would give him. It wasn't the first cash advance he'd taken on Baumann's card, and, as long as he got the desired results, his boss would never even notice the transaction.

Vince found an empty stall in the men's room and changed into a fresh white shirt, hoping he could make it back into town without the meddling blonde or her companions seeing him. He stepped back out into the heavy, humid afternoon then dropped into the passenger seat of the first cab in line.

"Where to, *amigo*?"

"Where can I charter a boat?"

"What kind of boat? Fishing? Diving? I got a cousin knows the best spearfishing..."

"Deep water, long distance."

"But chu just got here. Stay a while. See our beautiful island and our beautiful women."

Vince peeled a twenty from a thick stack of cash. "Just help me find a boat, or I'll find another driver." The cabbie snatched the twenty, popped the clutch, then lurched out of the cab stand. He sped down the terminal drive while tapping his phone and spitting rapid-fire Spanish into his Bluetooth headset. On the third conversation, the cabbie hit the mark.

"I got chu a big boat. She is docked not far from here. I take you there now." Five minutes later, he jerked the car into a gap barely large enough to call a parking space against the curb. The cabbie jumped out and led Vince down a dock to a huge shirtless man in ratty blue cargo shorts. Further along, Vince saw a cluster of teenage boys in matching navy blue t-shirts and loose khaki shorts beside three large sportfishing cruisers tied up side by side. "This is Manuel. He can help you with your boat." The cabbie scurried back up the dock, wiggled his car away from the tiny spot, then disappeared.

"*Buenas tardes.*"

Vince nodded at the man and walked down the dock to admire the boats.

"This first one, the red one, she is *Mariella*. Forty-five foot, five-hundred-mile range, depending on the weather and sea conditions. How long will you be needing her?"

"I think a week. I'm planning to cross to Havana and spend a few days cruising and fishing along the coast. I'd also like to hire one of your boys there to help crew her."

"Julio tells me you come from the airport. May I ask, *amigo*, why you do not sail directly from Florida? It would be much closer, no?"

Vince quietly walked along the dock, pretending to examine the boat and trying to come up with an answer to satisfy the man so he'd hand over the expensive cruiser.

"She runs smooth? She's reliable?" Vince tried to look skeptical.

Manuel took the bait. "Sí, *señor*. Very. Listen." Manuel hopped down into the cockpit then scrambled up the ladder to the boat's soaring flybridge, where he flipped the blowers on. The big fans spun to life. Then he hit the ignition. A deep, smooth rumble growled from the rear of the boat. He hollered to the group of boys. "Jesus! Ramiro! Come here!"

Two boys trotted over to the boat and spoke softly to their boss for a moment. Vince caught the eye of the younger boy and waved his money clip. The boys both scurried into action, preparing the boat for the unexpected charter.

Manuel turned back to Vince. "She's good, no?"

Vince nodded. "She'll do."

"Let's step into my office and write up the paperwork, then." Manuel started toward a small shack on stilts where the dock met the shore.

"I'll be right behind you," Vince shouted, then walked around the dock, pretending to admire the boat. As the boys scurried around loading supplies on the boat, he slipped the dock lines from their cleats, leaving them lay in place unsecured. The engine idled, and the boat quietly rocked in its slip, swaying with the rise and fall of the gentle water.

Vince glanced back down the length of the dock. Manuel's shack stood at least thirty yards away, and the man didn't seem like the running type. He casually strode around the boat, gaze darting while his head stayed still. Then he leaped from the dock, scrambled up the ladder to the flybridge, slammed the boat into reverse.

The older boy toppled from the dock into the water in the open slip beside the *Mariella*. The boat bounced back and forth as the props engaged and pushed it backwards.

"Hey! HEY!" Manuel ran down the uneven dock toward them, then launched himself off the dock into the water in a valiant effort to catch his boat, but the *Mariella* was already clear.

Vince watched the ruckus on the dock from the corner of his eye as he threw the starboard throttle forward, spun the boat around, then matched the port throttle. The big boat sped away from the shore toward the north point of the island.

CHAPTER THIRTY-ONE

KATE SLALOMED across the avenue between careening taxis and motorbikes. After checking around corners and up alleys, she returned to the corner then crouched, resting her elbows on her knees and catching her breath.

Steve stood with his wife near the corner, shaking.

"He's gone," Kate panted. "You okay?"

Steve rolled his shoulders. "Eh. I've been worse. I'll just be a little sore in the morning, is all."

She reached up and brushed a bit of gravel from his shirt. A tear in the sleeve caught her eye. Habit had her licking her thumb to wipe a bit of dried blood from his elbow.

Steve hopped back a step. "It's fine. Really."

Kate stared down at her thumb, damp with spit. "Sorry. My mom used to do that to me, and I always hated it."

"We all turn into our parents eventually."

She flinched, turned away from him, and busied herself with scanning the crowded street. "He could be anywhere."

"He could. But he's not. He's somewhere specific. This island is crowded, but it's also very small. There are only a few marinas with a boat big enough for what he needs." He playfully punched her shoulder. "Buck up, soldier. We'll get our man."

"What if we don't? What if Baumann takes Shark Key? What will happen to Chuck? To Babette? To us?"

"That won't happen. We can't let it happen."

"We will find him. But we need to keep moving." William's reason pushed the other three into motion. They jogged across the street. On the sun-soaked sidewalk, Steve pulled up short, then dodged around a pair of teenagers taking photos of each other perched on the white wall separating the avenue from the beach.

They walked south along the sidewalk. Over the squawk of seagulls and the laughing visitors, Kate heard William's phone trill. He dropped back a couple steps to answer it while Susan checked the map on her phone. "Our first stop is a couple blocks up on the right."

A white taxi jerked to the curb then a family spilled out, laden with beach gear and already sunburned.

"Grab that cab!" William shouted and turned back to his phone.

Kate hopped in the front, and Steve and Susan slid across the back leaving room for William. The taller man dropped into the car, curled his long legs against the back of Kate's seat, and rattled off a location to the driver. The cab lurched through traffic, stopping just a few blocks south of the cruise terminal.

Steve and Susan climbed out after William unfolded his lanky frame from the tiny seat. Kate paid the driver, then joined them. As the cab sped away, the four of them headed down the long dock.

William waved at someone and led them toward a huddle of local men scrambling around. He pitched his voice over the din and called, "Manuel!"

A soaking wet, broad-shouldered man broke from the group. "You must be William."

He nodded. "The dockmaster from the Yacht Club filled you in? It sounds like we have a mutual problem."

"Gringo just jumped on my boat and took off with my sister's boy on board."

Kate's head cocked to the side. "Wait, if one of your people is on board, why doesn't he just take over and bring the boat back?"

"That would work if it was my Alejandro or his brother here, but Ramiro? He'll work for the highest bidder. As long as he thinks he'll get paid, he'll do whatever he guy wants." He shrugged. "Honestly, I assigned him to crew to get them off my dock for a week. I should be more careful what I wish for."

William pointed to the two boats floating side by side. "Which one is better?"

"*Isabella* is nicer and has a longer range, but *Sofia* — the white one here — is faster. He ripped out of here about twenty minutes ago, so he's got a good head start. You'll need her speed. The *Mariella*, she has GPS tracking, so you shouldn't lose him."

"What's *Mariella*'s range? Might we have a better chance overtaking her if we've got more distance to do it?"

"*Sofia*'s reserve tank is greater than *Mariella*'s. You will catch her."

While the three men debated speed versus range, Kate pulled Susan aboard the white boat and waved to Manuel's two sons. "Run across the street and get whatever food you can find. And extra drinking water. Enough for five. One of you is coming with us."

The boys looked to their father, who shrugged and waved them toward the little store.

"Sí, Papa." The boys both took off down the dock.

Manuel climbed the ladder to the upper bridge. The two men followed while Kate and Susan listened from the boat's roomy cockpit.

"To the left here, this screen has your GPS, chart plotter, and radar functions. And all your engine stats and onboard systems, they are over on this right screen. Keep an eye on the starboard engine, she sometimes burns a little hotter than the port after she's running a while."

A metallic *click* sounded, followed by a heavy *clunk*. "Paper charts for most waters in the Gulf and western Caribbean are in this locker. The newer GPS run on Windows, and it sometimes freeze up. I been meaning to install a Garmin, but just no time."

"Yeah, I had that problem our first time out with the *Knot*. Thing rebooted itself every forty-two minutes, like clockwork. I replaced it as soon as we got back to port." William's deep baritone drifted over the rail.

Susan climbed up and slipped her arm around Steve's waist. Kate ascended halfway, just enough so her head poked up into the bridge. Manuel turned from an unlatched cabinet holding a selection of navigational tools to the features behind the wheel.

"All your system switches are along here. I think everything is marked and pretty standard. And she's ready to go." Manuel pointed to a tiny LED on the instrument panel as it turned from red to green. When he pushed the ignition button beside it, the twin engines rumbled to life. Their low growls vibrated under Kate's feet.

Steve whistled and squeezed Susan's shoulders. "She's beautiful, *Señor*. When all this is done, we'll come back over for a long vacation on this sweetheart."

Manuel blushed, then scurried down the ladder, beckoning to Susan. He pulled another set of keys on a white float from his pocket, unlocked the wide glass door, then slid it aside. He showed the women the richly-appointed salon and the large galley. His sons dropped in behind them to stock the full-sized refrigerator with bottled water, beer, juice, and fruit.

"You've got a queen stateroom here, another two twins back there, and the head is here. Alejandro can help take watch and will make sure you know where everything is."

Susan helped the boys store the provisions while Kate climbed back up to the bridge, Manuel following close behind her. William and Steve were discussing the instrumentation and drooling like little boys.

"You take good care of my girl here, okay?"

William clapped Manuel on the shoulder. "I couldn't hurt this lady if I wanted to. She's beautiful. And we'll get the *Mariella* and your nephew back safe for you, too."

"You'd better." He winked, but his eyes were troubled. "My sister will kill me if harm comes to that boy. But it's okay if you teach him a little lesson once you've got him safe."

William's cheek twitched, and he looked down at his feet before meeting the man's gaze.

Steve stepped towards the boat's helm. "We'd better push off if we're gonna catch up before dark. I don't want to have to try to board him at night if we can help it."

Manuel extended his hand to Steve. "Good luck, *señor*." He hugged Alejandro, hopped back onto the dock, then untied all the lines. Steve gently nudged the boat out of its slip. As they nosed past the dock, he dropped the port engine into neutral a few seconds early, and the bow drifted around to starboard. He nudged the starboard throttle up a hair to stop the spin, then matched the port and pushed the boat forward through the no wake zone near shore.

As soon as they cleared the shallow harbor, Steve called out. "Everyone hang on! Let's go get this bastard!" He shoved both throttles forward as far as they'd go. The twin diesel engines roared and the stern dipped low in the water. The bow climbed as they sliced through the thick salt water, pitching higher and higher until the boat leveled off. Then they shot forward faster than Kate imagined a boat could fly.

CHAPTER THIRTY-TWO

THE HORIZON STRETCHED A SHARP, straight line as far as Kate could see in every direction. A few soft, puffy clouds dotted the infinite blue sky before it faded to meet the deep cobalt sea. She could stare at the horizon for hours and never tire of it.

The *Sofia* flew on an east-northeast heading at its top cruising speed, skimming the water and lightly bouncing on each swell. Kate's blonde hair flew in tangles away from her face. She leaned over toward the instrument panel in front of Steve's seat.

"How long until we catch up with them?"

"A while yet. We're gaining on them, but not by a lot." He pointed to two dots on the bright LED screen covered in thin, crooked lines and tiny numbers. "They're over there. We're here."

Kate looked at the throttle handles. "It looks like they're not all the way down. Can't we go any faster?"

"We could, but I don't want to push the engines any harder." He tapped a gauge labelled *Starboard* with its needle twitching just below the redline. "We'll catch up before they get close to Cuban waters, but it'll still be a couple more hours. Why don't you go below and get a bite to eat?"

Kate stood. The momentum of the boat and the wind coming across the bow pushed her body toward the back of the bridge. She planted her foot and caught her balance, grabbing the back of her seat for stability.

"Watch your step."

Grabbing the railing before letting go of the seat-back seemed prudent. Kate clutched it as she inched her way to the ladder. Just before her head dropped below the deck, Steve called out "I'll take some pineapple and a cold beer while you're down there, if there's any left."

"Not your waitress, Capt'n!" The tip of Kate's middle finger was the last part of her to drop below the deck of the flybridge, but Steve's laughter followed her down the ladder. She ducked into the galley. A minute later, she brought him a container of fruit and a *Cerveza León*.

Back in the cockpit behind the wind block of the cabin, Kate rested in calm air. She leaned against a deep fish box and took in the boat's wake extending behind them. An inflatable dinghy was tightly lashed against the transom, its tiny outboard motor tucked into a customized mount to the port side. Two fighting chairs rested on post mounts in the center of the cockpit, offering a perfect view as the sun began its slow plunge toward the horizon.

She hoped they could catch up to the scum and secure him and the boat he rode in on before the sun hit the horizon.

Inside the cabin, William chatted with Alejandro in Spanish while Susan's snores rattled from the master stateroom.

"Kate, come join us!" William slid around to the center of the u-shaped dinette. Alejandro bounced out of his seat, pulled a plate of fruit and meats from the refrigerator, then set a fresh beer in front of Kate's spot.

"Thanks, this looks delicious."

"You're welcome. I take to Captain now." The boy pulled another plate and another bottle from the fridge and danced out of the cabin.

"I just—"

"Let him take it up. Steve'll still eat it."

Kate peeled slices of salami and swiss cheese from the plate then rolled them together.

"Good kid." William nodded after the boy. "His brother Diego, who we met on the dock, is sixteen, works for his dad full time, and loves running the charter business. But Alejandro" —William nodded toward the cabin door — "is more interested in moving to the mainland for college next year. He's planning to study entrepreneurship and economic development."

"Two different kids, eh?"

"For sure. Same parents, same upbringing, totally different goals. And I'm sure Manuel is just as proud of both of them."

Kate's breath caught in her throat. She pinched the rolled snack between her fingers so tight, the swiss cheese tore.

"What?" William leaned toward her.

"Oh, nothing. Just wondering what it would be like ... Never mind."

William raised an eyebrow. "We have all the time in the world, and I'm curious. What are you wondering?"

Kate shook her head.

"What it'd be like to have someone be proud of you?"

Kate fought to hold her face neutral.

"You don't have to talk about it if you don't want to. But can I try to guess? Parents aren't thrilled with your choice to live on a broken-down houseboat in Key West? Expect you to settle down and get a job and get married and —"

Kate grabbed her beer bottle, stormed into the twin stateroom, then slammed the door behind her. She collapsed on the bed as William tapped on the door. "Kate. Kate, whatever I said, I'm sorry. I shouldn't have pushed you. Please, forgive me?"

Kate pulled a pillow against her belly, wrapped her body tight around it, and cried until she fell asleep.

She woke when her body lurched toward the starboard bulkhead. The light in the stateroom was dim, the pale dusk sky fading through the small porthole in the wall. The boat heeled hard to port as she fumbled toward the cabin door. After wrenching it open, she spotted William's feet disappearing through the hatch as he climbed to the cockpit.

Kate heard shouting from the deck above.

"Man Overboard! Man Overboard! Man Overboard!"

She tore open cabinets and lockers, quickly locating the emergency kit and a few spare towels and blankets. Then she tossed them on the settee before dashing to the cockpit.

William stood at the transom holding a white ring, a thickly coiled rope on the deck at his feet. The white fiberglass glinted under the clear moon as the boat bobbed and lurched in the sea. All the men shouted and scanned the water for Alejandro.

Suddenly, a shout came from the bridge. "Wait ... There! Four o'clock, about twenty meters out falling astern! Get that life ring out to him. I'll come around and keep him to starboard. William, get ready!"

Kate looked over the starboard rail and saw nothing. William nudged her out of the way, took position at the widest point of the boat, then leaned over the rail with the life ring in his right hand. She still saw nothing when he sent the ring sailing like a Frisbee across the dark water. He shouted a rapid string of Spanish words, too fast for her to try to decipher. A moment later, she spotted splashing and a darkened figure tugging at the ring as it drifted back and the line pulled taut.

The boat took a slow, wide turn to starboard, keeping the line clear. Then they drifted toward the boy clinging to the life ring.

William frantically pulled in the line. "Cut the engines!" His deep baritone carried through the thick night air.

A moment later, the boat lurched as the engines shifted quickly into reverse then fell silent.

Waves and lingering wake rocked the drifting boat from all directions. Kate grabbed a rail and hung on. The men slid down the ladder to pull the ring toward the boat's swim platform. She carefully climbed down to the cabin, gathered the supplies she'd laid out, then returned with two large beach towels and a blanket.

When the men pulled Alejandro aboard, Kate wrapped him in the towels, then they settled him into one of the fighting chairs mounted in the center of the wide cockpit. His body trembled, and William rubbed his arms and legs to warm him.

Kate braced herself against the lurching and waited as the men dried Alejandro. She traded a fresh, dry blanket for his wet towels while Steve left them for the cockpit.

As the engines fired up and the boat nudged its bow back to the east, she scrambled to the transom rail then threw up.

CHAPTER THIRTY-THREE

Perched in the port seat on the flybridge, Kate stared into the inky distance.

"Sea legs coming back yet?" Steve asked. His features were shrouded in red highlights and deep black shadows, the bridge lit only by a dim red light.

She nodded as both of them scanned the area lit by the boat's bright forward-facing floodlights for any debris or hazards too small for the boat's radar to have displayed.

Kate moaned. "The Coke is helping. Watching for junk is helping more."

"Good. You can take first watch, then. We lost a lot of time back there. We were almost upon him when I saw something fly off their stern and hit the water. I swerved, Alejandro went over the gunwale, and here we are. Unless they stop for fuel, we probably won't catch up with them until close to daybreak. We should be just off Havana by about that time."

Kate gaped at him. "Wait, what? You want me to drive the boat? All by myself?"

Steve laughed. "Yeah. But not all on your own. The autopilot is set to match their current course, so really, you just need to keep an eye out for anything that might go wrong. Debris in the water, they change course... You know, anything out of the ordinary." His hands rested naturally on the boat's wheel.

"You know my boat doesn't have an engine, right?"

"You'll be fine. You've piloted the *Island Hopper* plenty of times. Just give William another hour or so, then he can come up and take over when you need some sleep. Susan and I'll get up a bit before sunrise, then we can figure out where we are."

"Aye, aye, Capt'n." Kate filled her voice with fake confidence. The extent of her boating experience was holding the wheel of his boat for three minutes at a time while he used the head and paddling her kayak between Shark Key and the beach on the other side of her little channel.

Steve patted her shoulder then climbed down the ladder.

She settled into the seat in front of the boat's wide instrument panel and popped the cap off a fresh bottle of fully-sugared Mexican Coke.

"Fishsticks!" She wrapped her lips over the top of the bottle and held it as far away as she could reach as

226

amber foam gushed up the neck of the bottle and flowed down the side, dripping on the brown turf covering the deck. She slurped the foam, let out a loud belch, then quickly looked around, suppressing the urge to excuse herself. There were advantages to the solitary watch.

Within a few minutes, a routine formed. She scanned the limit of the lights from three o'clock at starboard to nine o'clock port, and back again, then conducted quick spot-checks behind at five and seven. Followed that with a quick look at the GPS to check to be sure they were still both on course. Ended the cycle with look at the radar to see if anything else was in front of them, then back to the swath of sea ahead of the bow.

Her stomach finally settled. She started to feel lulled by the wind swirling behind her and the steady drone of the boat's engines. Three o'clock. Nine o'clock. Five, Seven, Dash. Repeat.

Kate's gaze was skimming past ten when a hand rested on her shoulder.

"About earlier." Even at its quietest volume, William's deep voice filled the bridge. Kate continued watching the sea. "I'm sorry. I didn't mean to pry."

She shrugged.

"I just know a little bit about the fallout from choosing an uncommon path."

Kate shook her head.

"I also know a little bit about how it can rot you

from the inside if you don't deal with it and talk to someone."

Moonlight sparked on the low swells in the water ahead of them.

"I was the first in my family to have a chance at graduating from college. When I dropped out to start my own business doing maintenance on boats, my mother flipped out. 'William, your mama did not work three jobs so you could drop out of school to scrape barnacles off no white man's sailboat!' But I needed to be outside. And I did use what I'd learned in my business classes. I built up a network of good clients. Marinas, private yacht owners, and the like. I studied for the Captain's test and passed it on my first try. Bought a boat, then a second one. Grew a successful business, received awards from the community. But Mama still saw me as cleanin' up after The Man. She was ashamed and always changed the subject when her friends asked how I was doing. My biggest regret when she died was that she never understood my definition of success was different from hers."

Kate pulled her knees close to her chest and rested her forehead on her folded arms. "But you have Michelle."

His quiet affirmation drifted across her shoulder.

"I was supposed to have Danny. But that didn't work out the way it was supposed to."

"I don't mean to pry, and you don't have to answer if you don't want to. But sometimes ..."

"He was a cop. A rookie, but still a cop. I was supposed to be ready, to know every time he walked out the door, he might not come back. The other wives gave me all the tips. 'Tell him you love him. Don't hang up the phone mad.' All that stuff. And I was okay with it. But nobody told me to expect him to bleed out in the doorway to our bedroom."

"Oh, Kate."

"Yeah. I had run to the store. I wasn't gone for long, but it was long enough to lose everything. When I came back, the front door wasn't closed all the way. There'd been a series of mid-day home invasions, but I never thought about it. It was a Wednesday, and Danny was off. But apparently, these junkies sat around neighborhoods waiting for someone to leave the house. They just walked onto the porch and tried the knob, thinking our house was empty and, lucky them, I hadn't locked up. They walked right through the front door. But Danny surprised them. So they cut him. Bad. He was gone before the EMS got there."

William's huge, warm hand gently squeezed her forearm.

"Thanks for not saying you're sorry, or he's in a better place, or you can't imagine. I get that people mean well when they say that, but ... this is why I don't talk about him. I can't take being pitied."

"There's a difference between the pity of strangers and care from your friends."

She pulled her arm out from under his touch and

229

started scanning the ocean again. "It's easier just to keep it between Whiskey and me."

"Maybe easier, but it gets pretty lonely. I'm —"

A sharp cackle from the VHF interrupted him.

"*M/V Mariella* hailing *Astillero Mariel*. Wake up, you old man!" The voice repeated the request.

A sleepy Cuban accent cracked through the speakers. "*Mariella*, this is Mariel Fuel Dock. Go to twenty-three. Two three."

Kate flipped the radio to channel twenty-three and glanced at her own fuel gauges, showing nearly a quarter of their main fuel tank remaining and the reserve tank full. On the new frequency, Kate's radio remained silent.

She sighed and checked the fuel gauges again. Just before midnight, the *Mariella* had veered east away from Key West, heading straight up the Gulf Stream toward the Bahamas. The boat would need fuel somewhere near Havana. Steve had predicted the captain would try to go unnoticed and blend in with the shrimp boats coming back toward the rising sun after a night of fishing.

Steve was wrong.

Kate tapped an intercom button marked *Master Stateroom*. "Uh, Captain? This is the bridge."

"Yeah, what's up, Kate?"

"They just radioed in to Mariel. I lost them on the radio, but they have to be going in for fuel."

"Oof. I'll be right up."

Moments later, Steve joined them on the bridge. Susan handed up a Thermos and coffee mugs a moment later.

William checked the GPS. "We're still about fifteen miles short and twelve off the coast. They're not angling into Cuban waters yet, but we'll have to be on our toes when they do."

"Let's think about this a minute," Steve said. "They clearly don't realize we're following them. We're good on fuel. We could still head north and get back home on what we've got with plenty to spare. What if we overshot Mariel and caught him as he comes back out?"

"First problem — his fuel tanks will be full. He could draw us out and run ours dry."

"He could, but we've still got a couple hours of fuel before we would have to abort and head for the nearest fuel dock in the Keys. We'd have to do a little fast talking to explain Alejandro, but we can deal with that when the time comes."

"Ambushing him sure beats chasing him all over the Strait."

"And it'll certainly catch him off guard." Steve tapped new coordinates about thirty miles to the north-east of Mariel into the GPS and set the autopilot. "Y'all go get a little more sleep. I'll wake you when they clear Cuban waters."

CHAPTER THIRTY-FOUR

As the northern tip of Cozumel fell off to starboard, Vince angled the large cruiser toward the east, tweaked the throttles, then set a course in the autopilot.

"Ramiro!" Vince shouted into the small microphone. His voice screeched from every speaker on the boat. The boy scrambled from the cabin and up the ladder to the bridge.

"¿Sí?"

Vince leaned back in the captain's chair with his feet resting on the corner of the instrument panel.

"You understand English?"

The boy nodded.

"Good. This trip could go really great for you, or it could be terrible. It's your choice."

Ramiro's hand inched up, his forearm close to his body and his hand stopping just above his shoulder. "¿Señor? Sir, where are you taking me?"

"It's not where I'm taking you, son. It's where you're taking me. We'll end up in Key West, but I don't want to attract any attention coming in, if you know what I mean. So we'll cruise with the gulf stream along the Cuban cost, then slip up into the Bahamas before coming back across toward Miami, where we'll get lost in traffic. Everything goes smooth, you'll get a full tank of fuel and a nice cash bonus in Key West, and this never happened. "

"What if ...?"

Vince shrugged. "You will want to make it go smoothly." He dropped his feet to the fiberglass deck and leaned forward. "Now, how 'bout you show me around this beauty?"

"But, *señor* ... what to keep watch?"

Vinced rolled his eyes. "Auto. Pilot. Auto means it's automatic."

Ramiro's eyes widened, and he started to shake his head.

"You don't want to make trouble, kid." He pointed two fingers at his eyes then toward the boy. "I'm watching you." He hopped off his seat and waved Ramiro down to the cockpit.

As Vince started down the ladder, he clearly heard the boy mumble, "Yeah, I make good trouble, asshole." In English.

Vince followed Ramiro down to the cabin. The boy turned. "Why I don't take boat back to home now?"

"Because if you take me where I need to go, you'll

get more cash than you ever imagined you'd see at once." Vince pulled out a wad of cash then handed Ramiro ten twenty-dollar bills. "There's plenty more when we get to Key West. You can take the boat back to Manuel then. Tell him you overpowered me, or you attacked me while I slept, I don't care. Tell him anything you want, except where I went."

Ramiro eyed the cash. "*Sí, señor.*"

"But if you try anything funny, I'll feed you to the sharks."

The boy knew the boat well, and his charter guest tour was well-rehearsed. But Vince sensed he was rushing through it. *Here's the galley. Here's your stateroom. Here's how to operate the marine head. Let's go back up.*

Ramiro's gaze constantly flicked to the water outside the windows in every cabin. When he wound down and started for the bridge, Vince opened the door to the cramped engine compartment. "Show me around the mechanical systems."

"Oh, sir, you don't need to worry about any of that. I will take care of everything and get you where you're going."

"How much fuel does this baby have on board?"

The boy's eyes flicked upward for a second while he searched his memory. "This boat, she carry over two thousand liters diesel fuel. She make it to Key Largo, no problem." He glanced at a small gauge mounted on a panel on the port bulkhead. "But Bahamas? No."

"Don't you keep reserve fuel on board?"

"Sí. But not enough to get to Bahamas. If the seas and the winds are just right and we go slow and burn less, we might get close to Andros. But this boat, she won't make it all the way."

"Slowing down is not an option." Vince glanced at his watch and thought for a moment. "I know a guy at the shipyard in Mariel. We should get there just before dawn. We can slip in, fuel up, then get out before anyone realizes we're there."

"Is dangerous, Cuba. No passport."

"No problem. You just stay hidden while we're in port. I'm just a guy taking a vacation on his very nice boat."

Ramiro's eyebrow popped up, and his glance fell down toward Vince's bulging pocket.

"You want more money? Fine. Two hundred to stay out of sight."

"Sí, señor. Mariel should be very good, then. No problem."

"Good, good. Now, I have an important question. I need you to think carefully before you answer, and you will want to be honest." Vince's stare bored into the boy. "Do you have any weapons on board?"

Ramiro's eyes flicked back and forth.

"Anything that could be used as a weapon? Anything at all..."

"There's some fishing gear in the rear cockpit

locker. Maybe a knife to clean fish." His shoulders seemed to relax a bit.

"Anything else?" Instead of waiting for his answer, Vince began rummaging through toolboxes and lockers in the engine room. "What's this?" He pulled a bright red object shaped like a pistol with an unusually wide barrel.

"Just a flare gun, *señor*. Emergency equipment for, um, emergencies."

Vince grabbed the boy's shirt, pulled him close, shook him. "What else is on board?" He snatched a deep canvas bag then dropped the flare gun into the bottom. "Everything. In this bag. NOW."

Ramiro spent the next half hour going through every locker and hiding spot on board. The canvas bag slowly filled with a random assortment of items Vince imagined could be used as weapons.

Finally satisfied all threatening items were stacked safely in the bag, Vince led the boy to a large fish box in the cockpit. "Give me the keys."

Ramiro handed over a small ring with three locker keys on a red float.

Vince rooted through the bag, pulled out a wide knife in a leather sheath, then locked away the bag containing the rest of the weapons. He crammed the keys into his pocket and waved the knife at Ramiro. "Everything goes smoothly. Right?"

"*Si, señor*. Smooth."

"Good. Now go up there and keep watch since you

seem to think that's important. Come get me when we're twenty miles from Mariel." He stepped into the master stateroom then slammed the door behind him.

Vince tossed and turned on the soft king bed, a hard lump from the fishing knife tucked under his pillow making him uncomfortable. Just after four, he gave up. After a quick exploration of the cabin, he found a hidden panel in the built-in nightstand, hid all his cash inside, then climbed the ladder to the bridge. Stars dotted the inky sky.

Ramiro slouched in the captain's chair, his face barely visible by the dim red light of the instrument panel.

The boat was thirteen miles off the Cuban coast, just barely into international waters. Vince picked up the mic, flipped the VHF to channel 16. "*M/V Mariella* hailing *Astillero Mariel*. Wake up, you lazy old man!"

Moments later, a voice cracked over the speaker. "*Mariella*, this is Mariel Fuel Dock. Go to twenty-three. Two three."

Vince flipped the VHF to channel 32. A simple security protocol he'd used with the Cuban before. "Go for *Mariella*"

"¡*Amigo!* I was not expecting a call for two more weeks. Your boys were just here a few days ago."

"I know, this trip was unexpected. I'm just passing through and need to fuel up. Four hundred gallons should do it. I'll be there in about an hour, but I'm in a hurry. Can you open up for me?"

"Of course, of course. I'll meet you on the west pier."

"*Gracias. Mariella* out."

Vince switched the VHF back to sixteen, the hailing channel, then dropped the mic back into its slot. He elbowed Ramiro. "Go below and stay there."

The boy scrambled out of his seat then down the stairs.

Vince flipped off the autopilot and stared across the water toward the dark horizon. The radar showed a few fishing boats puttering toward the Mariel Harbor. He relaxed, seeing nothing on the screen to his stern. Approaching the waypoint he'd set, Vince gently guided his vessel to starboard into Cuban waters.

Half an hour later, he entered the channel, dropping in ahead of a slower shrimp trawler then easing into the harbor. A lone man stood near the end of the pier holding a fuel hose. Vince eased the boat alongside the pier.

The dockhand tied it off then started fueling.

Vince climbed down. "Coffee."

The dockhand pointed to a small shack with peeling white paint.

He made his way there. Worn hinges squeaked as the door swung open. The dockmaster's office reminded him of a 1950's schoolroom. A heavy, metal desk filled the back wall, its corners curved, its edges marked by rough patches where the salt air had eaten away the metal faster than the men could spread on more industrial gray paint. Stacks of file folders covered the desk and the floor beside it, clipboards with rust-eaten clips hung from open wooden framing on every wall.

An old electric percolator dominated a tiny table against the south wall. Simple, colorful coffee mugs hung from nails on the wall above it. Vince selected a bright aqua mug then filled it with thick, steaming coffee. He sat in a worn wooden chair and took a sip.

"It's good to see you, *amigo*. It's been too long. I was beginning to think you were too good for an honest day's work anymore."

"Not at all, old friend. Just diversifying, that's all. Not seeing me is a sign of trust."

"So what does it mean, seeing you now?"

Vince laughed. "It just means I need fuel."

The old dockmaster's eyes quickly flashed to the clock above the door and then back to Vince. "Fish don't get caught in deep water..."

"I trust our arrangement has been profitable for you?"

"*Sí*. Very."

"We've been experiencing some growth lately. We expect to increase our business within the coming weeks. Will you be able to grow with us?"

The man twitched.

Vince spun on his chair just as the door swung open and slammed against the wall.

Two huge men in olive green military fatigues burst through the door. The first man through the door — the one with sergeant's strips on his shoulders — pointed a gleaming Kalashnikov directly at Vince while the other blocked the doorway.

"*¡Manos arriba!*"

Vince fought to hold a blank expression. "*No comprendo*, man. You speak English?"

The soldier jammed the barrel of his rifle into Vince's shoulder and motioned to put his hands up.

He fought the urge to grab the barrel, twist the weapon out of the man's hands, pound the butt into his nose, then turn it on his friend. Instead, he set his coffee cup on the dockmaster's desk before slowly lifted his hands up over his shoulders.

"*¿Qué es tu asunto aquí?*"

"He wants to know what your business is here," the dockmaster whispered from the corner.

"I figured that much, asshole. I pay you to prevent these little interactions, not translate them. Tell him the truth. I'm just taking on fuel, then I'll be on my way."

The dockmaster opened his mouth, but the soldier raised a hand to silence him.

Vince watched through the shack's tiny window as four more soldiers passed down the dock. One stood watch on the pier while the other three boarded *Mariella*.

"What we find aboard your boat, *señor*?" The soldier's English was passable.

Vince grinned. "Nothing. I'm just a guy on the way from Mexico to the Bahamas for a little vacation. I've got one crew member aboard, but nothing out of the ordinary."

"Please do not make us destroy such a beautiful craft. Tell us where to look, and we will not damage anything."

He shrugged. "Tear it up. You won't find anything. I don't even have enough cash to pay for my fuel."

The dockmaster's eyes widened.

Vince glanced over at him. "What, you don't take American Express here?"

His so-called friend hung his head.

"Guys, I'm serious. I don't even have enough cash aboard to offer you a respectable bribe." Out the window, soldiers were leading the Mexican boy up onto the pier and securing his hands behind his back.

The lead soldier motioned to Vince with the barrel of his rifle. "Get up." His partner let his rifle dangle from its strap across his shoulder and pulled a zip tie from a cargo pocket on his thigh. He secured Vince's hands then shoved him out of the tiny shack and into the back of an open army-green Jeep. Moments later, Ramiro appeared at the end of the dock, herded from behind into a second Jeep.

From Vince's vantage point in the dirt lot that served as a parking area, he watched his boat rock as the men searched it from bow to stern while the sun climbed up over the horizon.

Two hours later, the sergeant shoved past his guard posted at the door to the dockmaster's shack. Then he heard muffled shouting. The longer it continued, the wider Vince grinned, knowing the soldiers had come up empty and the duplicitous dockmaster would pay the price. The shouting continued as three soldiers climbed off the boat, marched up the dock to the Jeeps, then cut the zip-ties from Vince and Ramiro's wrists.

Vince climbed out and stretched, rubbing his wrists. He waved Ramiro past the weather-beaten shack and down the dock. They untied the boat, jumped aboard, then shoved as hard as they could away from the pier.

As soon as the boat cleared the channel, Vince opened the throttles all the way. The boat shot northeast away from the Cuban coast toward freedom.

CHAPTER THIRTY-FIVE

KATE SQUIRMED in the narrow bunk. William tried to insist she take the master stateroom, but Kate refused. He stood a full foot taller than her, so it seemed disrespectful for her to take the huge bed and leave him to fold himself into the smaller cabin. Now she kicked the covers tangled around her legs and stared at the low ceiling. She missed Whiskey's heavy weight and steady breaths.

Thanks to the wide stateroom windows, the cabin slowly brightened until Kate was able to make out the pattern on the bedspread and then titles on the books lined up on a rack above the door. The boat rolled in the low waves, and the previous day's clear sky had been replaced by a pale haze dotted with dark clouds. Giving up on sleep, she wiggled back into her khaki shorts. Then she popped into the boat's small but well-appointed head to splash water on her face.

"Morning! Sleep well?" William's cheerful voice annoyed Kate. He sounded well rested and ready for a perfect day at sea.

Kate expected the opposite. They should have been back to Shark Key with the book last night. Now they were bobbing in the middle of the ocean just off the coast of Cuba with no real idea how or when they'd get home, or even whether they'd be able to get the book back.

This whole trip was a complete fiasco, and she regretted agreeing to help at all.

"Like a baby," Kate lied. "Do I smell coffee?"

"Sure do. I just made a fresh pot." William pulled out a heavy mug, filled it, then handed it to Kate. "Cream or sugar? They only have powdered creamer on board." He grimaced as he reached for the sugar packets.

"Neither. Black is fine, thanks." Kate closed her eyes and swallowed a gulp of the dark liquid, savoring it as she waited for the caffeine to find its way into her bloodstream. "Where are we?"

"Still waiting a few miles outside Cuban waters, a little bit east of Mariel. When I took fresh coffee up to Steve and Susan a few minutes ago, the signal showed they were still sitting at the fuel dock. Should have been in and out of there in under a half hour, but they've been there over two."

"Looks like the weather is starting to turn. I hope

we can get this over with before a storm hits." Kate flopped down in the dinette and wrapped her hands around the warm mug.

William sat opposite her. "I don't mean this to be rude, but you look tired. Are you sure you slept okay?"

She shook her head. "If you want to know the truth, no. I didn't sleep at all. This whole thing is ridiculous. We're chasing a complete stranger across the Caribbean for an old book that may or may not have a map to a hidden treasure. For real? I don't know why I'm here. And for that matter, I really don't know why YOU are here. At least Steve and I have an interest in keeping Shark Key the way it is. You're just passing through. Shouldn't you just be swimming or fishing or relaxing with your wife? What does any of this matter to you?"

The corner of William's mouth turned up slightly. "It matters because it matters. What Chuck has built on Shark Key is pure. It's beautiful. And what Baumann wants to do to it is wrong. Whether I stay on Shark Key for a day or a year, I'm here now, and I have the ability to help, so that makes it my responsibility."

"You're crazy."

"Maybe, but here's the thing. When I lived for myself and worked for vanity — for accolades and recognition and awards — I was constantly chasing the approval of people just like Baumann. People with money and power who were ultimately only out for themselves. And after Michelle sold her app, it got worse.

"We attended fundraisers for everything. But it finally clicked for me when we paid five thousand dollars for an event to save the everglades, and every major Miami developer was hosting a table. Heck, Baumann was probably there. These were the very men who lobbied for environmental waivers and variances, who brought in truck after truck of fill dirt and concrete to pave over the land we were there to protect? I realized that night how hypocritical we all were. Michelle had always been reluctant to join the society circles and had questioned the authenticity of purpose. We had a long talk. She'd been prodding me for a while to step back and evaluate how we were spending our time and our resources. So she was all over it when I called a realtor. We moved onto the boat and made an intentional choice to travel with no plan. To be fully part of wherever we stopped for however long we were there. And to trust that when we arrived where we were supposed to be, we'd know. I think Shark Key is that place."

"But you've only been here a few days."

"Yes. We've been a lot of places and made a lot of friendships. Shark Key is special. Chuck is special. Steve and Susan are special. You and Whiskey, even though you won't accept it, are special. Speaking of Whiskey, I hope you don't mind, but Michelle slept up on your roof deck with him last night, and Chuck gave her all the leftover grouper for him after the restaurant closed. She said he was pretty antsy without you there. Anyway, you have a special community, and it's worth chasing some jerk across the gulf to keep it safe."

"How ..."

William laughed and held up a small phone with a thick antenna. "I've lived in the Caribbean long enough I don't go anywhere without a sat phone. I talked to Michelle about a half hour ago. Also, Babette should be getting out tomorrow, if not later this afternoon."

Kate took a sip of coffee and leaned back, relaxing just a tiny bit. "Thank you. Thank Michelle, too. With everything else going on, I didn't want to make a fuss, but I was worried about Whiskey. I knew Chuck had my spare keys and figured he'd make sure he got food and bathroom breaks, but I feel awful just taking that for granted."

"It's not taking it for granted, Kate. It's what friends do. We all watch out for each other. It's not quid pro quo, either. When one of us needs something, we all jump in. We don't have to be asked or begged, don't need to strike a deal. We just do. And whether you realize it or not, it's why you're here right now."

"I still—"

"They're coming out and they're moving fast." Steve's voice crackled over the boat's intercom. "All hands on deck!"

Kate wiggled out of the soft seat and poured the rest of the coffee down her throat. "I'll wake him."

William climbed the stairs to the rear cockpit while Kate opened the door to the crew quarters to wake Alejandro.

CHAPTER THIRTY-SIX

THE PLATE of steaming shrimp and grits landed in front of Tina with a thud. Two thick pats of butter lay melting in the center.

"You want another order of these for your son? No pressure, but we're almost out of today's shrimp." A group of tourists stood at the edge of the deck. The teenaged waitress waved them in. "Y'all sit anywhere you like. View is best over on that side. I'll be over to you with coffee in just a second."

Tina leaned forward on the bar and shoveled up a scoop of grits. "Dated a guy once who always said, 'Ya snooze, ya lose.' Guess that finally applies. The boy wants fresh shrimp, he can get his ass out of his sleeping bag earlier." She shrugged and ate.

The waitress seated another couple near the edge of the deck, then bustled around the tables, filling coffee cups and taking orders. The door from the kitchen opened, and the hair on Tina's neck tingled. A barrel-chested fifty-something man with thinning hair pushed under a faded Mercury hat limped out on a pair of crutches. She nodded at him. "You're the owner here, right?"

"Am for now, anyway. Chuck Miller." He reached across the bar, and Tina shook her cousin's hand for the first time. "You and your boy are in site forty-seven, right? Sorry I wasn't here to welcome you personally. Are you finding everything to your liking?"

"It's a damn sight better than the car. Thank you for your hospitality. We'll get something a little more permanent as soon as we find some work. How long you been here?"

"All my life, and then some. I was born here, and my dad was born here before me. My Gramps came from up north during the Depression."

"Wow. Unusual to meet another native down here."

"Ayup. Gettin' more transplants every day. Few of 'em are suited for it, but most of 'em ain't. Were you born in the Keys?"

"North Miami. Spent my summers working on Key Biscayne." Scrambling over security fences at the resorts and lifting whatever she could from the pockets of sunburned tourists.

"That area sure built up over the years. Gramps used to tell stories of how beautiful South Florida was before. Then it was all about who could build the tallest condo or the most prestigious golf course. Nothing's sacred to those greedy—" He shifted on the crutches and adjusted his cap. "Sorry. I just get a little ..."

"I know what you mean. At least you're safe on your little piece of heaven here."

Chuck looked down at the bar. It took him a minute to answer. "Not really. I'll be honest, this place has been in my family for three generations, and I'm about to lose it to one of those slime-suckers. The investors and tourists run up the property prices to a point where honest, hard-working people don't have a chance anymore. The people who keep those air conditioners running and the lawns mowed and put fresh fish on every plate on Duval Street? Most of us can't afford to live any closer than Big Pine."

"That sucks. Ain't you got any way to save it?"

Chuck bit his bottom lip. "Not that I've found yet." His shoulders drooped lower with each word. She almost felt sorry for him. But if she didn't find an angle, there might be nothing left. Pity could wait.

"How long you think you got left here?"

"End of the month." He glanced at his watch. "About ten days, I guess. Might squeeze a few extra days in before they pretend to run an auction and the developer buys it for the loan balance, which is about a tenth of what it's worth, and leaves me with nothing."

"Why didn't you just sell it?"

"Didn't think it'd come to this, really. I've always

been able to make it through off-season. Would have this year, too, if that bastard Baumann hadn't set his eye on stealing it from me. And now that I'm in the hole, why should he buy it for market value when he can get it on the cheap?"

The sap's eyes were getting watery, the rims turning red. He slapped the bar and shook his head like a dog.

"Sorry to hang a rain cloud over such a beautiful day." He waved his hand toward the clear sky. "I'm covering a charter for one of the dive boats based here. Perfect day to enjoy what's left under the water here."

She looked at the brace on his knee and shrugged. "I hate to ask, you bein' down on your luck and all, but do you happen to know anyone looking for help? I got bartending and waitressing experience, and Lucas is a solid busboy. Never complains."

"If you don't mind drunken tourists or working late, you might try the Electric Eel down in Old Town. Owner's name is Janet. Tell her you're stayin' here and I sent you down."

A party of three lumbered up to the bar and settled in on stools. Chuck held up his index finger to them then disappeared into the kitchen. All three men were sunburned under the straps of their Salt Life tanks. One carried an iPad in a sturdy waterproof case, and the other two carried cameras encased in waterproof housings with elaborate light rigs.

"Even on nitrox, we won't have a ton of bottom

time. He said visibility has been around eighty, so I want to make sure to get a few wide shots as we're coming in." The man poked at his tablet, dragging items on his shot list around.

Chuck emerged from the kitchen with a sack slung over his shoulder. He paused to shake hands with the three newcomers. "Welcome to Shark Key. We've had a little change in schedule, but we'll be ready to shove off in just a few minutes. Captain Steve spent the night on the other side of the Gulf Stream, so Justin and I are going to be taking you out on the *Island Hopper* today. First two dives will be nitrox on the Vandenberg, then we'll take a surface interval and do some snorkeling around the Sand Key lighthouse. After that, we'll drop you down over two of our most photogenic shallow reefs, and wrap up by bagging a few lobsters for dinner. Sound good to you fellas?"

"Perfect. You sure you're up for the ride?"

"Takes more'n a sprained knee to keep a Conch down."

"If you say so. You got lunch and beer, too, right?"

"It's being loaded now." He pointed to a faded blue cooler disappearing through a break in the seagrape hedge across the parking lot. The men all fist bumped then turned back to the tablet.

Tina waved Chuck over. "I couldn't help but overhear. I've got some serving experience. Do you need a hand with them? I'd be happy to come along and keep the food and drinks flowing."

"That's kind of you, but this ain't our first rodeo. I think we'll be okay."

"What happened with the Captain? The other side of the Gulf Stream is Cuba, isn't it?"

"There's a little water in between. It's nothing, just a slight change in plan."

Tina noticed he was biting his lip again — a tell if she'd ever seen one.

"Her husband with him?" Tina pressed, tilting her head toward Michelle, who was sipping coffee in front of a fruit plate at a table a few feet away. "Didn't see him around last night."

Chuck glanced toward the kitchen door, then tapped his hand on the bar. "I need to—"

"Of course, get going."

"Hey, we've got live music out here tonight for sunset. It gets busy, so make sure to come early if you want a spot on the rail." Chuck tapped the bar again then disappeared into the kitchen.

Tina had finished the hearty breakfast along with two more cups of coffee when Lucas plopped onto the stool beside her. "Whatcha eatin'?"

"Was shrimp 'n' grits, but they're gone."

"Why didn't ya save me none?"

"'Cause you're twenty-five years old, and if you want breakfast, you're big enough to get your ass up and git some. I may be your mama, but I ain't your keeper."

"Dammit, mama."

"You're cute, boy, but don't you disrespect your mama like that." Tina pinched his cheek, pulled him toward her, kissed his forehead, then shoved him back into his seat. She waved to the waitress. "Can he get a mountain dew and a couple eggs?"

CHAPTER THIRTY-SEVEN

A DEEP RUMBLE rolled across the water from the dark clouds clustered on the southeastern horizon, and tiny goosebumps rose on Kate's skin from the wind finding its way through the high flybridge. The red marker showing the *Mariella's* position on the GPS screen began to turn onto an easterly course.

Steve leaned back against the wide vinyl seat. "At least this guy is predictable."

"Stupid, more like. He's coming straight at us." She dragged her finger across the screen. Its course would carry the stolen vessel no more than a mile from where Kate and the *Sofia* idled a wide, slow circle.

William raised an eyebrow. "Maybe he just doesn't care. Underestimating this man could get us all killed. Don't forget that."

"I think we should intercept him as soon as he clears Cuban waters and wrap this up." Susan pointed to a spot on the screen. "If we shoot across his path then double back, we might still be able to surprise him."

Everyone agreed. Steve pulled the boat about and shoved the throttles forward. The big cruiser's stern dug deep into the choppy sea, shoving the heavy boat up onto plane.

Kate monitored the screen as they careened west, closing the distance between the two dots on the chart. The *Mariella* sped directly toward them. When just two miles separated them, William picked up the VHF.

"M/V *Sofia* to M/V *Mariella*. You have entered international waters, and you are not authorized to be operating that vessel. Slow to a stop and prepare to be boarded."

"Think he'll answer?"

"Of course not, but we need to at least give him a chance. We're not pirates, are we?"

"Arrgh!" Kate scrunched the side of her face together in her best pirate impression.

"Not that kind of pirate, Kate. Modern pirates in the Caribbean would kill me and William, feed us to the sharks, and sell you and Susan on the dark web before the sun reaches noon."

William pressed the microphone's button again. "M/V *Mariella*, stop and prepare to be boarded."

The boats were less than a mile apart.

"We'll meet them in about thirty seconds. Everyone strap in!"

Alejandro crouched low on the boat's bow and clipped a tether to the railing.

"There." Steve pointed to a spot just off their port bow. "He's veering off." Steve turned the boat hard to starboard, bringing it around to parallel the *Mariella*'s new course. "I thought we'd get a good game of Chicken out of him. Looks like he's a little more chicken than I expected."

The GPS screen showed the dot arcing away from the pursuit and straightening out to the north. Steve pulled off toward starboard, punched the throttle, and set a parallel course. The *Mariella* pulled further west, expanded the gap between the boats, and then eased back toward the north.

Steve tapped the radar screen, "Maybe if we're lucky, we can just herd him back and let the Coasties deal with him."

"But we need the book!"

William rested a hand on Kate's shoulder. "One thing at a time, Kate. We'll be there when they board him."

The boat took a big rolling wave to the port side bow. Kate slid into Susan on the wide seat, then grabbed the seatback to keep them both from falling to the deck.

"Sorry, girls. Between the weather and his wake, it's getting rough. Maybe you should go below."

Kate's cheeks burned hot. "Below, my stolen donkey! I should have ended this before it even started. I'm here to finish it now."

The two boats danced for nearly an hour as they raced north until the bow of *Sofia* was nearly even with *Mariella*'s stern. Suddenly, a sharp crack sounded from the other boat.

"Kate, DOWN!" Two more cracks echoed over the water.

While Susan scrambled to the safety of the cabin below, William crouched against the fiberglass and pushed Kate into the protected nook beside him. In his hand, Kate recognized the polished wood handle of a Colt 1911 from a story on gang violence she'd worked on back in the city. Her ears rang at the loud explosion as three quick shots roared from the gun.

The other boat straightened out and took off at full throttle away from the *Sofia*. Steve adjusted and pushed the *Sofia*'s throttles all the way forward. The boat's engines screamed.

"We can't stay wide open for long. I just hope he overheats before we do." He tapped the starboard engine's temperature gauge. The needle was already nudging into the red zone.

Alejandro scrambled up the ladder, shouting rapid Spanish over the scream of the boat's engine. William nodded, then the boy disappeared below deck.

"Steve, can you help Alejandro in the engine room? I'll take the helm. I want to stay to his starboard and keep herding him north. Just a little farther."

Moments later, they saw a cloud of dark smoke puff from the rear of the *Mariella*. The boat drifted to a stop, dropping lower in the water as smoke billowed from the engine compartment.

William pulled the *Sofia*'s throttles back to neutral and let their bigger boat sink down into the water and drift toward the other's stern. In the deafening silence, shouts in both English and Spanish echoed across the water.

The greasy thug who'd attacked Babette shouted frantically from the boat's helm. "You!" He pointed at the teenager in a dirty blue t-shirt — the same shirt Alejandro wore. "Get that engine started, Now!"

The boy scrambled around the cockpit to release the *Mariella*'s dinghy, then he leaped out onto the boat's swim platform. He was chased by a string of English profanity and racial slurs Kate hoped he didn't understand. Then she glanced toward the ladder.

Alejandro's head had just appeared above the flybridge deck. He shrugged and gazed across the water at his father's burning boat. Smoke poured from the back of it, so black and thick it blocked the name "*Mariella*" from view. The boy balanced on the rocking swim platform, engulfed in smoke, scooping seawater over the transom.

"What in the name of Pete is that boy doing?" William flipped the radio to PA and raised the micro-

phone. "*Mariella*, we can assist." His voice boomed
from the forward speakers and echoed across the water.
William dropped the mic. "Kate, take the helm and get
us over there. He's doing more harm..." He scrambled
down the ladder and beckoned for Alejandro and
Steve to follow him to the bow.

As the *Sofia* neared the billowing smoke, the thug
leaned across the rail of the flybridge and shouted,
"Stay back!"

When William stepped over the bow rail with
Alejandro right behind him, the man pointed a
handgun down at them. His arms swung wildly as his
boat rocked in the surf. Alejandro scrambled back up
to the helm.

A shot rang out. William dropped to his belly on
the deck as the wide sliding door to the salon shattered. Pebbles of safety glass rained down on the
deck then scattered as the boat rolled in the
stormy sea.

"Miss Kate. He say you ..." the boy pointed toward
the cabin.

"Not a chance, my friend." Kate scrambled to the
bow as rain pounded on the fiberglass deck. "I'll cover
you." She took the Colt from William, crouched
behind the gunwale, then aimed up at the man with
the slicked back hair, ignoring the fat drops pelting her
face.

He held his own gun steady in both hands.

William climbed across the bow rail. "Put the gun

down, man. We're only here to help. Put the gun down."

Another shot rang out, and the fiberglass on the *Sofia*'s starboard gunwale splintered in a puff of white.

"*Papa's querido...*" Alejandro hung his head.

"Look out!" Kate shouted.

Three things happened at once.

Vince jumped from his sheltered spot on the flybridge and fired toward the *Sofia*.

William leapt from the bow toward the *Mariella*'s cockpit.

The *Sofia*'s bow rammed the other boat.

William landed in the cockpit with a thud. Steve's body flew forward against the bow rail from the impact, and a shot rang from the Colt in Kate's hand. The glass window on the *Mariella*'s flybridge shattered.

Alejandro swore and tweaked the throttles to pull off the *Sofia*'s stern.

The thug screamed from the flybridge. He waved his gun down at Steve in the bow like he was objecting to a bad call at a Dolphins game. The wind whipped up, blowing the black smoke off to the west and clearing Kate's view of the *Mariella*'s starboard side. But smoke continued to pour from beneath the swim platform.

"Alejandro!" Kate shouted up from the bow. "Get us back over there!"

William waved for Alejandro to bring the boat

closer as Kate started screaming and waving her hands at the man on the other boat.

He pointed his gun at Kate again.

The boats had drawn close enough for Kate to see his crazed look. He had deep dark circles under his eyes, and the whites surrounding his beady brown irises were well exposed. His greased hair flopped down across his forehead, and he looked like he was running on coffee and candy bars. Maybe even a few lines of cocaine.

And then in a flash, she saw William's strong arms swipe down over the man's shoulders, capturing his wrists.

"All clear! Come on over, guys! And bring some zip ties!" William pushed the thug down to the deck of the flybridge.

Alejandro feathered the throttle and pulled the boats side by side. He spoke to his cousin in the cockpit in rapid Spanish.

Kate thought she saw the other boy rub his fingers together, as if to say "money."

After a brief talk, the two shook hands then disappeared into the *Mariella*'s engine room.

Kate slid aft along the starboard gunwale.

Susan, several thick white zip ties in her hand, had just joined Steve in the rear cockpit when the boat rolled, causing her to stumble. A shard of glass embedded into her left heel. The zip ties fell to the deck as she grabbed her foot. Blood gushed from the wound. She hopped to keep her balance, but the glass was everywhere. She screamed louder and fell against the starboard rail, another wide cut opening in the sole of her right foot. Her arms swung wildly, then in what felt like slow motion, Susan's body folded at the waist and toppled into the roiling sea.

Kate shrieked. Steve dove over the rail, and she quickly lost sight of him in the rough waves. Susan's white shirt made a stark contrast to the dark waters. The heavy waves had already pulled her several yards away from them.

"Man overboard! Man overboard! Man overboard!" Kate shouted the alert three times, scrambled around the corner to find a life ring, then repeated the call.

Susan screamed and flailed in the water, drifting further from the boat.

A heavy splash from behind the *Mariella* caught Kate's attention. William stood at the transom, dumbfounded, watching the thug in the green shirt swim toward the screaming woman. Then all heads turned toward Alejandro's shout from *Sofia's* flybridge.

"Shark!"

The thug was still fifteen yards away from Susan when a fin pierced the surface of the water. It circled between them, then pivoted.

Kate watched in horror as the beast stretched its maw wide. Susan thrashed between the waves, bobbing right into its path.

Its jaws snapped shut.

As it rolled to its side, Susan's leg, trapped between its teeth, pointed toward the sky. Her body did a macabre cartwheel before the shark plunged into the Strait, taking her deep into the drink.

Shots rang out from the cockpit of the other boat before Kate remembered the Colt in her hand. Through streaming tears and a seizing chest, she aimed at the beast and fired until the slide locked open.

But the carnivore was already well beyond her reach.

She fell to the deck, her tears splashing on the deck and swirling in Susan's bloody footprints.

CHAPTER THIRTY-EIGHT

KATE STEPPED across the *Mariella*'s soot-covered transom. Over the starboard rail, rain pelted a darker patch of water where scraps of fabric floated between the swells.

The drenched thug sat on a fish box with his hands tied behind his back. William had secured him and quietly swept the glass from *Sofia*'s cockpit. Then he led a glassy-eyed Steve into the salon to dry off, leaving Kate to deal with the thug.

"Talk."

The man stared at the fiberglass deck.

Kate pushed away the image of the dark stained waters and the wide, scarred fin. Her fists tightened as she paced the deck in front of him.

"You..." Her nostrils drew together, and she fought to breathe. She pulled the Colt from her cargo pocket and spun it around in her palm. "I should have kicked your ass harder when I had the chance."

When she cocked her arm back, the man's shoulders seized like he was trying to shield his face with his tied hands. He pulled his knees up and tucked his face down, balancing in a little ball on his tailbone.

"Wait!" His voice was hoarse.

"Hmm. You *can* speak." She grabbed his arm by the bicep and pulled his torso forward. "You getting scared? Give me a reason to not toss you overboard right here." She shoved him backward.

"Let's start with a name. What can I call you? 'Asshole' is getting a little repetitive, even though it suits you."

His legs uncurled. He planted his feet wide, then stumbled across the cockpit into the rain, trying to catch his balance. "Vince."

"Vince what?"

A wave hit them on the port side, and the boat rolled hard to starboard. Vince stumbled toward the gunwale, face planting on the rough deck just short of the rail.

"Holt. Vince Holt."

He rolled onto his shoulder, tucked his knees under him, then crawled forward toward the sheltered area near the cockpit door. The rough deck tore the skin from his knees. Streaks of dark blood appeared on the white fiberglass behind him, then washed down toward the scuppers with the beating rain.

Kate stood, feet planted wide, knees loose. She rocked with the boat. "Okay, Vince Holt. Start with the book. Where is it?"

"What book?"

"I'm not in the mood for games right now. We both know what book. First edition, *Treasure Island.* The one you stole from us two days ago and nearly killed its rightful owner for."

"What do you mean, nearly killed him? I just knocked him down."

"And cracked his skull on the pavement."

His eyebrows softened a little, then the hardness returned to his beady eyes. "Collateral damage, I guess. What's it matter, anyway? He'd be fine if he'd just get with the program and do what he's supposed to do."

"And what about ..." Kate's voice caught in her throat. Shaking her head, she continued. "What Chuck's supposed to do is be able to run his business in peace, free of harassment by thugs and criminals."

"And I'm just doin' my job, lady. A man's gotta eat."

"Your job. Just like any other hardworking fisherman or tour guide or schoolteacher? Come on. You hurt people for a living. Your job is illegal. Your boss is corrupt. How can you even look in the mirror?"

Kate touched a nerve. The man twitched and closed his eyes.

"You can't, can you? That's why you've got days of scruff on your chin. You step up to the mirror and spread lather over your face, and then you see those little black eyes staring back at you. The only eyes who know everything you've done. Everyone you've hurt and killed. All for what? Greed? Power?"

She inched closer to him. His body was shifting, tensed muscles releasing and ready to pounce.

Kate circled around, leaned close to his ear, and whispered, "For what? For a crappy little trailer by the dry dock and a beat-up Hyundai? For friends you can drink with, but who disappear into the shadows when—"

"Ma- ma- master suite. Closet."

She grabbed a rope, strung it between his wrists, then tied it to the ladder. "I'll be right back." The rain beat down on Vince's head, plastering his hair to his forehead and across one eye. "You better not be lying to me."

He shook the hair from his face and slumped down onto his side.

Three hours later, Vince Holt was tucked into the u-shaped dinette of the *Sofia*. He wore fresh clothes and had a towel draped around his neck. His hands were still secured with zip ties, but now they rested in front of him on the table. Alejandro sat perched in front of the tall interior helm across the salon, the big Colt in his hand.

Kate stepped out into the cockpit into the after-noon sun. The storm had moved off to the west as they'd motored north, and the clear skies had made the rest of the crossing bearable. Holt had only puked once.

The *Mariella* lay fifty yards astern, attached to a set of tow lines Steve and William had rigged up. Kate checked the lines then climbed the ladder to the flybridge.

"We're getting close. Michelle is waiting right here." William tapped a dot on the radar screen. "She's got Chuck's Whaler. We should have her on the horizon in just a minute or so."

"Great. I'll be glad to get this book back in his hands so we can get this whole thing over with. How much did you tell her?"

"It was a quick call. Just gave her the GPS numbers." He paused, choosing his words. "Look, when we get there, I'm gonna need your help. Steve's a mess, and he needs a little time to sort through everything before he talks with the authorities. We'll move you all over to the Whaler. I need you to help keep them separated. The boys will tie you all up to the *Mariella* and work on getting her secured a little better while I run in and refuel the *Sofia*. Between the main and the reserves, she'll have enough in the tanks to tow *Mariella* back home, but it'll be a slow trip, and it'll take at least three aboard to keep watch. So I'll go back to Cozumel with the boys and then fly home tomorrow. You can fill in Michelle while you all wait for us."

Kate watched the horizon until she spotted a tiny dot that became a little boat, and she wondered how the hell to explain the past two days.

CHAPTER THIRTY-NINE

KATE'S SHADOW stretched behind her as she pulled herself out of the little Boston Whaler and onto the weathered dock. She reached a hand down to Steve, but he turned away and yanked Vince out of the boat by his armpit. While Michelle tied up the Whaler, Vince stumbled over the planks, turning each time Steve pushed him one way or the other until they reached the front door of Chuck's little house. Steve pounded, and when Chuck opened the door, Steve shoved Vince through it and stalked back down to the docks.

Kate peeked around the hedge as he boarded the *Island Hopper*. He slowly ran his hand along the rail until he collapsed in tears on the dive deck. Kate started toward the boat, then she stopped.

When Danny died, people had crowded around her for days, never giving her a moment alone to wrap her head around what had just happened. How her life would never be the same. How the one person she counted on to always be there would never be there again.

The best gift she could give Steve now was privacy.

Kate turned and slipped back through the hedge toward the north point of the island. There would be plenty of time later to console her friend. Now he needed a quiet moment to let down his guard and feel.

She wouldn't mind a moment to herself, either.

As she climbed the deck, she spotted Whiskey. His ears perked forward, his entire body motionless except for his tail thumping the thick boards of the deck. Beside him, Babette was settled in a sturdy chair with pillows and beach towels tucked all around her. Her roommate from the hospital and the woman from the Historical Society fawned around her like a queen.

Whiskey quivered next to Babette, his eyes on Kate.

"Okay, c'mere boy!" Kate snapped her fingers at her side, then the dog bolted to her and jumped up, his enormous paws on her shoulders, licking her face. His strong tail knocked a chair over as it wagged.

Kate hugged him back and finally pushed him back to the ground.

"Kate." Babette's hand barely reached her shoulder, but the wave beckoned Kate to the chair beside her. The other two women disappeared into the kitchen. "William called. Where's Steve?"

Kate cocked her head toward the *Hopper*'s slip. "He needs a little time to himself right now."

"Yeah. When my husband died, I couldn't get a moment alone. I just wanted to wail and scream and swear at God for taking him so early. But I couldn't do that in front of everyone. I had to hold it together. I know they were all just trying to help, and I'm so grateful they were there. But ..."

Kate squeezed Babette's hand, and the two sat together and watched the sun drop closer to the horizon.

A few minutes later, the other two women emerged from the kitchen with a tray covered in red plastic baskets and a couple of galvanized buckets filled with ice and beer and bottled water. The shorter woman with the red glasses set the tray on a nearby table.

"Kate, do you remember Amy and Kara?"

"Of course." Kate pushed herself out of the chair and stretched her hand out to the broad-shouldered woman first. "Kara, it's good to see you up and about. I hope you're feeling better?"

"Still a bit tender in spots, but I'm getting by, thanks for asking." She glanced around the deck.

Amy reached forward and shook Kate's hand. "Good to see you again. I hope we're not overstepping by being here. After everything that happened, I felt like I could use a couple days off. Kara told me Babette was getting discharged. I figured, how better to spend my free days than by coming out here, giving her a hand, and getting a taste of what we're trying to save. And then when the phone call came in..."

"Oh, not at all. I'm sure Chuck is glad you're here. We've all got a lot to deal with right now." Kate glanced at the table. "Wait. Babette, are those your grouper bites and island tartar? You gave these two your secret recipe?"

Babette grabbed her side and winced, but kept laughing. "Who says I gave it away?"

Kara came to her rescue. "She had us help her to the kitchen and set up a stool for her to lean on. Then she ordered us out long enough for her to mix up the batter. After that, she left us to do the dirty work of coating them and watching the fryer."

Michelle crossed the deck to join them as Amy passed the baskets and bottles around, then they all watched as Babette tested the first bite and nodded her approval. Kate popped a chunk of fish in her mouth. She closed her eyes, savoring the flavor of fresh fish and nutty fryer oil. "Babette, how are you feeling?"

She smiled and waved at the darkening sky. "I'm alive, I'm not trapped in that grungy old hospital, the sky is clear, and the sun is setting in the west. All things considered, I'm great. Sure, it'll be better when this hurts a little less. I'm still pretty bloated from where they patched me back up, but that'll pass. Literally." She laughed at her own joke, grabbing her side and leaning into the pain.

"Do they have you on good pain control?"

Babette flapped her hand in the air. "They offered it, but fresh air and some Tylenol is really enough. Conchs come from tough stock. Besides, I need my faculties about me to decide what kind of beer I want." She raised her Kalik, and tipped the top toward the group. "To Susan."

"Susan." They all slowly clinked their bottles against Babette's. Babette took a tiny sip while the other three women drank in unison.

A few minutes later, Whiskey's head jerked toward the stairs. His hips slowly rose up, his hair on end, a low growl rumbling in his chest.

"Whiskey, no. Sit." He obeyed Kate's stern command, but his unblinking eyes never left the man who'd just climbed the steps.

Chuck led the new arrival to the table amid horrified looks and angry glares. Then he squeezed Babette around the shoulders before settling into a spot beside her. He took a beer from one of the buckets, clinked his bottle against hers, then paused to watch the sun slip under the horizon. Then he picked up a conch shell from an empty table and blew into it, playing a lingering mournful note.

As its low wail bid the day farewell, Kate could just barely see the rocking radio mast on the *Island Hopper*.

Chuck sat a little straighter and looked at the newcomer, who squirmed a bit in his seat. "You all know about Vince by now, but just to get the formality out of the way, this is Vince Holt." Heads around the table nodded, but no one shook Vince's hand. "Vince has been working for Marty Baumann."

Kate looked at the other women. Michelle held a neutral expression, but Babette, Amy, and Kara's eyes all narrowed at hearing Baumann's name. It seemed a common reaction among the locals.

Chuck continued. "Recent events have led him to seek opportunities outside Baumann's organization." He nodded to Vince.

"Miss Wilcox?"

Babette glanced down at her bandaged abdomen, then leveled her glare back at Vince. "We've met."

"Babette."

She swiveled to face Chuck. "How can you let it go? How can you let him get away with what he did? To both of us! To Susan?"

"He's not going to get away with it. But right now, we have a common interest. He can help us if we help him. We'll deal with the rest later."

"Every day he spends out in the sun is a day he should be in a cell. Or worse."

Vince broke in. "Miss Wilcox, I am truly sorry for what I did to you. I've been thinking about leaving this ... job for a while, and I just ... what happened with you and with Mr. Miller ... it was just ... I'm sorry. I'm glad you're recovering, and I'd like to try to make it up to you."

"Babette," Kate started. "None of us has a good reason to trust this guy. No offense, Vince."

"None taken."

"But I can tell you that what happened to Susan wasn't his fault. He jumped in and tried to help. I saw it." She paused. "I still don't trust him, but he's offering his help in return for a chance to get out and start over. I think most of us can appreciate that, even if we aren't sure about him yet. So for now, that'll have to be enough."

"It's enough for me, and I'm the one who has the final say," Chuck announced as Amy deposited several more baskets of grouper on the table. "As much as we'd like to press pause for a few days, the clock is still ticking. Baumann smells blood, and he will exploit every weakness he can find."

He turned to Kate. "Do you have it?"

She pulled the battered archive box from her bag then set it on the table.

Chuck continued. "Vince here is in the unique position to be able to feed Baumann information to keep him off our backs while we go through this to find the place where Gramps hid Capone's loot. He can buy me the time I need to save this place for all of us. Amy, I can't thank you enough for helping me get this book in the first place, and I promise we'll return it as soon as my business with it is done."

Kate looked across the table. "Michelle, your husband is a bit of a badass."

"Yes. Yes, he is. I think I'll keep him." She grinned. "You'd better fill me in on all of his accomplishments because he'll never tell me for fear I'll never let him go on any more adventures."

"Someday. Suffice it to say, William was amazing, and we never could have gotten the book back without him."

Chuck handed her a fresh bottle of water. "I know you two don't really have a dog in this hunt. We appreciate William's help, and yours, too. But I'll understand when the two of you are ready to move on."

"We've already talked about this, and we're not going anywhere. We haven't been here long, but we know home when we see it and Shark Key is it. You can count on us, Chuck."

He sat still for a moment, then reached up and scratched his eye. Kate was pretty sure she spotted a tear, but the old salt would never admit to feeling sentimental.

"Okay, let's get down to business here." Chuck pulled the small leather-bound book from the box and opened it flat on the table.

Vince squirmed in his seat. "I don't want to be a downer on my first day on the team, but all's in there is a bunch of notes about fish and tides scribbled in all the margins. I stared at it for hours after—"

"It's a fishing journal, Vince. There are supposed to be notes about fish and tides." Babette's sharp tone told everyone she wasn't ready to forgive him just yet.

"How about we take a deeper look." Chuck flipped

a few pages. "Like here." He pointed to one of the notations.

12.7.39 — *Storm blew in from the southwest. Baby cried all night. Gigi took the car into town to get medicine for him and didn't come back.*

"That's from about six months before she disappeared for good."

Babette rested her hand on Chuck's arm. He flipped page after page, reading the rare personal notes to the group.

3.28.60 — *Winds still high, viz 20 at KK.*

4.9.60 — *Wedding.*

"That's my mama and daddy's wedding date. Then there are a bunch about fishing ... then, here." He pointed.

8.2.60 — *Finished house.*

He pointed to the roof of his house just beyond the restaurant. "My house. He built it for them as a wedding gift."

Chuck turned back to the front of the book and read.

8.24.40: *Alone with P two months now. Offered a Negro widow and her children to live in the bunkhouse. James 1:27.*

4.17.41: *Visited KK. Planning a dock with rental slips for next tourist season.*

12.5.41: *Rental slips sold for the whole season.*

"They go on like this. Fishing notes and tides several times a week. Little notes every few months."

He closed the book, his finger tucked between its pages to hold his place. "I remember Daddy talking about Ophelia when I was little. It was during the war. Her boys were a few years older 'n him, and he worshipped them like they were older brothers. I think she married a man from the mainland and moved off the Key not long after Daddy started school." He flipped deeper into the book. "Yeah here's one from a few years later.

5.2.43: *Wedding of Ophelia and Curtis. Paul was ring bearer. KK set them up in Montgomery.*

"Your grandfather may have been a man of few words, but it sounds like he had a big heart." Michelle sighed. "Not many white men would help a black woman in that time, even down here."

"Just doin' what's right."

Kate glared at Vince. He seemed engrossed in the history, but she wasn't convinced he was worthy of the fresh start Chuck was offering him. "What else does it say?"

"A lot more of the same," Chuck said.

Her shoulders sagged as the last shred of hope abandoned her. She glanced around the group. Their furrowed brows and downturned lips mirrored her own mood. She felt her own fresh start slipping away.

Time was running out fast, and they had no idea where to look for the treasure.

CHAPTER FORTY

Kate stepped down off the dock onto the aft deck of *Serenity*. She slid the door free and a gust of chilled air enveloped her.

"What do you think, Whiskey? I hear the right words, but he looks like the type who would say whatever he needed to say to get out of hot water." Kate scratched the dog's head. "I'm all for fresh starts and second chances, sure, but I'm not buying his story."

Look at me, trying to have an in-depth conversation with a dog.

The curtains swayed with the gentle movement of the water. Through a narrow gap, the dock lights cast an amber strip of light across the dark room.

Kate flopped over the length of the couch, body aching from the stress of the past two days. Whiskey squeezed into the narrow gap between her and the cushions. She fell asleep on the couch to the soft sound of water lapping against *Serenity*'s flat hull.

> *Kate leaned far out over the polished port rail, the sky above her ablaze with purple and green light. She watched the blue sun climb higher in the sky. Something pressing into the small of her back told her the sun wasn't supposed to be blue, but it looked simultaneously ordinary and stunning. It captivated her, so she didn't notice the massive swell until it slammed the starboard side of the hull, sending her flying over the railing toward the roiling water eight decks below.*
>
> *She fell in slow motion, inch by inch, or maybe her mind just sped up to record every millisecond—*

She awoke with a start, her hands making contact with the carpet a split second before the rest of her body hit the deck. Whiskey lay snoring on the couch, all four legs stretched into the center where Kate had just been sleeping. She pushed up to her knees then rubbed her left elbow.

"Jerk." She kissed the sleeping dog between the ears before dragging herself down the narrow hall and into her bedroom. Both hands on her watch pointed down. Almost five-thirty. Too late to go back to bed, but too early to get up. She stripped out of the clothes she'd been wearing for two days, climbed into the tiny shower, and let the hot water pound the top of her head and run down her back.

How did any of this get to be my problem?

They'd practically stolen an antique book from the historical society, immediately gotten it stolen from them, then chased the thief across the Caribbean and back. All for nothing. No map to the hidden money. No clear directions of where to look. Not even a viable clue.

People were hurt. Susan was dead. And Shark Key was three days closer to becoming a gated resort, with all its current residents out on the street.

She'd come to the Keys to get away from reality. To escape the trappings of conventional life. After Danny, deadlines were meaningless. News stories were irrelevant. Everywhere she turned, the world looked upside down. Corruption and greed ran unchecked. The innocent sat in cells while the criminals ran free. Danny's death looked like a simple home invasion. Like one of thousands, and like no other one in particular. No evidence. No arrests. No accountability.

Shark Key was supposed to be a haven from the broken world, but the same old brokenness was encroaching again. Sure, the story of a legendary gangster and his lost treasure held some appeal. And the idea of sticking it to a corrupt developer and winning one for the little guy felt noble. But reality was manifest in the bruises darkening her skin and the indelible memory of Susan's body toppling over the port gunwale into the cerulean water. Life and death decisions. Nightmares.

No, this was not what she signed up for. But this time Kate had a choice. She scrubbed the crust of Mexican dust and Caribbean salt from her short blonde hair, then toweled off, grabbed her laptop and started typing:

HOUSEBOAT FOR SALE.

It might take a little time to sell a houseboat with no motor, but affordable housing in the Lower Keys was hard to find. Someone was bound to want it. Chuck would surely tow *Serenity* out for them, and she could easily fit her essentials in the car with plenty of room left over for Whiskey. One former classmate was living in Belize and another had settled in Cartagena after covering the recent economic recovery in Colombia. She'd take it slow, head west, and camp along the way where she could. Maybe she'd even write a book about it.

The irony of taking a month or more to drive to almost the exact place she'd left on a boat not thirty-six hours before struck her, and Kate laughed loud enough to wake Whiskey. She nudged him and hopped to her feet.

"Let's go take some pictures of the sunrise, boy."

CHAPTER FORTY-ONE

VINCE CLUTCHED his coffee and lowered his aching body to the dock. So much had changed in three days, he took comfort in reclaiming his morning routine. He sat, legs dangling, waiting for the sunrise. A sharp chirp from his phone snapped his attention back from the eastern horizon.

"Yeah?"

"Where have you been?"

Vince held the phone at arm's length and could still hear every word. When Baumann's swearing finally showed signs of slowing down, Vince pulled the phone closer.

"You wouldn't believe me if I told you." He glanced around to be certain he was alone. "The details aren't impor—"

"Like hell they aren't!"

Vince sighed and started over. "Hear me out. I tried it the usual way. But the dude has some relentless friends. They caught up with me in Cozumel, and I had to improvise."

"Improvise?" Baumann's growl hung in the air while Vince chose his words.

"It was my only option. But in the end, it all turned out better than we could have hoped."

"Better how?"

"They think I'm on their side. We're working together now."

Silence.

"Look, they had me dead to rights. I whacked one of them and tossed her overboard." He crossed his fingers. Perhaps taking credit for the woman's accident would buy him some credibility. "'Stead of scarin' 'em, it just pissed them off. They cornered me. Threatened to toss *me* overboard in the Gulf Stream. Even if that was an empty threat, they were gonna turn me over to the cops when we got back. So I sold them a story they couldn't resist."

A sigh through the tiny speaker was the only reply.

"What do they want more than anything, Boss?"

"I'm not in the mood, Holt."

"But it matters."

"Fine, they want me to back off."

"No."

"Excuse me?"

"That's not it. If you just back off, you could

come back. They want you gone for good. So I told them I wanted out. I told them I was planning to double-cross you — to take the money and take you out. I begged them to cut me in on the deal. To give me enough to get away and get set up somewhere new. They're suckers for a second chance, and I played them hard. They're going to lead me straight to it. And then I'm gonna take it all and bring it to you."

"Why would they trust you?"

"Because they're naïve, bleeding-heart suckers? Because they love a good story? I don't know. I just know they do. I sat out there with them all night, poring over that stupid book and listening to the dude's stories about his grandfather and his childhood. I swear when this is over, you're paying for me to spend a week at a resort where the drinks and the women—"

"When this is over, we are going to have a long talk about my expectations. A member of my organization is to keep me informed of every step in an operation. Is that clear, Holt?"

"Yes, sir." Vince rolled his eyes. The thick seagrape bushes on the opposite shore rustled as an iguana or maybe an alligator slunk through in search of breakfast.

"Good. So, in your little ruse, when do I find out you've betrayed me?"

"Hopefully not til we've got the money."

"And I just sit tight until then?"

"I've got it all under control, Boss."

"Sure you do. Just so you know, when I *hear* about this? Nothing's personal."

"Of course. This is all gonna work out. You can count on me."

"That's yet to be seen. Until this is over, I need to know everything you know, the minute you know it. I don't care how you manage, but I want phone calls every hour from you, and if I don't hear from you on time, I'll assume you've bought into your little redemption story, and I'll adjust my plan accordingly."

"That won't be necessary. I'll call every hour, and I'll get you everything."

The line went dead, and Vince tucked the phone back into his pocket. The last time one of Baumann's men betrayed him, the guy's body turned up jammed behind a dumpster in Miami.

He sat on the end of the dock, sipped his coffee, and watched the sun ascend into the morning sky.

When the dock's planks grew too hot to sit on, Vince walked back to his place and locked the door behind him. Behind the false back in the closet of the spare room, Vince unlocked a shallow case. He selected a tiny .25 caliber Baby Browning and filled two magazines with six hollow point bullets each, which he dropped into a deep cargo pocket. He strapped the Browning to his left ankle, then chose two small smoke grenades and a can of tear gas, which he dropped in the other cargo pocket.

After locking the compartment, he grabbed a deep

mesh bag. Packed his faded buoyancy compensator, regulator, mask, and fins. Pulled his wrist-mounted dive computer out, tapped the power button. Nothing. Tried three more times, but the screen stayed blank. He stuffed it in his pocket, hitched the bag over his shoulder, then hauled everything to his car.

CHAPTER FORTY-TWO

KATE HEARD SLOW, uneven steps on the dock behind her as she strapped the dripping kayak to the pilings at the end of her dock. She spoke without turning around.

"Good morning, Chuck."

"It's a perfect morning for a paddle around the cove, isn't it?"

She turned toward him, her camera dangling from her wrist. "Perfect. All wrong. Both. Neither."

"Yeah. I guess it won't feel perfect for a long time, will it? Look, I want to say thank you. I know it feels like it was all for nothing now, but I appreciate what you and the guys did for me. Really. And I know there has to be something in that book somewhere. I'm gonna get a little breakfast and start fresh. I'd love your help, if you've got the time."

"Chuck, I know you believe your grandpa's story,

but I just see you getting deeper and deeper into a problem you can't solve. The cost is too high now. You're gonna lose this place, and I can't stick around and watch it happen. I'm sorry, but I'm putting *Serenity* up for sale, and Whiskey and I are gonna hit the road again."

"Is that really what you want? To always be packing up and moving on? Constantly looking to the next shore and never really being present where you actually are? To always being an outsider, a tourist that locals depend on for dollars, but never really accept or trust?"

Kate shrugged. "Better than getting dragged into local land wars where good people end up dead."

"Some things are worth fighting for. Worth dying for. This place is one of them."

"Maybe it is for you. You've lived here all your life. You have no idea what it's like out there. How cruel people can be to each other. You've never been out in the real world. I did all the things I was supposed to do. Went to college, got a job, got married. And it all got ripped away by some asshole who wanted our DVD player. Is a DVD player worth dying for? I'd say no. But it's what Danny died for. I think I've paid my dues to this world already."

Chuck stared off the end of the dock, toward the tiny green island across the channel. His voice sounded a million miles further away. "You think you're the only one who's paid a price, Kate? You think you're the only one who wants to be free from the bull crap of the people who were supposed to love you and protect you but didn't?

"My daddy died when I was six years old. He died because he stepped up to fight in a war we never should have been in. But we were. And once we were, he said that serving and leading those boys who never asked to be there but got sent into hell anyway seemed like the right thing to do." He swatted at a gnat beside his ear.

"My mama, she took it hard. And she tried to run, like you're trying to run from the memory of Danny. But she had me, so instead of packing us up and running for real, she ran in her mind. And no matter how far she ran, how much she drank or smoked or shot up, the world was still the same when she landed. Until one day she ran too far. She died trying to run from something too big to run from — reality."

Kate rested a hand on Chuck's shoulder, but he shrugged it off and glared into her eyes.

"I was nine. So don't try to tell me about paying your dues. Don't try to tell me about what price is worth it and what isn't. Don't try to tell me I haven't seen the world enough to know it's not worth saving. You with your fancy college degree and that trust fund you refuse to touch. This is all a game to you, and you don't even know it. You're slumming it. Living in a

CHRIS NILES

rundown boat, driving a beat-up car, packing up and moving on when it gets a little too real. You're running away from everything being human is all about, Katherine Kingsbury. You're fighting, but you're fighting the wrong battle in a war that's already decided. Stop already. Smell the ocean. Taste the salt-water on your lips. Sit around a table and drink a beer and savor the reason we live."

Chuck started back toward the seawall. He tossed these parting words over his shoulder as he walked away. "Or you can tow away that hulk and let people like Baumann and your father pave over our haven to build tennis courts and ten-bedroom houses. As for me, I'll die trying to stop it."

When he was gone, Kate pulled out a scrub brush and attacked the siding of her boat. Fifteen minutes later, she flung it into a bucket. Every muscle in her body screamed as she stood up and stretched out the hose that dangled from the piling. While she sprayed the suds from the walls over the side and into the water, Whiskey leapt and bit at the stream of cool fresh water.

"Cut it out." She directed the water away from him, and he chased after it. "Whiskey, I'm serious. Stop it."

"He's just having a little fun."

Kate jumped at William's baritone, then quickly wiped a tear from her eye before turning to meet him.

Michelle stood beside him, her fingers interlaced with his.

"Sorry, I didn't mean to scare you."

"It's okay, I just didn't realize you were back yet." She dropped the hose sprayer back onto its hook. "He just...he doesn't understand."

Michelle wrapped her arm around Kate's shoulders. "He's not supposed to understand. But I'm sure he senses that you're sad, and he wants to make you laugh."

"It's not just that, though. Chuck was just here. He tried to convince me to stay. Kept talking about how this place is all he has left. How there's a price to everything, and how his parents died when he was a kid. Yeah, it's sad. I get that. But we all have our own issues. Maybe my parents are alive, but they may as well have died. Hell, life would be better if they did. They're out there stealing people's lives, no different from what Baumann does. And as many times as I've tried to fight them, I always lose. What makes this any different?"

William leaned against the weathered piling and stared until Kate met his gaze. His eyes were gentle, but firm. "Who do you think lives here at Shark Key? Do you think you're the only person who doesn't pay rent?"

Michelle smiled — somehow her eyes were soft and kind, but also disappointed. "Kate, haven't you ever wondered why there are so many single moms living at the campground? Do you even know Linda in the

Beneteau over on the east dock? Her husband died in Afghanistan. Or Evelyn—"

Kate whirled out from under Michelle's arm. "So now I'm the selfish one?"

"That's not what we're saying at all. I'm just trying to tell you that no matter what he says, Chuck doesn't want to save this place for himself. Losing Shark Key means putting all those people he's been helping out on the street, too. Susan understood that. It's why she and Steve came along when Chuck couldn't go to Mexico. Baumann is hurting more than just one man who likes his space. At least twenty women will be homeless if he gets his way. A lot of them with kids. Think about that, Kate."

William took Michelle's hand and led her past the seagrape hedge then across the crushed coral parking lot to the deck.

Kate slowly walked back to the end of her dock. She sat, feet dangling just above the shallow water. A small skiff slowly explored the waters across the channel. While a woman piloted the boat, a small boy, maybe six or seven, ran along the gunwales, pointing out the wonders he saw darting between the surface and the sand. The small boat rounded a point on the island revealing her name — *Bonnie J* — emblazoned on the hull.

Why are boats always named after women? She went back to spraying down the dock. And the nerve, the nerve. Talking to me like a child like that. Calling me by ...

Kate froze.

Katherine Kingsbury. *Katherine K.*

It wasn't a person at all.

Kate ran inside for her laptop. She opened up a browser and typed "Katherine K."

CHAPTER FORTY-THREE

Kate sprinted past the mourners on the deck, the crushed shells and gravel in the parking lot shredding the soles of her feet.

She burst through his door. "Chuck, give me that book!"

He didn't question her. Just crutched toward the door, the small novel in his hand.

Kate snatched it from him then ran to Gramps's room, flipping pages.

Chuck followed, but much slower.

"Look!" she cried. And when he finally caught up, she turned to him and pointed at an entry in the book. "Here. Just before he built the first docks." She pointed at what she wanted him to read.

6.4.53: Went to see Katherine K. Beautiful day.

"And here." Kate indicated another line of text.

7.15.53: Poured pilings for new docks on east shore.

She flipped more pages, rattling off entry after entry. They were often separated by many lines of the mundane — weather, tide, catch records — but the pattern was clear. Every reference to Katherine K in the book was followed by a significant investment in the marina.

"Katherine K wasn't a person, she's a boat! It's been under our noses this whole time."

She pointed to a bronze ship's placard on Gramps's dresser. The left half was missing, and the engraving was worn from years at sea.

—herine K

K marks the spot. *Katherine K.*

"Sometime in the thirties, your Gramps found this wreck, and that's where he hid Al Capone's gold."

She flipped open her laptop and showed him the page.

Katherine K (SP-220) *was built in Baltimore, Maryland in 1894 and was purchased by the United States Naval Coast Defense Reserve in 1917.* Katherine K *patrolled the waters around Key West and served as a patrol and harbor tug. She was swept away from Key West Harbor in the Hurricane of 1919 and the wreck was never found.*

"Your grandfather went to visit *Katherine K* just before building new docks." She ruffled through the pages. "And here. *Katherine K* gave Ophelia and her new husband a generous wedding gift. So where is it?" Kate frantically flipped through page after page of the book, opening it to random pages, flipping back and forth and holding a finger in the page for each *Katherine K* entry until all her fingers were taken. She snapped the book around her fingers, gripping it with her thumb. "Bring the biggest chart of the Lower Keys you've got, then meet me up on the deck." Halfway to the front door, she spun around, ignoring the pain shooting through the balls of her feet. "Hurry up, my friend. Everyone's depending on you!"

As Chuck limped to the office, Kate ran out the door and up the back steps to the deck. She spotted an open table along the edge near the kitchen door and plopped into a seat. A moment later, when Chuck made his way up the steps with a rolled up navigational chart, Kate's nose was buried in the book.

He unrolled the chart on the table and weighted the corners with an empty beer bottle, two conch shells, and an ashtray. She sent him back for sticky notes and paper.

Deep in concentration, she sensed rather than saw the people who'd joined her, their black t-shirts and shorts lurking in the corners of her vision.

"Look, here, he talks about fighting a blackfin tuna south of Sand Key Lighthouse on the same day as it looks like he went to *Katherine K.*"

Steve leaned over the chart and silently placed a

salt shaker just below the marking for Sand Key Lighthouse.

"Wait, what?" Kate looked up at her friend, his face raw and swollen. "You shouldn't..."

"Kate, I..." He coughed and wiped his eyes. "I can't be anywhere else. Can't sit at home feeling sorry for myself while you all push forward. I won't let Susan's death be for nothing. I have to help."

Kate reached out with her free hand to squeeze his fingers. Then she flipped to the next entry. "Where's Chuck with those stupid sticky notes. I need better bookmarks than my fingers!"

"Here." Steve chuckled weakly and handed her a pile of napkins. She stuck them between entries then shook out her hand.

"Okay, here's another. Marquesas Rock." Another salt shaker.

"And here, put one two miles south of Half-moon Sho— These are all right in the same area. South of the quicksands, right?"

Steve dropped another salt shaker on the map. He took the book from Kate and flipped to the beginning, slowly turning pages and scanning the margins of each one carefully. "There are lots of other locations noted in here, but you're right. It looks like every time there's any mention of the *Katherine K*, the locations around it are out in this area."

"Then let's get more salt shakers!"

They started at the beginning of Thomas's book,

noting every location he mentioned and marking it on the chart. Kate read the entries while Steve and William raced to find the spots. If an entry coincided with a mention of *Katherine K*, they placed a salt shaker. If it didn't, it got a pepper shaker.

"East of Raccoon Key, permit running. Caught four for dinner."

"North of No Name Key. Fought huge tarpon five hours. Hook slipped and lost him just before sundown."

"On the way to see Katherine K, saw a hammerhead south of Cosgrove in 60 ft of water."

"Hammerhead, eh? I've seen a few out that way with divers from time to time." Steve dropped a salt shaker on a sixty-foot notation. "Kate, did I ever tell you about the charter I did for Fisher Platt?"

"The news anchor?"

"That's the one. It was maybe ten years ago. For the twentieth anniversary of Shark Week, his producers wanted a puff piece of him diving with sharks. I took him and his crew out to Hogfish Horseshoe. I had frozen a couple amberjack for bait, figured we'd see the usual black-tipped reef sharks who hang around waiting for the easy meal. So, I get them all settled down on the bottom, and then one of his cameramen wants to sit with a camera on top of the reef. On top of it. Can you believe that? I kept pointing up at the reef and shaking my head, then back down to the sand and nodding really big. The dude still shoved off, stirring up a cloud of sand and going for the reef anyway. I cut him off and led him to a little overhang near the top of the horseshoe, low enough to keep his back protected by the rock. It took him a while to figure out how to hover without letting his breath pull him up and down. And I was still worried he was too close to the bait pulley, so then I had to put Jonathan— Chuck do you remember Jonathan? I wonder what he's up to?"

"Oh, yeah. He had a way with the lady divers, didn't he?"

"That, he did. Anyway, Jonathan had to hover next to him and try to watch everyone else below ... I don't know what I was thinking not taking at least three extra dive masters to wrangle that bunch. Live and learn, I guess. So, Jonathan is up there, and I do a final okay for all the guys on the sand, then I tug the bait line for Susan—" Steve's voice hitched, but he took a breath and continued the story. "She drops the amber-jack shawarma over the side of the boat, and I start pulling it down. Damned if the biggest scalloped hammerhead I've ever seen didn't show up. I think Platt pissed himself right there on camera. It was the BEST!"

"Oh, no. The best one was that kid — the son of a dive shop owner from like Wisconsin or somewhere. Remember him?"

Steve burst out laughing. "The octopus kid? How could I forget?"

"Guys. Pepper in Jewfish Basin west of Coon Key, please?"

Steve pulled a shaker from the box then dropped it on the chart. "It feels good to laugh."

"Then let's laugh, my friend." William squeezed his shoulder as he readied himself with another set of salt and pepper shakers.

After three hours of fish stories, they reached the final page of the book.

"Gentlemen." Kate laced her fingers behind her head and kicked her feet up on the chair beside her. "I think we have a search area."

The chart was covered in dark containers, except for a four square-mile area of white salt shakers south of the Marquesas Keys, right at the boundary of the National Marine Sanctuary.

Michelle joined them, bringing with her a huge bowl of cut pineapple, mango, and watermelon.

"Tomorrow morning, we search from this salt shaker here" — William tapped on the shaker closest to Chuck then the one farthest east — "to about here." He popped a chunk of pineapple into his mouth.

"These salt shakers are making me want a Margarita." Kate glanced over at the empty bar, then at her watch. "It's a little early, though."

"It's five o'clock somewhere." Chuck bounced up toward the bar.

William looked perplexed. "It's four o'clock here. How is that early?"

Kate tried to stop Chuck. "I was kidding."

"Margaritas are no joking matter. And if my crew of heroes wants a pitcher, then I'm happy to oblige. Besides, if this all goes south, we'll be happier if we drank through the whole stock before that rat bastard Baumann gets a chance to lay his hands on a drop of it."

A few minutes later, he returned. The thin redhead who was staying with her son in Michelle and William's tent followed him with a sweating pitcher and tray full of frosty, salted glasses.

Chuck turned to the newcomer. "Thanks for helping out. I'm a little short-handed today"

"It's the least I could do after you've been so kind." She set the tray on the table. "Hi, y'all. I'm Tina, and I'll be around all night. Just let me know if you need anything." She wiped her hand on her narrow black apron then shook hands with each of them.

Chuck poured a round of margaritas, and over the next hour, the deck began to fill with friends.

William snapped several photos of the marked nautical charts before returning the shakers to their carriers. Then he and Michelle helped Tina distribute salt, pepper, hot sauce, and silverware to each table on the deck to get ready for the dinner crowd.

On her way past, Tina patted Chuck on the shoulder. "I'll drive Babette up in the golf cart so she can join you guys, and my boy is gonna help in the kitchen.

You just stay with your friends and relax tonight, okay? We've got dinner covered."

"Thanks again." He reached for the empty pitcher. "When you get a chance, can you whip up another pitcher?"

The afternoon faded to evening. Branson Tillman, the guitarist, joined them. He wasn't scheduled to play that evening, but he pulled his guitar out and started to strum a few chords. Justin dropped into a chair beside him after he cleaned up from the day's dive charter and tapped out a beat on the picnic table. Kate and Michelle sang along, and soon the whole deck was working the through the entire collection of songs every islander knows by heart.

CHAPTER FORTY-FOUR

TINA ROLLED over and pressed her thumbs against her temples. She'd skimmed enough from bar sales the night before to get a nice hotel room and a hot shower, but why pay for it when there were tourists willing to share? The party had gotten rowdier than she thought laid back island folks could get, especially considering the circumstances, but of course they'd started drinking in the middle of the afternoon. Cousin Chuck regaled them with stories of the Keys in the seventies and eighties, and a few from his grandfather, but as much as she tried, and no matter how many margaritas he put down, he didn't leave a hint of what they thought they'd find when they found the wreck of the *Katherine K.*

She crept out of bed, slipped on her shorts and tank, then felt around for her phone. The battery was dead, so she stuffed it in her back pocket and looked around the room. The guy, she thought maybe his name was Joey, snored loudly. She pulled three twenties from his wallet before slipping out of the room.

Outside, she looked up and down the road, trying to remember where Joey had driven when they left Shark Key. She was on the north side of the island, standing in front of one of the new hotels finished not long before the last hurricane passed through. She remembered hearing about them all filling up with FEMA residents until they got thrown out in favor of paying tourists. Mother nature's a bitch.

The sun was already climbing above the trees. Tina headed toward it. The airport was just around the bend on the south side of the island. It would be easy enough to turn up there and offer her services as a spotter for Chuck and his friends. He had seemed a little wary around her last night, and if she just happened to be around again, he might grow suspicious. Instead, she'd have to rally what little patience she possessed.

She hopped aboard the island shuttle bus. "This goes up the road, right?"

"Ayup."

"To Shark Key?"

The driver shrugged.

"Shark Key. You know where that is?"

The driver shrugged again.

"It's up the road just a few miles. You go there?"

"I go up Highway 1. If it's on 1, then I go past it, yeah."

"Well, which stop is it?"

The driver pointed at a faded route map. "You off or on, lady? I got a schedule to keep."

Tina handed the driver a twenty.

"I don't make change."

"Are you kidding?"

His third shrug really pissed her off. She dug in her shorts pocket then pulled out three crumpled singles.

"It's four dollars."

Clenching her teeth to keep from screaming, she pulled out a fistful of coins, dropped them in the driver's lap without counting them, stomped to a seat near the back of the bus, then stared out the window. The bus passed the hospital, community college, and a golf course her Fort Lauderdale clients wouldn't set foot on. When it turned back onto US 1, Tina felt like she'd been transported back to the center of the mainland. Scrubby trees. Sandy lots. Hand-painted concrete block buildings surrounded by chain link fences. Broken-down cars in various states of disrepair. But only if central Florida was surrounded by clear, turquoise water that stretched to the horizon.

The bus passed the Navy base at Boca Chica to the right, then the glittering water filled the view on both sides of the bus. After driving through a small town marked Big Coppitt, they stopped at a Circle K gas station with a wide wooden front porch. It looked like it was trying hard to be a house instead of a run-down convenience store. The bus continued on across a short causeway, then Tina spotted the entrance to Shark Key on the left. She stood up, but the bus continued on down the road as nothing but shallow ocean spread to either side of the road, and then filled the space below it, too.

"Hey!" Tina shouted to the driver. "That was my stop."

The driver pointed to a sign above his head. DRIVER MAY NOT SPEAK WHILE THE BUS IS MOVING. The bus continued across the bridge.

"Hey! Stop this thing!"

An elderly black woman about the size of a key deer tapped Tina on the arm. "Honey. Ain't you never ride a bus before? You gotta go to the next stop at Sugarloaf. And you gotta pull this before your stop so he knows you want to get off."

"But I just told him I want to get off now."

"That ain't how the bus work, baby. Bless your little heart." The woman pulled the chain and the STOP REQUESTED light lit up at the front of the shuttle. A few minutes later, the bus rattled to a stop just past a tiny bus hut on a barren strip of land in the middle of the ocean.

Tina stormed up to the driver. "I need to go back to that last stop."

"Next southbound shuttle will be here in maybe

forty-five minutes. It's another four dollars, though. And he can't make change, either."

"This bus sucks."

"You might prefer walking, then."

"Take me back there."

"I'll be back to that stop on my southbound run in about three hours. But it's another four dollars if you ride it back south. "

"What?"

"I'll stop long enough you can go buy a Gatorade and get change at the end of the line if you want. But I gotta keep moving. Off or on?"

"For the love of all that's holy ... I'll just walk." Tina climbed out of the bus then stomped down the path, the sun at her back.

CHAPTER FORTY-FIVE

KATE PARKED her Civic next to Chuck's Waggoneer in front of the General Aviation terminal. Two years in the Keys without setting foot in this place and now she'd been there twice in a week. But the excitement of looking for the *Katherine K* overshadowed the worry Kate had about losing the home she'd come to love.

Kate strode across the tarmac toward William's airplane. The little single-engine Cirrus gleamed in the sun as William polished its hull while doing his pre-flight inspection.

"Your baby is seeing a lot of sky this week."

He turned his back to the sun and propped his sunglasses up on the bill of his hat. "Better in the sky than sitting on a sweltering tarmac."

"Hot as hell, for sure, but no wind means calm water and clear visibility. We might have half a chance of finding this wreck before lunch!"

"Don't count your chickens, young lady."

"Anyone wants to count chickens, they just need to go down to the post office. There were at least seven standing in the parking lot when I went by the drop box this morning. Pretty soon, they'll declare independence and incite an avian revolution."

"Fish is a healthier meal, anyway. Hey, I'm about done and ready to fire her up. Chuck and ..."

Kate waited for William to finish his thought, but all she got was a shrug. "Vince? Yeah, I'm still not okay with all this. But Chuck of the Second Chance wants his help, so what can I say?"

"He seems sincere, I suppose. And if we can't give him a second chance, then are we really any better than the folks we're fighting against? So if his answers were good enough for Chuck, they're good enough for me. Anyway, they're inside with the cooler. Do you mind letting them know we're ready to roll?"

Kate sucked in a deep breath then counted to five while slowly releasing it. Then she plastered a smile on her face and skipped back to the small terminal building. Chuck was rattling through all the native Conchs he knew, trying to find someone he and Vince had in common.

"Guys. The plane's ready." She twirled her finger in the air and pointed out toward the airplane.

Chuck pushed up out of the torn vinyl chair then pointed to the handle of his rolling cooler. He tipped his head to Vince, letting the younger man follow behind him with the supplies.

Vince's bright green polyester shirt screamed as he emerged from the shade of the terminal. Palm leaves and bright parrots painted a random pattern across his torso. The light-hearted shirt did nothing to soften his sharp features, and his slicked black hair practically dripped New Jersey on the Florida collar.

William helped Chuck up to the right seat and directed Vince across the back, thrusting a pair of binoculars into his hands. Then he and Kate loaded the cooler behind the wide seat. Kate climbed in beside Vince, and pulled another set of binoculars from her bag. She strapped in as William boarded. Moments later, they were taxiing down the runway and then climbing into the morning sky.

William banked the plane and set a heading west toward the outer Keys. "I want to find the east end of the grid and start a creeping line search from there so we're working away from the sun. We know the *Katherine K* is resting somewhere along the narrow drop-off between flats and the deeper straits, so I can keep the pattern pretty tight. I'll fly two-minute arcs, which will cover the whole area and give you two in back a chance to rest your eyes during the turns. It'll use a little more fuel, but we're not in a rush. I've got it all programmed into the GPS, and it says we'll be on station in about five minutes."

"I can't thank you enough, William." Chuck's voice

shook. "I always thought this was something I could look for more as a hobby when I got older. Now that I'm running out of time, I don't know what I'd do without you. Without any of you, really." He looked back at Kate, and his eyes filled with tears.

"It's a good thing I've got the binoculars, old man!" Kate waved them at him, winked, and patted his shoulder. "Now, let's saddle up and find this girl!"

William banked, and the little plane dove down to their search altitude. "Ready up? Turning into the first search leg."

Kate held her binoculars close and leaned her forehead against the windows, scanning the clear water below. She could see wide natural reef formations of dive sites she knew were nearly sixty feet to the bottom. The *Katherine K* was bound to be heavily encrusted, but from this altitude, her shape would be unmistakable, coral or no.

After nearly two minutes, the dark blue of deeper water had gradually given way to the light turquoise of her beloved sandy flats. William's voice snapped Kate out of her trancelike scan.

"Clear of the pattern. Turning for the next run. Blink your eyes and take a drink, kids!"

"You are having far too much fun with this."

"What's the good of life if you can't have fun?" His face scrunched behind his mirrored aviator sunglasses. Kate thought he was winking until he reached up behind the lens, a tear sparkling on the back of his finger.

After forty minutes of arcing back and forth across the same line of the sea, finding only wrecks that Chuck confirmed on the charts, Kate's eyes burned and her shoulders ached. On the next turn, she stretched her arms up overhead and asked the question.

"Are we there yet?" All three men burst out laughing.

"Don't make me stop this plane, young lady!" William waggled the wings and pulled the plane's yoke gently back. "But seriously, I'm sure you're both getting pretty tired. I'll pause the pattern. We can climb and take a little spin around the crater to give you two a longer break. Kate, can you grab some drinks from the cooler in back of you?"

"Gladly." Kate unsnapped her seatbelt and climbed up onto her knees, stretching down into the cooler behind her seat. "We got choices, people! Orange, green, or blue. What the hell flavor is blue, anyway?"

"I'll take a green, please"

"Blue for me."

Vince rolled his neck and stretched. "Got any Budweiser?" Kate choked back a swear and handed an orange bottle over the seat to him. She chose an orange for herself, too, wrangled herself back to her seat, then cracked the seal.

"Heading back into the track. Heads up, y'all." William banked the plane and continued talking. "We've got about an hour left on this grid, then if we don't have any hits, we'll head back to the airport, refuel, maybe take a little nap, then we'll come on back out and start from the west and work back toward the middle. We'll keep that up til we hit something. But I feel good about this morning."

Four turns later, just as they entered an inbound leg, Kate's shout startled even herself. "I think I've got something! Ten o'clock, closing in. Can you get lower?" She pulled the binoculars to her eyes and scanned for the shape deep in the water.

"Where, Kate?"

"Coming up on it now. Can you circle? Get lower? You're passing it ..."

Kate heard Chuck fumbling with a chart up in the front seat. "Katie, honey, I think that's the *Edgar*."

Kate slumped in her seat. "Don't call me Katie."

William flew two circles around the coral covered wreck as Chuck called Steve on the sat phone to confirm the coordinates. The reef Kate had gotten so excited about was, in fact, the *M/V Edgar*, a 1950s tugboat that had run around during a storm and had finally been cleaned, towed, and scuttled in seventy feet of water as an artificial reef. The coral growth on her was still new, and Kate hadn't led any dives on it yet, but Steve had taken a group out to it just a few weeks before, and he confirmed the coral growth was thickening up and fish were finding it.

324

"The *Katherine K* is going to be a lot more encrusted, and based on Gramps's notes, I think it'll be a little shallower. He wasn't as good at free diving as he thought he was — I beat him every time we went deeper than fifty feet when I was a kid."

"Chuck, he was in his seventies when you were a kid. Of course you beat him."

"Heh. Nothing slowed that old man down, and if he thought he couldn't win, he didn't bother. He put up a fight, for sure." Chuck's voice softened as he remembered the grandfather who raised him. "Everything he did, he did for dad and then for me. I wish I'd have realized it at the time."

William waggled the plane's wings. "Ready to go back in?"

"Is it lunchtime yet?"

"It will be after we finish this grid."

"Then I'm ready."

William guided the plane back in line to restart the search track where Kate had spotted the Edgar. Chuck flipped the satellite radio to Radio Margaritaville to help everyone relax. As they flew a track, banked to the west, blinked a few times, then flew another track, everyone on board hummed along to the familiar tunes.

"I think ..." Vince's voice barely rose over the drone of the engine. "Can we go back over that last line again?"

Kate looked across him out the starboard window. "Did you have something?"

"I'm not sure. I think maybe, but I'm not sure. It was nearly straight under us, a bit more than halfway down."

"Okay, I'll adjust a little to the east and see if Kate picks it up. Chuck, anything on the charts here?" The papers already rustled in the right seat.

"I don't think so. If something's there, it might be clean."

William brought the plane around in a tight circle, lined up a hundred yards east of the center line from the last track, and dropped his altitude to five hundred feet. Thirty seconds later, Kate yanked her binoculars up. Five more seconds, she began to hum, and five after that, she shouted, "THERE! Fifty yards ahead and just off port. See it?"

"Roger ... got it. Circling."

"That's about fifty feet of water, heavy coral. Looks like natural reef on both sides, so it doesn't look like a boat at all. It's no wonder no one has found it yet."

Kate pulled a camera with a telephoto lens from her bag and began snapping pictures.

"Call Steve and give him the GPS numbers. We're going diving!"

CHAPTER FORTY-SIX

KATE SMELLED the red snapper before she saw the tray piled high with sliders. After shoving one in her mouth, she grabbed a second on her way to *Serenity* to collect her gear. She returned with a mesh gear bag on her shoulder and Whiskey on her heels.

"...anchor up to the west of it and let the current hold us right over the top. Then we can set a guide buoy once we see what's down there."

"Steve, are you sure you're up for this?" William asked.

His face looked rested but still a bit puffy. "Absolutely. It's better if I keep busy."

"Just let us know if you need a break, okay?" He glanced at Kate, his eyes filled with concern.

She knew her responsibility — stay close and keep Steve grounded.

Chuck said, "From what we could see, Steve, it

looks to be around fifty feet down and dropped right on the reef. Hard to tell, but I reckon it'll be pretty torn up. It barely even looked like a hull — I'm surprised you saw it at all." He clapped Vince on the back.

Vince glanced around the group. "Uh, yeah. Thanks."

"Chuck, you're not going, are you?" Kate tapped his crutches lying on the deck beside his chair.

"It'll be fine with just a brace. In the water, it doesn't have to carry my excess weight around."

"Great, then, don't you guys think we'll learn more by getting out there and checking it out than by speculating? Let's get the propellers turning."

"Patience, grasshopper!" Steve crouched and whirled his hands in his best "wax on, wax off" Karate Kid impression. "Let's say we roll out there in the *Island Hopper*, and we hit the lode on the first dive? Then what?"

"Then we pull it up and come home."

"Kate, do you think we're talking about a little trinket you can carry up and dangle from your weight belt during your safety stop?" Steve rubbed his eyes then continued. "We could be looking at several heavy cases. We need lift equipment, guide lines, storage space ... and security. Til now, no one has had any clue this stuff was down there, but as soon as we start raising stuff up, we'll need protection."

"Whiskey is all the protection we need."

"He'll be useful, for sure. But this is gonna be more

involved than you're imagining. And if we don't find what we're looking for pretty quickly, then we have a different set of challenges. Once we're on the reef and confirm it as the *Katherine K*, I'd like to stay there until we're sure one way or the other. Depending on her condition, we may not be able to do that in one afternoon. It's been thirty years since anyone was in there, so there's thirty years of growth. We'll have to be careful of the reef, the hull might have eroded. We might need cutting tools. Salvage operations are a lot different from recreational sightseeing dives, kiddo."

"We could sail the *Knot* out for support. We've got two extra staterooms, full kitchen, and some storage lockers we could empty out. And freshwater showers." Michelle smiled.

William added, "We just can't get under any of the bridges, and the wind has been flat for days, so we'll have to motor out around the island and through the shipping channel."

Vince waved his finger and gulped down his mouthful of snapper. "What if ..." He shook his head. "Never mind. It'd be perfect, but it's too risky." He took another enormous bite of sandwich.

Steve perked up. "What are you thinking?"

His eyes flitted from side to side. Finally, he swallowed and met Steve's gaze. "What if we borrowed the *Tax Shelter*?"

Steve's eyes bulged. "Borrowed?"

"I've skippered it before. Baumann thinks I'm still

on his side. You guys can take off in the *Hopper*, then I can call him in a panic saying you all look like you found something and I need to follow. I'm here, the boat is here. It'd be almost stupid to not take it, right?"

"That's almost brilliant. What's the risk? What'll trip us up?" William looked skeptical.

"He's pretty OCD about the damn thing. He will probably want to send another of his guys to crew her. I'll say I have someone here. Tell him I'm ready to go and can't wait for him to send someone down. But he might pitch a fit. He knows I love that boat and might think I'm just making up a reason to take her out. But ... yeah, this might actually work."

"Can he track its location?" Steve asked.

Vince laughed. "The tech is there, but he wouldn't know how to check. He can't do anything himself. Couldn't find his junk without a hooker to do it for him." Several heads turned. "Sorry. Too much? I forget you people are little more refined than my usual companions."

"Refined?" Chuck pointed to the holes in his t-shirt and the frayed hem of his cargo shorts. "We drink our beer from the can and we clean our own fish. But do we try to treat the people around us with respect and keep the conversation appropriate for mixed company. I'm not a prude, but I do feel like certain things should just be ... private."

Vince's cheeks turned red. "I get that. My normal

crowd, you gotta talk like that to fit in, you know? I'm sorry."

"Forgiven. Just keep it in mind."

Kate scanned the table. While everyone was distracted, she dropped a whole slider to Whiskey, who swallowed it in a single bite. "So Steve, you're coordinating surface support. Make sure we have plenty of straps and lift bags and sacks. I can run the dive plans — we can use nitrox for better bottom time and shorter surface intervals. If we need to, we can set a hot mix at least for the two of us. Chuck, is your gear oxygen clean?"

"No, I'm still using that old regulator you tripped over in the shop the other day."

"Jeesh, Chuck. Maybe once your ship comes in, you'll get a new setup. You'll have to surface more often and take longer breaks, but we can deal with that. Steve, how many lift bags do you have? I've got two pony tanks we can use for those."

William chimed in. "We've got extra pony tanks, too. Neither of us is nitrox certified, but we do have wreck certs so we can help look, and I can help lift and stow at the surface so Steve can stay on bottom longer."

"Great, so we've got William, Michelle, Steve, me, Chuck, and Vince, right?" Kate's gaze bounced from one to the next as she counted in her head. "Steve and I on nitrox, the rest of you on air ... the *Hopper*'s compressors will keep up fine, I think. William, have you ever mixed enriched air before?"

"Not yet, but I have a feeling I'm going to learn."

"It's definitely an art, so we'll make sure one of us is with you, and I'll mix myself if we need to go hot."

William raised an eyebrow at her.

"That's a more concentrated mix of oxygen than normal enriched air. Gives us even longer times underwater, but it's a little riskier, and you've got to get it just right."

Steve pushed his chair back. "I think we have a plan. Michelle, why don't you come out on the *Hopper* with Kate, Chuck, and me, and William can stay with Vince on the *Tax Shelter*. William, you cool with that?" He glanced at William's waistband.

"Completely." William inched closer to where Vince was sitting, his lean form towering over the smaller man.

"Vince, can you get me on board now? I'd like to see what we've got to work with there..."

Vince led William past a table where Tina, the redhead who'd helped with dinner last night, and her son were finishing their lunch. They headed down to where *Tax Shelter* was docked. The others gathered the rest of their gear then started loading the *Island Hopper*.

CHAPTER FORTY-SEVEN

"Drop here, then let out about a hundred and fifty feet."

"Aye Aye, Capt'n!" Kate peered over the bow through the clear water to the sandy bottom fifty feet below. She crouched beside the anchor well and counted as the anchor rode reeled out.

The sun sparkled on the surface of the Florida Straits, and the boat bobbed in the low ripples. Once the anchor was set, Kate climbed around the wheelhouse into the aft cockpit, wove around the long dive benches, then adjusted the arms of her thin wetsuit. She pulled a wide blue Bimini awning toward the stern, creating shade over most of the dive prep area.

"Thanks. The air is so still out here, I think I'd be baked like a soufflé in the first ten minutes." Michelle wiped a bead of sweat from her temple.

"It helps when the tanks don't explode, too."

Steve chimed in from the front, "That's actually a myth, Kate. Even with hot nitrox fills, the worst that could realistically happen is the tank's burst valve could pop and lose the seal. These puppies are tough. But we don't know what we're gonna find down there, and I don't feel like servicing a bunch of perfectly good tanks. So, let's pretend it's good for the tanks." He strapped a buoyancy compensation vest onto a tank wrapped in green and yellow stickers.

"Chuck, is that Jacques Cousteau's original dive gear over there?"

"Ha ha." He slid to the end of the bench, then began to rummage in his faded mesh bag.

"I'll set you up here." Kate heaved a plain tank into the cradle beside Chuck. "You're on the end so you can backroll right over the starboard gunwale here." She turned back to her own gear.

Michelle hovered at the edge of the dive deck. "I feel a little useless here. What can I do to help out?"

"You could raise the flags and toss out a current line? You'll find everything you need in the locker on the bow."

"Aye, aye." Beneath a two-fingered salute, Michelle winked at Kate then started up toward the bow. She met Steve near the back of the dive deck. Her soft voice carried in the still afternoon air. "Are you sure you're up for this?"

His tight smile didn't make it to his eyes, but he

nodded and started toward his gear. Michelle touched his arm as he passed.

At the aft camera table, Kate unloaded her electronics onto the rubber mat then began checking all the housing seals.

Steve dropped his own small camera housing beside hers. "What all did you bring?"

"Everything. I just got a new head-mount for the video camera with an extra mount for a light." She picked up a chunky plastic housing connected to a web of straps. "I also brought the housing for my phone for quick snapshots and peeking around corners, and then of course, the big high-res with strobes. If she's really been undisturbed for this long, I'm sure it's a gorgeous site. I want to get some really good shots before we start lifting anything. If there's anything to lift, of course."

"There will be." Chuck kept his eyes on his gear.

"I think it's best to do a complete circuit around her, both to make sure we're in the right place and to identify all the possible penetration spots. Then we can start back at the deepest end and look for any areas where the coral looks thinner or younger than the rest."

Steve and Chuck nodded agreement. Kate peered over the edge and surveyed the coral formations beneath their stern, comparing them to the aerial photos from her tablet. "This looks different from down here, but I'm sure we're close. I use less air than either of you, so let me drop in first. I'll stay shallow and have a look around to make sure we're in the right spot. If we need to move, I'll come back up. Otherwise I'll throw up a little marker buoy, then you guys can hop in with the big camera and join me."

"Sounds like a plan. Good diving!"

The three fist-bumped. Kate slipped on her fins, shrugged into her buoyancy compensator, then pulled the straps tight.

Steve double checked her gear.

She emptied a bit of air from her BC then rolled off the port gunwale into the water. After the initial splash, she signaled okay to the boat.

Steve helped Michelle lower Kate's cameras to the water's surface.

Kate secured her gear, rolled in the water so she was facing the sea floor, then stretched her body flat. She drifted gently deeper, pinching her nose and clearing her ears as she scanned the coral. At twenty feet, she added a quick burst of air to her BC to stop her descent.

She paused to hover in the warm blue water, isolated from the sounds of the surface, surrounded only by the familiar hollow hiss of each breath pulled from the tank on her back and the soft gurgling of the bubbles as she exhaled through her regulator. She carefully finned away from the *Island Hopper*, searching for the distinctive lines of the *Katherine K*'s twisted hull. Every breath calmed her nerves, and she took a moment to appreciate the beauty of a healthy reef in a calm sea on a sunny day. Below her, schools of fish flitted this way and that, searching the reef for food, their scales glittering in the filtered light.

There's nowhere on Earth more peaceful than under water.

Kate glanced at the dive computer on her wrist and took a quick heading. The sea floor fell off to the south, dropping from sixty feet at the ledge to over four hundred in the center of the Straits a few miles out. While the Keys didn't offer dramatic wall diving like some other popular Caribbean spots, it was still easy to lose track of depth.

Not long after she'd earned her dive master certification, she'd seen two inexperienced divers go deeper than the dive plan. One kept signaling his buddy to ascend, but the other kept descending. Kate went after him at one hundred five feet and found the diver erratic and incoherent. Narc'd. She guided him slowly up to sixty feet before he shook his head and looked around as if he wasn't sure how he'd gotten there. She never wanted to see another case of nitrogen narcosis, and she certainly didn't want to experience it. On nitrox, she could go deeper for longer with lower risk, but she wasn't planning to stay down by herself for very long.

She continued along at twenty feet for a few more minutes, drifting back and forth above the reef, hoping to catch her first glimpse of the *Katherine K.* Finally, she passed over a tall formation of stony coral. The reef dropped down then opened up onto a flat area that could only be *Katherine K*'s deck. Grinning around her regulator, she pulled a fist pump to a nearby goliath grouper who'd been lazily swimming along beside her.

Kate slowly rolled over and spotted the *Hopper*'s hull a few hundred feet to the west. They could let out another couple hundred feet of rode to get close enough for their first dive. She started the video camera, then rolled back over and finned a wide loop above the wreck, comparing the structure and size to the details they'd been able to find for the *Katherine K*. The hull was twisted in the center, with the bow listing to starboard and pointing southeast toward deeper water. The stern had torn away amidships. It listed to port and rested atop a coral formation with its transom facing northeast.

Kate dumped air from her BC and dropped twenty more feet until she was hovering just above the *Katherine K*. She dropped two bright orange foil bottom markers, then pulled a neon inflatable sausage mounted on a small reel of fishing line from her pocket. She pulled her alternate from its clip and rolled it so air flowed to inflate the sausage. Filament unspooled from the reel as the sausage shot to the surface to mark the location for Steve and Chuck to move the *Island Hopper* and join her.

Markers dropped, Kate checked her computer. Plenty of air. She needed to start getting photos, but she paused to hover above the old tugboat, listening to the quiet rhythm of her inward breath and the gentle gurgle of bubbles pouring through her regulator with each exhale. Every surface of the *Katherine K* was encrusted with thick coral growth, their bright colors slightly muted in the deep water. Blue tangs, huge queen angelfish, and schools of tiny sparkling French grunts darted in and out of the wide gash in her hull. But as Kate swam closer to the torn boat, she realized more than the grunts were sparkling.

CHAPTER FORTY-EIGHT

KATE EXHALED. Then she pushed even more residual air from her lungs. Her body dropped three feet deeper, hovering just inches from the reef supporting the *Katherine K*. She sipped air from her regulator to stay in position in front of the gash separating the boat's bow and stern. The reef's fish, unaccustomed to divers, had given her a wide berth and clustered in deeper waters behind what was left of the wheelhouse.

The dark area belowdecks beckoned to Kate. She knew she should let Chuck be the first to find his grandfather's legacy, but the temptation was too strong. With a flick of her fins, she slowly floated into the darkness of the big tug's hull and shone her dive light downward. Behind the crust of coral along the edges, the tug's darkened bilge was loaded with metal cases and rotting crates. Bright flecks glimmered in the beam of light. She pulled more air into her lungs and rose a foot, then two, and finally paddled herself backward to open water.

Kate repeated the process, carefully penetrating the bowels of the *Katherine K*'s stern, where she found more cases and crates. She gently pulled away the top of one of the wooden boxes, revealing a cascade of gold coins covered in light silt. She replaced the cover then inched away from the ship's hull.

Once she was clear of the bow section of the hull, she swam a few feet north from the coral head, rose about ten feet above the bottom, then floated. In her excitement, she'd already used far more air than normal at this depth. She focused on controlling her breathing while she waited for Chuck and Steve, who were descending along a weighted line Steve had dropped from the stern to guide the lift bags.

When Steve reached the bottom, she waved him around to the side of the wreck to start taking photos. Then Chuck dropped down in front of her. She pointed toward the wreck, grinned, and beckoned him to follow. At the gash in the hull, she pointed her light into first the bow section, then the stern. Among the cases and crates, loose gold and jewels glistened in the darkness.

Chuck's body began to shake. He buried his mask in his hands and sobbed.

Kate tapped his inflator, and the two of them rose a few feet. As she held him in a hover over the wreck, she tried to imagine finding something so important to a beloved relative — tried to imagine even having a relative who had sacrificed so much for her. She didn't have to imagine the relief Chuck had to be feeling because she felt it, too. Shark Key was finally safe from the hands of Monty Baumann.

When Chuck collected himself, the hug he gave Kate around all the gear was really more like patting her on both shoulders, but his joy was obvious. He twirled his finger in the water and pointed it straight at the *Katherine K*, grinning around his regulator.

Kate looked at his pressure gauge. He was already below two thousand pounds. She waggled two fingers at him then pointed at the instrument.

He grimaced and gently finned a quick circle around the tugboat.

Steve came around the bow of the ship, camera flashing. He waved Kate and Chuck over to a spot along the side of the wheelhouse then pointed to a crusted bronze placard. Beneath the layer of growth, the letters K A T were visible.

Steve and Kate worked with Chuck to count and photograph the cases, chests, and as many of the loose articles as they could before Chuck ran low on air. The three finned together back to the stern line and communicated in crude signs. Chuck would ascend while Steve and Kate began removing cases and attaching the lift bags to the stern line. Once on the surface, Chuck would gather some extra collection bags, weight them, then send the bundle back down to them.

Kate gently backed into the bow compartment, then chose the sturdiest looking case. She cradled the straps of a lift bag around it before gradually adding air with a small inflator hose. The case began to rise from the place it had rested for eighty years, stirring up silt and clouding the water. She guided it out toward Steve, who floated it free of the hull then swam it out to their impromptu staging area below the *Island Hopper*.

Chuck's feet dangled from the swim platform fifty feet above them. Steve rigged the case to the stern line with a carabiner, added more air to the lift bag, then watched the first case of treasure make its way to the surface.

Steve and Kate repeated this process with several lesser-weathered cases, then they gently coaxed a few of the rotting crates into bags and sent them to the surface. Kate checked her pressure gauge and signaled to Steve that they needed to ascend. The two friends swam to the guide line then slowly made their way thirty-five feet up. As they floated beside the line for their safety stop, the colorful fish began to return to their home on the wreckage of the *Katherine K*.

Kate surveyed the scene below her and smiled as her breath passed through her regulator, into her lungs, and back out in soft bubbles rising to the surface.

CHAPTER FORTY-NINE

Tina revved the engine and yelled out the window. "Lucas! Lucas, get your fat ass out of that tent and get in the car!" She tore out of the parking lot the second her son's butt hit the seat. A hundred feet out of the driveway to Shark Key, she whipped the car onto the shoulder behind an old gray Chevy. A fat man in a threadbare red hat stood at the railing of the low bridge holding a fishing pole.

Tina leaned across Lucas and shouted out the passenger side window. "Can't catch anything if your line ain't in the water."

The man fumbled in his tackle box.

"Look, you ain't no fisherman. And if you ain't fishin', you're watchin'. I need to talk to your boss."

"Lady, I don't know what you're talking about."

"Some asshole just took off in his three-million-dollar yacht. I can get it back for him. With a hold full of money. Now call your boss."

Fifteen minutes later, a sleek silver Mercedes skidded into the lane leading to Shark Key. Tina met Baumann on the dock where the *Tax Shelter* had been tied up.

"Have we met before?"

Tina pulled her shoulders back and arched her spine to take full advantage of Baumann's leer. "Briefly. I seen you at the big fundraiser on the bay last weekend."

His brow furrowed.

"I wasn't a guest. I brought the special refreshments ... in the second-floor lounge?"

"Ah, yes. Right, right, right. Refreshments." Baumann nodded, his gaze scanning the sky as if he might find a clearer memory of the night within the puffy white clouds. "You'll forgive me if I've forgotten your name?"

"I never gave it."

"Then you have me at a disadvantage, Miss ..."

"Ransom. Tina Ransom." She held out her hand, but Baumann had turned to scan the horizon beyond where his yacht should have been. She dropped her hand.

"So, where's my boat?"

"We need to get something clear first. Charles Miller's my first cousin. My Grandma Gigi was married to his grandfather, so she was the original owner of this land. We ain't got no other cousins. So I'm entitled to half this place, and half of whatever else they find out there. What happens between you and Chuck for his half? Well, that's between the two of you. I'll help you get it, long as you guarantee me my cut."

Baumann spun on his heel. "You're a white trash waitress from Miami who's dealing drugs on the side. Why on earth would I believe you?"

"Because I know what's under that water. In 1931, the night Al Capone got sent up the river by the tax man, his secret vault in the basement of the Lexington Hotel in Chicago was emptied. Millions of dollars' worth of gold and jewels disappeared into thin air. Except it wasn't thin air. My grandma and Tommy Miller took it. When they got to the Keys, Miller hid it. He hid it from his own wife, and he left it to rot. And now my cousin has found it for us."

He stared at her, blinked. Remained silent.

"What does this mean for you? I hate to tell you this, but Holt is screwin' you over. They picked him up in the middle of the ocean a couple days ago, and he's flipped. He's helping them, and using you to do it."

"Unlikely. My business is under complete control."

"If you believed that, you wouldn't have sent Mister Fake Fisherman to keep an eye on him." She rested her hand on her hip. "Who, by the way, you should fire for gross incompetence. Not only did he not see your greaseball leave, I made him the minute he showed up on the bridge."

"Thank you for the unsolicited advice, but my business is my business."

"Holt tell you they found the wreck?"

Baumann froze.

"Yeah. Hours ago. Things are movin' fast, but not so fast your boy didn't have time to call you. They all came skiddin' in here this morning and a bunch of them loaded up that little dive boat then booked out of here like it was on fire. Your boy rolled out of here with the black guy on your boat a couple hours later after one of them got a phone call."

"How do you know all this?"

"I got eyes. I got ears. And I know how to be invisible. They're planning to use your boat to carry it all. So not only will you get your precious *Tax Shelter* back, it'll be loaded with millions of dollars of untraceable assets. You just gotta guarantee me my half."

Baumann's fists tightened at his sides. He sucked in a deep breath, then popped the trunk of his car. "Fine."

"Good. Glad that's settled." She dangled a set of keys on a red float. "I lifted the keys to a pretty little Bayliner from the office while they were loading."

Baumann raised his eyebrows. "You might be smarter than you look. Now help me with this." He pointed to a case deep in the trunk. After they dragged it forward, he opened it, handed her a pistol in a waist holster and two extra magazines, then tucked extra ammo into his own pocket.

"Lucas! Help the man. Carry that for him."

Lucas climbed off his perch on a nearby picnic table and stuffed his phone in his back pocket. He hoisted the plastic case from the trunk then followed his mother down to the dock where she was pulling the cover off a bright red Bayliner. Baumann stepped into the boat's cockpit.

Tina tossed him the keys. "You got GPS tracking on that beauty of yours?"

Baumann tapped his phone and handed it to her. She zoomed the image in and out a couple times, then fiddled with the menu on the Bayliner's Garmin. "Lucas, get over here! How do you work this damned thing?"

"I don't know, Mama." The boat rocked as he dropped from the dock, rocked a little more when he dropped the case below the gunwale.

"You kids are supposed to know electronics and crap, right? Figure it out."

"But, Mama..."

Tina's blood pressure shot up, and her eyes bulged at her idiot son. "I swear, you've been nothing but trouble since the day you was born."

Lucas poked at the Garmin until he found the right option to enter destination coordinates. Tina shoved him astern then untied the boat from the dock. "Now sit down and shut up."

Baumann goosed the throttle to back away from the slip, spun the boat south, then guided it down the channel and under the bridge. Once they were clear of the shallow water, he opened it up and followed the GPS west toward the Marquesas Keys.

CHAPTER FIFTY

"THESE PILES OVER HERE," Kate pointed at a dark area near the top of the screen, "They'll be the hardest. It's tight in there, and the crates look pretty rotted, so they'll disintegrate the second we try to strap them in. We'll have to bag everything. There's not really enough vertical space for the lift bags to lift, and it's so narrow, we'll stir up all sorts of silt, too. We'll lose visibility almost instantly."

Chuck leaned against the camera table. "Let's leave those for last. Get everything that's easier, and then we can rig exit lines. Kate, you can wiggle in there with a pony tank and load up whatever you can. Just keep the sacks light."

"I wonder how your Gramps got them back there in the first place?"

"The crates weren't rotten then." Steve chimed in. "He probably put a few down, then pushed them back as he added more and more cases. They probably still had some residual air in them so they would have been a little buoyant and easier to move. Not easy, but easier."

Kate flipped to a wide photo of the dive site. "It's a wonder no one has found this yet. It's a beautiful site. Look at how the hull and the reef have joined together. You can't really tell where one ends and the other starts."

"Once we get this all out, we can set a mooring buoy and I'll add it to my itineraries as an exclusive for as long as we can keep it quiet. It's a little further out than most of the half-day charters, but it'd be perfect for an afternoon dive after the dark, deep Vandenberg."

"And the treasure story is certainly a great angle." Kate put on her best TV announcer voice. "'Ladies and Gentlemen, legend has it that the lost treasure of Al Capone was hidden near this site. Keep your eyes open — you might find a gold coin or a loose emerald or ruby!'"

"Hell, they might. With all that silt and growth, I'm sure we'll miss some. But I think my Gramps would like it that way."

Steve glanced around the dive deck. "We're gonna need a bigger boat."

Kate scratched Whiskey behind his ears, then pulled her mask and cameras out of the rinse tub and hung them on a hook beside her rig. At the sound of a low rumble, she looked up to see the giant *Tax Shelter* zooming toward them from the eastern horizon. She hopped down off the bench and waved toward the approaching yacht with a flourish. "Our cargo ship approaches!"

Chuck glanced up toward the horizon. "I've got a weird feeling about this. I know the *Island Hopper* isn't big enough or secure enough to bring all this back in one trip, but that boat belongs to the man who's trying to steal my home."

"That's what makes it poetic, Chuck. I don't trust Vince at all, so we'll put him in the water where we can all keep an eye on him. I'll send Whiskey over there to guard the *Tax Shelter*, and you know William will keep everything running smoothly."

"Speaking of ..." Steve climbed out onto the swim platform and heaved the first case they'd sent up over the transom. "I want to put these up in the bow storage locker, just to get them out of the way and keep them out of sight." Michelle and Kate helped him wrestle the heavy cases into the forward compartment.

Chuck was still glued to the computer screen. "I can't thank you all enough. These past few days have been the worst I've ever felt. I thought I was going to lose Shark Key forever. Now it looks like I'll never have to worry about losing it again. That couldn't have happened without all of you." A tear dripped down his cheek, sparkling in the light.

"Ahoy!" William's deep voice carried across the water from *Tax Shelter*'s sweeping flybridge. He guided the boat alongside the *Island Hopper* then dropped the engines to idle.

Steve shouted over the starboard gunwale. "Set anchor with your stern about here. We'll pull ours and raft up to you. Our last tank is almost full, so we're about ready to go down again."

William piloted around to the west, set his anchor, then began to let out the rode. The yacht drifted into place just above the reef. As William backed down on the anchor, Steve eased up to his port side. Kate dropped three fenders and tossed spring lines across to Vince, who quickly tied them off.

"That good?" William's voice crackled over the short-range walkie-talkie sitting on the table.

Steve grabbed it. "Perfect!"

A moment later, both men clambered aboard the smaller dive boat. Kate briefed them on what they'd found so far and the process they'd set up for raising the cases. With extra hands and more gear, they agreed they could probably get most of the cargo loaded before dark. Kate, Steve, and Chuck would stay on station at the *Katherine K*, rigging lift bags and pushing them and crates out to Vince, who would clip them to the line then send everything to the surface, where William and Michelle would be waiting to load everything into the lazarette between the *Tax Shelter*'s swim platform and engine room.

Kate glanced at Steve. "The boat will be right on top of us, and we're not super-deep, so I'm okay with pushing the safety limits a little bit. Instead of ascending at a thousand pounds of air, let's stretch that to five hundred. We can clip a pony tank to the line at fifteen feet for the safety stop, just in case. Chuck, you'll probably run low on air first. When you hit five hundred, signal one of us then just go on up alone. We'll keep an eye on you through your safety stop."

She paused to screw her regulator to a tall tank covered in yellow and green stickers.

"Steve and I both have high capacity Nitrox tanks, so we've got plenty of air and plenty of time. Unless the current shifts, we should stay right on top of the site. Vince, it looks like you can probably just hover above the reef at about thirty-five feet. Catch the packages as they raise up then clip them to the line. As long as you don't go crazy, you should be able to get an hour, maybe more. Just don't forget to watch your air. Five hundred pounds, ascend slow, and don't skip your safety stop. We can't risk a trip to the chamber for anyone."

Michelle raised the *Island Hopper*'s red and white diver down flag while the four divers geared up. For the next hour, they tugged and strapped and lifted cases and boxes and bags, sending them toward the surface for William and Michelle to lug each bulky package out of the water and haul it through the hatch on the transom into the yacht's roomy lazarette.

As Kate floated out a small bag filled with heavy gold coins, Vince waved and tapped his pressure gauge.

She repeated the ascent sign — a thumbs up — signaled okay, then pointed back and forth from her eyes to him. *I've got my eye on you.*

Vince collected a load of bags and crates, then slowly made his way up the stern line. Midway up, he paused to send the load to the surface. He waited long enough to catch the next batch of bags that Chuck clipped to the line, and with his safety stop complete, he pulled those to the surface with him.

Kate waved at Chuck, tapped her pressure gauge, pointed to him. He checked his air and waggled four fingers at her. Kate sucked in a deep breath and bit down hard on her regulator. He should have already surfaced. Four hundred pounds of air was barely enough to get safely through his stop. She jabbed a finger toward him, then pointed at the surface. Chuck shrugged and clipped two more cases to the stern line before starting up.

She glanced over at Steve, who indicated he still had plenty of air. When Chuck stopped, Kate checked her watch and began counting to time his safety stop. Anger would use extra air, so she tried to ignore it while she clocked him.

Kate and Steve hovered above the opening to the *Katherine K*'s hull. She looked down on the wreck and strained to see through the murky water. Their work had raised years of silt and sand, and the clear, eighty-foot visibility had dropped to around ten feet around the hull. They had most of the treasure raised, and now it was a matter of waiting for the gentle current to clear the silt away so they could look for anything they might have left behind. As they hovered above the wreck, they heard a low hum resonating in the water — the unmistakable sound of a boat motor.

The boat could be a half-mile away, but she could only see a hundred feet, maybe less. Nevertheless, she rolled toward the light and scanned the surface fifty feet above her. Without signaling to each other, Steve did the same — human nature. She didn't see a shadow of another hull, and he didn't indicate seeing anything, either. So they both rolled back toward the reef then finned back to the edge of the hull.

They sifted through the silt and sand for a few more minutes as the engine drone grew clearer. Finally, Kate tapped Steve on the shoulder and pointed at the surface. The shadow of *Tax Shelter*'s sleek hull sat straight above them, and the smaller hull of the *Island Hopper* sat alongside to the south. But a third shadow appeared to the east, approaching the *Tax Shelter*.

Kate's eyes widened and quick, short bursts of bubbles shot from her regulator. Steve nodded, then motioned for her to focus on his eyes. He breathed slowly and Kate counted the spots on the lens of his mask until she matched his calm breaths. He signed for her to wait while he collected the lift bags and other gear, bundled it all up, then tucked it all into a niche in the *Katherine K*'s hull. After that, he checked his and Kate's air, waggled his fingers in a swimming motion toward the *Tax Shelter*'s bow, then made the sign for ascent.

Kate shook her head and swam toward the yacht's stern. Steve grabbed her ankle and pulled her back toward him. She fought his grip, thrashing her legs. Her foot struck the side of Steve's head, and she felt his fingers release. Kate started toward the surface again. She rose a few feet, then looked back.

Steve was in trouble.

He groped for his mask, but it was dangling behind his head. Kate flipped over and kicked hard toward him. She helped him reposition the mask, and he quickly cleared it and glared at her. He jabbed her in the shoulder, then jabbed his own shoulder and pointed to the anchor, nodding once for emphasis.

She blew a long string of bubbles and nodded, then the two headed west, slowly ascending as they made their way toward the *Tax Shelter*'s bow.

CHAPTER FIFTY-ONE

VINCE TUCKED the last sack filled with their find behind the engine room ladder then tapped the hatch above his head. He glanced around the sparkling engine room. The pristine runs of piping, hoses, and wires contrasted with the dull metal and rotting wood crates they'd brought up from the hull of the *Katherine K.* But they'd looked inside enough of them to know the contents sparkled. Just a short run back to Shark Key to unload, and he could take his share then slip away to a new life somewhere Baumann could never find him.

The engine room and the storage area behind it were full of cases, crates, and bags. Only a narrow path was left between the aft hatch that led to the swim platform and the forward bulkhead of the engine room. The giant twin Caterpillar engines sat in silence flanking the priceless treasure. Vince climbed over the crates then scrambled up the ladder into the luxurious dinette in the boat's cockpit. Chuck stood near the port stairs, dripping salt water all over the teak decking that someone else would have to clean and varnish.

"Is that all of it?" Vince was in no mood for surprises.

"All we're getting tonight. Anything that's left is strewn on the bottom, and we've kicked up so much silt, there's nothing more we can do until it clears up." Chuck tilted his head to the side and shook it.

"Good, because we couldn't fit much more down there and still get to the engines."

William poked his head out of the main salon. "We don't need to get very far. We're floating pretty low, so I'll take the scenic route around to the west of the quicksands, and then east through the gulf. Then we'll drop down through the flats on the rising tide. No more than an hour, I wouldn't think."

"Chuck, would you like some pineapple?" Michelle's voice drifted out from the galley. Chuck stuck the corner of the ship's fluffy towel in his ear, tilted his head to the side, and hopped on one foot.

William turned back inside. "I think that's a yes."

Vince flopped into the wide banquette, his back to the ocean. He picked at the nail on his pinky finger. "I want to thank you guys."

Chuck stopped his ear water dance and met Vince's gaze.

"I hurt you. I stole from you. I led you on a chase

360

across the Caribbean. One of your people..." He paused. "You all had no reason to forgive me. But you did. You're giving me a chance for a fresh start, and I'm ... I appreciate it is all."

William rested his hands on the back of a white captain's chair and leaned in. "All that is true. You did give us more trouble than we were expecting. And yeah, I knew you could've been feeding us a line to save your own skin out there after Cuba. But you also risked your life to try to save Susan. And you've been helpful. You've kept your word."

"And we'll keep ours," Chuck added. "When we get back and get all this unloaded, I'll make sure you have enough to start over anywhere you want to go."

"Thank you."

Michelle set a huge bowl of cut pineapple and mangos on the table between them. "Who's that?"

"Who's who?" Vince spun around and saw a small boat speeding directly toward them.

"I don't like how fast they're approaching with the whole ocean to themselves. We have divers in the water and our flags are still out." William grabbed a set of binoculars. "Michelle, come with me." He dropped the field glasses on the table then pushed his wife into the cabin, slamming the sliding door behind him.

Vince picked up the binoculars and trained them on the approaching red Bayliner. A tall pale man stood at the helm. A small woman sat in the captain's chair beside him, her red hair flying behind her in the wind.

He handed the glasses to Chuck and ran into the salon. He met William coming back up the steps with Michelle and the giant German Shepherd on his heels.

"...not stuff me in a corner to hide—"

"Whiskey, stay with Michelle—"

"Hey. Sorry to interrupt, but what kind of weapons do we have on board?" Vince fought to keep his voice steady

"You know the boat better than I do. What does he keep?"

"Not much outside of fishing gear. There's a spear gun buried under all that stuff we just loaded, but nothing else I know of. I meant what did you bring?"

"I've got a .45, but I wasn't expecting to run into any trouble, so no extra ammunition, unless Michelle thought to toss a box in her purse."

"I didn't even bring my purse. We've got Whiskey, right boy?" She scratched the dog behind his ears, but they both looked like they'd shatter at the first touch.

Vince glanced out the sliding doors. The Bayliner was nearly on them, slowing and approaching their starboard side. Baumann had a shotgun slung on a strap across his chest and a pistol holstered on his side.

"We're gonna have to talk our way out of this. Whatever I say next, know that I meant every word I just said to you out there." He pointed to Chuck, standing in the center of the aft deck. "Tell him. Every word." Vince opened the sliding door and stretched his arms out wide.

"Vincent."

Vince's blood froze at the sound of Baumann's voice, but he fought to keep his body loose and his voice warm. "Throw me that line. You're not going to believe what I've got for you, Boss." Vince tied the line to a cleat amidship then scrambled aft to tie the speedboat's second line to the *Tax Shelter*'s swim platform. He held out a hand to steady Baumann as he jumped from the small boat, then led his former boss up the starboard stairs to the main deck.

"Hey, asshole!" Tina's shout rose from the Bayliner. She scrambled over the gunwale onto the *Tax Shelter* then up the stairs behind them.

"Vincent, why is my yacht in the middle of the ocean and why are these ... *people* on it?" Baumann looked like he was smelling hobo feet on his three-million-dollar showpiece.

"I told you they were after something. They found it. And it's all loaded in your storage locker below." Vince tapped the hatch to the engine room at his feet. Chuck shot Vince a look of agonized betrayal. When Baumann crouched to look through the hatch, Vince met the gaze, tilted his head to the dinette where he'd just confessed his gratitude, and gave an earnest nod, silently begging Chuck to believe him.

"Mr. Baumann," Tina's shrill voice sliced through the tense moment. "You know he's playing you, sir."

"I smell a lot of something that's not my sparkling clean boat down there."

"I've been watching him at the marina for the past two days. He's one of them now. Plannin' to take his cut and run. I heard him talking about it."

Baumann looked up from the engine room hatch and stared at him.

Vince smelled his own sweat through his wetsuit and fought to steady his breathing and hold the taller man's glare.

"Is this true, Vincent? Are you double-crossing me?"

His gaze flitted up to the left then back to Baumann. "Not at all, sir. The opposite. I'm double-crossing them. I even got them to load it all on your boat for you."

"Vincent, I've known you a long time. We've worked together on countless occasions. We've played cards at the same table. I know your tells. I do appreciate you loading everything, though. It'll make it all far easier to take with me. As for you, your journey ends here." He pulled the handgun from his hip and waved Vince toward the port steps.

"Please. I wasn't. I didn't. I—"

Crack!

Time stopped, then everyone moved in slow motion.

Michelle stood in the wide gap of the open sliding glass door, clutching William's arm, her face buried beneath his shoulder in horror.

William stared at Vince, his face filled with pain and empathy.

Chuck launched toward Baumann, too late to stop what had already begun.

Whiskey flew through the air behind William.

Lucas appeared up the starboard steps to see his mother standing at the side of a murderer.

The force of the gunshot propelled Vince backward. He toppled over the railing, tumbled down the stairs. A deep sensation of emptiness radiated from the left side of his chest.

He hardly felt the impact as he landed in the warm swells of salt water.

CHAPTER FIFTY-TWO

KATE AND STEVE leveled out at seventeen feet under the surface, hovering below the three hulls tied together in the rolling ocean. Three more minutes remained to wait while the excess nitrogen worked its way out of their bloodstreams. They'd spent more than their allotted bottom time on the wreck of the *Katherine K*, and cutting short the safety stop was more than either of them was willing to risk.

They hung in the dark water, gesturing, planning. Kate pointed to the bow of the *Island Hopper*, walked her fingers forward, shrugged. Steve shook his head and pointed to the wide swim platform of the *Tax Shelter*, motioning a surprise attack.

With one minute of their safety stop left, they began to slowly swam aft, staying in the shadow of the huge boat. Ahead, a heavy splash broke the calm. A dark object plunged below the water, then rose back toward the surface. A thick, dark cloud spread around the form. Kate kicked hard toward the area, but another large form plunged into the water, grabbed the body, then dragged it aboard the *Island Hopper*. She turned and began finning toward the smaller boat. Glancing back, she saw Steve thrusting his arm toward the stern of the *Tax Shelter*.

Stick with the plan.

Their heads breached the surface almost touching the edge of the swim platform. They hovered, their ears just above the surface. Kate heard Tina screaming. "Lucas. Lucas, you leave him and get back over here right now!"

Over the sound of water slapping against the hull and the screaming from the aft cockpit above them, she thought she could hear crying from the direction of the *Island Hopper*.

An unbidden thought flashed through her mind.

Can Steve handle this right now?

She looked over. Through his mask, she saw only determination in his eyes. He was starting to twist out of his BC when someone stomped down the port steps. They ducked around the opposite corner of the hull between the *Tax Shelter* and a red speedboat just in time to see Baumann marching William and Michelle down to the swim platform, their hands bound behind them with thick white zip-ties, his gun pressed against the small of her back. He pushed them to the edge of the swim platform then over the gunwale onto the *Island Hopper*.

The two boats slammed against each other in the swells of the open ocean. A series of low voices, grunts, and thumps sounded from inside. A minute later, Baumann hopped back onto the *Tax Shelter* then scurried up to the main deck. Kate and Steve quickly slipped off their BCs, clipped them to a cleat, then hauled themselves up onto the swim platform. As they pulled their fins and masks off, Chuck limped down the stairs, his hands tied in front of him. They scrambled to hide against the opposite rail, then as Baumann cleared the last step, Steve launched across the swim platform, lowering his shoulder to jam it into Baumann's kidney.

All three men toppled over the side and onto the aft deck of the *Island Hopper*.

Baumann slammed Chuck in the back of his head with the butt of his pistol, then rolled forward down the deck with Steve, out of Kate's view.

Kate started up the stairs but paused when a woman screamed, "Lucas, get your ass back here now!" She crept up two more steps then peeked around the safety rail at the top of the staircase.

It was the redheaded woman, Tina, from the campground. She was leaning over the port railing and bellowing at her son.

From the boat below, a young man shouted through sobs and hiccups, "No, Mama. These people are hurt and need help. You hurt them, Mama. They need help."

Kate tucked her feet up under her and coiled to jump.

"Shut up, you useless waste of air." Tina pulled a gun from her waistband, pointed it down toward the *Island Hopper*, fired.

"That was your son, you bitch!" Kate screamed and dove at the woman, knocking the gun from her hand. It splintered the smooth teak as it hit the deck then spun away from them.

Tina rolled, curled her legs, then thrust them, kicking Kate in the gut.

Kate slid to a stop. On the other side of the sliding door, Whiskey snarled and threw himself at the glass. She pulled the door open, releasing the dog. He lunged at Tina.

She ducked and rolled under his body, popping up between him and Kate, then ran at Kate, her shoulder low. Whiskey took two strong strides before launching at Tina. The momentum caught both women, then all three flew over the railing onto the bow of the Bayliner. Whiskey was thrown toward the stern. Kate's head slammed against the edge of the helm. Her vision went blurry.

Tina was dragging her into the forward cabin when three unmistakable blasts sounded. Kate smelled saltwater and gasoline. And as everything went dark, she felt Whiskey's wet fur against the side of her face.

CHAPTER FIFTY-THREE

KATE CAME to when she crashed against a bulkhead in the Bayliner's tiny cabin. Whiskey, silhouetted in front of the hatch, fought to keep his balance. Beyond the sound of water against the gunwales, the boat was silent. It rolled unevenly in what should have been a calm sea.

They must be untying it from the yacht.

She glanced around the dim cabin. The boat was listing slightly to starboard, and water sloshed below her in the bilge. She could stop the leak, restart the pump, then limp to shallower waters. If she could move.

She couldn't have been out for long, but it was long enough to lose everything. Again.

Three shots.

Her friends were gone. If she got to land without drowning, it would just be her and Whiskey. Alone.

She'd started over before. She could start over again.

Kate crawled to the port window. The *Tax Shelter* was drifting away, or maybe she was drifting away from it. Either way, Baumann's lean form stood in the high flybridge, directing Tina as she prepared to raise the boat's anchor. Kate could just make out the stern of the *Island Hopper* on the other side, drifting away from the *Tax Shelter*. It listed heavy to port, the opposite corner of its transom high in the water. It would be on the bottom in less than ten minutes.

Kate rolled back over, rubbed her head. Felt a sticky wetness. She pulled her hand back to examine her own blood. It would be so much easier to just go back to sleep and let the boat sink. She closed her eyes.

They jerked open again as the boat rolled over another swell and Whiskey scrambled to keep his position.

Whiskey.

He couldn't swim far enough to survive. She could accept this as her end, but she couldn't let him drown. Her breath quickened. Her gaze darted around the cabin. She counted seams in the paneling until she could think straight again.

Kate pushed herself up. Found an oily rag to wipe the blood from the back of her head. Tore a wide strip from another rag, tied it tight around her head. She opened the hatch to the engine compartment. A series of holes from a shotgun blast had ripped through the fiberglass hull, and the charred remains of the bilge pump sat in the deepening pool of oily water.

The speedboat was going down, and there was nothing Kate could do to stop it.

She peered out the porthole. The giant white yacht loomed over her. When she turned astern to see how much further the *Island Hopper* had sunk, she saw movement. Just a hand gripping the starboard gunwale near the transom. But a hand that hadn't been there before. A hand pulling someone up the side of the sinking boat.

Kate scrambled to the hatch then grabbed a set of fins lying in the cockpit. No mask or snorkel, but she'd have to make it without. She scanned the bilge of the small boat and estimated the time it had left.

She kissed her hand, then lay it between her dog's ears. After a moment, she whispered, "Whiskey, stay."

Kate scanned the hull of the *Tax Shelter*, made sure she was clear. She sucked in a deep breath then launched herself over the gunwale and under the surface of the water.

With no mask, everything under the clear water was blurry, just brightness and shadows, but the *Tax Shelter*'s keel was unmistakable. She finned hard toward it, her lungs screaming for fresh air. The drone of the yacht's idling engines grew louder, and Kate burst to the surface just inches from its swim platform. Two sets of scuba gear still dangled in the water, clipped to the cleat where she'd left them less than an hour before. She reached into the pocket of her BC, pulled out the KA-BAR knife she'd taken from Vince that first night, then tucked it inside the zipper of her wetsuit. Clinging to the edge of the boat, she scanned above her and prayed she'd stay hidden in the light surf.

She could see the top of Baumann's back in the upper flydeck.

From the starboard corner of the swim deck, she could see the *Island Hopper*. The bow was low in the water, but it was higher than she'd expected. Then she spotted the lazarette door in the center of the *Tax Shelter*'s transom. She kept her head as low to the water as she could and, hand over hand, pulled herself around to the center edge of the swim deck.

Kate pulled off her fins off then tossed them up against the transom. The moment Baumann leaned forward out of sight, she dolphin kicked hard, rolled up on to the swim deck, pushing fast against the fiberglass to stay out of sight.

She popped open the small hatch then slipped down the ladder. The compartment smelled of diesel fuel and rot. Crates and cases filled with treasure were stacked in every spare cubic inch. Kate climbed back into the engine room. The purring twin diesels vibrated the whole compartment. Hoses and valves and tubing stretched wall to wall. A huge white generator sat to the starboard side of the hatch, and a bright yellow walkie-talkie sat on top of it.

The walkie-talkies Steve and William had been using to coordinate between the boats. The walkie-talkie whose partner had to still be aboard the *Island Hopper*.

Kate grabbed it and mashed the button. "Kate to *Hopper*. Kate to *Hopper*. *Hopper*, can you hear me?"

She released the button and waited. Her heart pounded harder than the diesel engines. "*Hopper*, do you hear me?"

The walkie-talkie crackled then a weak voice crackled across the static. "Good to hear your voice. Where are you?"

"I'm on the *Tax Shelter*. What's your condition?"

"We could use a little help over here if you can spare it. We're all hurt, and we're going down fast."

"Chuck, I'm ..." Kate looked around. "Your money ..."

"Let it go, Kate. It's just money."

"How long ..."

"We're in bad shape. Vince and Lucas are dead. Michelle's been shot, and Steve and William are unconscious. I've only got one hand and one leg. When this boat goes down, we're all dead."

"How long can you hang on? I can't let him get away. He can't win."

"Let him win, Kate. Just help us."

Kate looked around at the crates and sacks filled with millions of dollars in gold and jewels. Treasure

Chuck's grandfather had risked his life for. Treasure that had built Shark Key.

Treasure that should have kept it safe.

"Okay, Chuck. I'm on my way."

The walkie crackled one more time, and Kate's brain lit up.

Three minutes later, the *Tax Shelter*'s engines roared to life. Kate folded the knife, tucked it back into her wetsuit, then slipped through the lazarette hatch. She glanced toward the ocean's murky floor, fit the fins onto her feet, filled her lungs, then dropped off the swim platform into the boat's growing wake.

Kate kicked across the choppy water until she reached the *Island Hopper*. She scrambled over the gunwale, just barely above the surface, then clambered up toward the transom. The *Hopper* rocked in the last choppy remnants of the *Tax Shelter*'s wake. The huge yacht was disappearing into the horizon.

"Chuck, where's that walkie? I need it now!"

"Help me get untied."

"Chuck, the walkie!"

"Right there. The camera rack... but we need help."

Kate ran to the camera table, rifled through the pile of electronics until she found the walkie. She checked the channel then mashed the talk button.

She stared at the horizon until a plume of black smoke rose toward the sky. A second later, the sound of the explosion reached her ears.

Then she leaned over the transom. "Whiskey, come here boy!"

The dog launched into the water. Kate pulled the knife from her wetsuit, cut the zip ties from Chuck's wrists, then deployed the *Hopper*'s inflatable life raft.

CHAPTER FIFTY-FOUR

APPLAUSE ROSE from the long picnic table when the flaming sun slipped below the ocean. The horizon in front of them glowed orange while a deep purple darkness stole across the sky from behind them. Tiny white lights draped above the deck twinkled as if the heavens had been lassoed and pulled close enough to touch.

Kate lifted her empty glass toward Amy, who was pouring from a pale green pitcher.

Steve stood and blew into a huge conch shell. A solemn blast wailed from it — the traditional farewell to the day.

Tonight, that farewell was for more than just the day.

From the head of the table, Chuck tapped his glass with a fork handle and cleared his throat.

"I want to thank you all for coming this evening to honor the life of our friend Susan Welch. Susan was family to all of us, and we will miss her. But tonight is about more than just mourning and sadness. It's about hope." He adjusted the crutch under his arm.

"This past week has been tense. Dangerous. Susan made the ultimate sacrifice, and many more of you made sacrifices, too, because Shark Key was in trouble. I was in trouble. But thanks to all of you, today, and for as much future as we have in this paradise, our little corner of it is safe."

Kate wiped a tear from her cheek.

"I met with the bank this afternoon. With Baumann out of the picture, they've been quite accommodating, to say the least. Without each one of you helping, none of us would be sitting here. So, thank you."

Chuck toasted, and glasses clinked around the table. Branson Tillman played Susan's favorite songs softly from the corner of the deck.

Michelle leaned over to Kate. "How did you get to us? I thought we were goners."

"Honestly, I did, too. I heard a lot of gunshots from the *Hopper* and assumed Baumann had killed all of you. I hit my head so hard, I thought I was gonna drown. My head was bleeding everywhere. It was Whiskey that got me up out of that sinking speedboat. I knew he couldn't swim to shore. And when I saw Chuck's hand on the side of the *Hopper*, everything changed ... I didn't have any other option."

At the sound of Whiskey's name, he leaned against

Kate and tipped his head backward to gaze at her. She scratched his head and continued.

"When I got aboard the *Tax Shelter*, I saw the *Hopper* wasn't as low as I thought. And I knew if Baumann got away, everything we had been through would have been for nothing. Worse than for nothing. I knew there was no way I'd win in a direct fight against the two of them, so I sneaked into the engine room. And when I saw the walkie-talkie, it just clicked. After I talked to Chuck and confirmed the other one was on the *Hopper*, I stripped the wires to the battery, cut a fuel line with my dive knife, then got out as they sped away. It killed me to sink everything we had worked so hard to find and Chuck needed so badly. But we've all lost everything before. I couldn't let that bastard get away with everything."

"You made the right choice, kiddo." Chuck limped up behind her and rested his hand on her shoulder.

She reached up and patted his hand.

"We had enough stashed in the *Hopper* to last me longer than I deserve. I'm paying off the note on this place, upgrading some of the facilities, and I'm going to dredge your slip and put a new motor in *Serenity*, if you'll let me."

Kate started to tilt her head back toward him, but the pain reminded her of the gash wrapped in gauze on the back of her head. She squeezed his hand and turned toward him, not even trying to hide the tear in her eye.

Amy leaned in to refill their glasses from the pitcher she carried around the deck. As she poured, she whispered to Chuck, "I'm releasing all of your grandfather's belongings back to you. Take your time and go through all of it before you decide what to send back to us. There's too much of your family's history here for you to just hand it over without knowing what's in it."

William wrapped his arm around Michelle's shoulders, and Steve sat on the bench opposite, taking in the group of mourners sharing stories about Susan and paying their respects. Babette sat encased in pillows with her legs propped up at the end of the table, sipping a virgin margarita.

"Snorkelers and divers will be pulling coins and gemstones out of those quicksands for years. Since it's all protected under the wildlife refuge, I've gotten a commitment from the park service that they'll never issue salvage permits for anyone to dredge or sift for it. But anything that a random snorkeler finds, they can keep. Tourism is gonna go through the roof when the story gets out."

"I'm gonna need a bigger boat." Steve smiled. "Who better to help find it than the people who put it all there?"

Kate couldn't disagree with her friend. "I can't wait to get back down to chart the rest of the *Katherine K*. There's a lot of history on that wreck, and the marine life that's made a home there is just amazing. Maybe I'll even take a few more charters when you ask."

On a TV behind the bar, news footage of the explosion ran on a loop. Kate scanned it as the captions scrolled across the screen.

Off the coast of Key West, an unusual find. Beneath the wreckage of a luxury yacht that exploded last week killing four people, recovery teams have found cases filled with gold and jewels that appear to date back to the time of prohibition. Key West was well-known as a bootlegger's paradise, with liquor being run between the Florida island and Cuba to the south throughout the thirteen-year dry period. The Mel Fisher museum will be assisting in determining the provenance of the unusual find....

Kate fingered a heavy gold coin, flipped it, then dropped it back into her pocket.

A gentle breeze drifted in off the flats in the darkening night. Chuck flipped off the lights, and the family of friends sat beneath the twinkling stars, just laughing, sharing stories, and pouring margaritas.

THE END

Thank you for reading LOST KEY. I hope you enjoyed joining Kate and the Shark Key family on this adventure.

I'm working on a shorter book that takes Kate and Chuck into the Keys backcountry where they run into just a little more trouble than they bargained for. I'll be sending that out entirely for free to my VIP Reader Group as soon as it's ready.

If you'd like to read that, please join my VIP Reader Group at chrisnilesbooks.com/vip!

ALSO BY CHRIS NILES

The Shark Key Adventures

LOST PALM

An extraordinary prize lies hidden in the remote Florida Keys backcountry.

When Kate Kingsbury finds a map tucked in the pages of a rare Hemingway novel, she sets off to discover a little more about the islands around her new home.

But in an instant, her sunny adventure becomes a dangerous fight for her life.

Can Kate survive the threat lurking among the mangroves?

LOST PALM is exclusively available to members of my VIP Reader Group. Join today for free at chrisnilesbooks.com/VIP

LOST KEY

It only takes a moment to lose everything.

When a corrupt real-estate developer sets his sights on Kate Kingsbury's marina in the Florida Keys, Kate and her neighbors must band together to save Shark Key. Their only hope is a lost treasure stolen from the infamous Al Capone. Can they find what's been hidden for almost a century before time runs out?

LOST RELICS

In the aftermath of a devastating hurricane, five long lost indigenous idols are linked to a series of missing teenagers in the Dominican Republic. And when Kate Kingsbury joins the search for the ancient zemís, the killer sets his sights on her.

Can Kate find the ancient idols before he kills again?

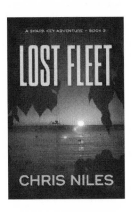

LOST FLEET

A shocking secret lies at the bottom of the Caribbean Sea.

When her journalism mentor is killed in a horrific plane crash off the coast of Key West, Kate Kingsbury travels to New York to lay him to rest.

At his funeral, she learns he might have found proof that a Chinese fleet arrived in the Caribbean nearly a hundred years before the Europeans. As she follows his leads, she meets the charming David Li, whose uncle — a powerful Chinese oil magnate — is searching for the fleet, too.

Is David searching for the truth, or is he a mole for his uncle? And will Kate live long enough to find out?

The Anna Mitchell International Thriller Series:

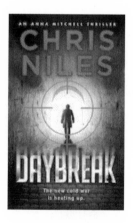

DAYBREAK

The new cold war is heating up.

Russian-backed terrorist Sasha Volkov plans to launch a series of attacks on American soil that will plunge the world into chaos. And only former CIA operative Anna Mitchell can stop him.

But when Anna uncovers a secret about her own past that ties her to Volkov, she must make an impossible choice: learn the truth about herself, or save innocent American lives.

Learn more at chrisnilesbooks.com

AUTHOR'S NOTE

I was eleven when my family moved to Florida's west coast. And while I never quite got used to Santa wearing shorts and shades, the Sunshine State burrowed into my blood. I've lived on the coast and inland. North, and ... less north.

But when my younger brother moved to Key West a few years ago, I found the place my heart felt at home.

Every region of the state is unique; each carries its own culture and vibe. From the pulsing nightlife of South Beach to the sleepy live oak canopies in Talla-hassee, Florida's got diversity covered.

Visitors typically only experience a tiny portion of what those who've built lives there know. My goal in this series of novels is to give my readers a glimpse of life beyond the vacation. To meet a character who's living the life most of us can only dream of. And to join in adventures around the Caribbean and beyond.

I mean...who doesn't want to cruise around on turquoise waters with only the sun to tell the time?

While I've done a lot of research and tried to keep all the facts straight, I will admit I've taken a few liberties with the geography to facilitate the story.

The biggest one? Shark Key itself.

Shark Key is a real island (and a beautiful one, too), but it was developed long ago and is now a gated community full of multi-million dollar estates. I rolled back the clock and gave the mile-long island a different history. I also deepened the water on the east coast of Shark Key by a few feet to allow access for bigger boats, and I added a bridge passage under the Overseas Highway just to the east of the Key.

In addition, I took some liberties with the Custom House and other locations as well...their staffs are far more attentive and adherent to policy than I make them out to be! If you notice any mistakes, they are mine and mine alone, and not the fault of the many wise and informed people I used as research slaves.

Finally, a word about Kate's German Shepherd dog, Whiskey. He's inspired by a real badass. The real Police Dog Whiskey is still on active duty. He chases bad guys in Western Australia, drives on the wrong side of the road, and barks with an accent. ;)

I hope these books offer as much escape and adventure for you as they've given me in writing them.

ACKNOWLEDGMENTS

If I won the lottery, I'd buy a shack on the beach and write the great American novel.

Well, I won the lottery ... the marriage lottery, that is. I'm blessed with a husband who supports my dreams and encourages me every day as I make a career out of my "lottery dream." It's not a shack by the beach, but to be honest, I'm really glad to have electricity and running water.

The first idea is easy. It's even not so hard writing the first few chapters. But after that, it takes a team of people cheering me on, kicking my butt, and checking my details to make sure I didn't get anything wrong that I didn't mean to get wrong.

I have so many people to thank, and even after I thank them all, I'm sure I'll have forgotten some. So of course, thanks to everyone I'm not mentioning here. I still love you and cherish your support.

I have to start with the many people who shared their knowledge and spirits and technical expertise. Special thanks to Julie for being the inspiration for many of Kate's best features (and none of her flaws!) and to Juliet for sharing her expertise about police dogs, and introducing me to the legendary Police Dog Whiskey. He's an amazing dog, and you have every right to be proud of him. Thanks to Barry for taking me shooting and answering every ridiculous law enforcement question, so I could keep the cops off of Kate's tail, to Bill for answering random airplane questions during his layovers, and to my buddy Cap Daniels for getting William's plane in the air.

Thanks to Amy for naming Babette (and Amy Johnson), for teaching me that you don't need white cotton gloves to handle antique books, and for helping untangle the knots in Tommy Miller's flight from the mob. And of course thanks to Mark for figuring out the treasure (both in the story and in real life).

I'd never get through a day without Ric, who names random bad guys after whoever's annoying him that week (and who chases me with his own astronomical word count and reminds me to keep writing when I don't feel like it). And to my unsung cheerleaders: Linda and Stacy for reading every word and loving even the terrible ones, Tammi for being Tammi and advising on #AllTheThings and fixing my brain when it gets caught in a downward spiral, Ernie for telling me to Quit F***ing Around™, and to Michelle Spiva for helping me understand what readers really want.

Finally, to Adam for being my secret muse, for living the life I can only dream about, for fact-checking AllTheThings, and for sending me random crime reports from the *Key West Citizen*.

But my greatest thanks go to you, my reader. In a world as crazy as ours, I'm humbled and privileged that you chose to read this adventure I created. I hope I've honored your time and delivered a great story, and I trust you'll join me again for LOST RELICS.

ABOUT THE AUTHOR

Chris(tine) Niles has been telling stories since she was a lying kid. Now she's figuring out how to make a career of it. Because she likes to eat, she tried for about fifteen minutes to write romance. But her characters kept killing each other, so she switched to thrillers.

Her heart is buried deep in the hammock north of Sugarloaf Key, and you can only find it from a kayak. Despite that, her body lives in northeastern Indiana with her husband, two mostly adult daughters, and a hungry four-legged sack of fur named Franklin.

You can find out more at chrisnilesbooks.com.